# BUBBLE

# FOR ME!

SIMON & SCHUSTER BOOKS FOR YOUNG READERS
An imprint of Simon & Schuster Children's Publishing Division
1230 Avenue of the Americas, New York, New York 10020
This book is a work of fiction. Any references to historical events,
real people, or real places are used fictitiously. Other names, characters, places,
and events are products of the author's imagination, and any resemblance to
actual events or places or persons, living or dead, is entirely coincidental.
Text copyright © 2016 by Stewart Foster
Originally published in Great Britain in 2016 as *The Bubble Boy*
Published by arrangement with Simon & Schuster UK Ltd.
First US edition 2017
Jacket illustration copyright © 2017 by Cathy Gendron
All rights reserved, including the right of reproduction
in whole or in part in any form.
SIMON & SCHUSTER BOOKS FOR YOUNG READERS
is a trademark of Simon & Schuster, Inc.
For information about special discounts for bulk purchases,
please contact Simon & Schuster Special Sales
at 1-866-506-1949 or business@simonandschuster.com.
The Simon & Schuster Speakers Bureau can bring authors to your live event. For
more information or to book an event, contact the Simon & Schuster Speakers Bureau
at 1-866-248-3049 or visit our website at www.simonspeakers.com.
Book design by Tom Daly
The text for this book was set in Adobe Garamond Pro.
Manufactured in the United States of America
0317 FFG
2  4  6  8  10  9  7  5  3  1
Library of Congress Cataloging-in-Publication Data
Names: Foster, Stewart, 1963– author.
Title: Bubble / Stewart Foster.
Other titles: Bubble Boy
Description: First edition. | New York : Simon & Schuster Books for Young
Readers, [2017] | Summary: Orphaned eleven-year-old Joe lives in a hospital due to
his autoimmune disease, interacting only with his sister, an American boy with the
same illness, and medical staff while dreaming of being a superhero.
Identifiers: LCCN 2016020200| ISBN 9781481487429 (hardcover)
| ISBN 9781481487443 (eBook)
Subjects: | CYAC: Autoimmune disease—Fiction. | Hospital care—Fiction. |
Brothers and sisters—Fiction. | Orphans—Fiction. | Friendship—Fiction.
Classification: LCC PZ7.1.F675 Bub 2017 | DDC [Fic]—dc23
LC record available at https://lccn.loc.gov/2016020200

# BUBBLE

## STEWART FOSTER

SIMON & SCHUSTER BOOKS FOR YOUNG READERS
New York   London   Toronto   Sydney   New Delhi

# ONE

## 11 YEARS, 2 MONTHS, AND 21 DAYS

"**I've got a tattoo.** Guess what it is?"

"A giraffe?"

"On my ankle?"

"Okay, an elephant."

Beth touches me on my arm.

"Come on, Joe," she says. "You're not even trying."

"Sorry. Show me it?"

She smiles then pulls up the right leg of the overalls that all visitors have to wear, even family.

"Last guess?"

"Spider-Man?"

"No." She laughs. "*You* can get that one when you're older."

We look at each other and say nothing.

She used to say she was sorry. I used to tell her it was okay, that it didn't matter. Now we just look at each other then look away, pretending nothing's happened.

She pulls down her sock and I look at the tattoo, which is gray and red with a bit of blue in the middle.

"Looks like a smudge."

"It's a turtle dove! . . . And it itches." She scratches the turtle dove so hard that I think it might come off. I shake my head at my sister. Beth covers her tattoo and gets up, and we stand side by side with the monitor beeping every thirty seconds beside us. We look out at the big gray building opposite with the sun shining on its windows and all the people inside sitting at their desks, staring at their computers. I see them come in and I see them leave, and during the nights and over the weekends I see the empty seats and the lights on dim until Monday morning when all the people come back again.

The air conditioner clicks, pushes cold air around the room, and makes me shiver. Beth asks me if I'm okay and I nod.

"It's too hot outside, but it feels cold in here."

"Is it hot enough to make asphalt melt?" I ask.

"No, not that hot." She smiles then puts her arm around me, and we stand looking out of the window, watching the planes as they fly above the tall buildings on the flight path in and out of Heathrow. It's the only window I can look out of, now. There used to be one that let me see into the corridor and watch the doctors and nurses walk by. But one day the maintenance man came to cover it up with a special white paint that stuck to glass. I asked them why they did it and they said it was for privacy. I told them I couldn't hear what they were saying. They smiled, said that's not what they meant. I don't want any more privacy, though. I have too much of it already.

Beth squeezes me very gently—any tighter and she would bruise me. I'm glad that she's not afraid to touch me. Whenever the doctors have to touch me because they're doing an examination or helping me, they hold me like I'm glass. That's why I'm so lucky to have Beth. She says she's lucky to have me too; that she wouldn't know what to do without me. Sometimes, just after she's left, I wonder what that would be like. She'd be able to get a boyfriend and stay with him, or she could go out more with her friends. She wouldn't have to worry when she's in her university classes. But she says she's happy spending her time in here with me.

Outside, a man in gray coveralls walks across the roof of the office building with a brown bag in his hand. He walks between the black poles and silver tubes, checking the pigeon traps in the gutters, then he takes a knife out of his bag, bends down, opens a cage, grabs a pigeon, and slits its throat.

Beth turns away.

"I don't know how you can watch," she says.

"It's not that bad."

We turn away and walk back to the bed, past the emergency oxygen tanks and the gray monitors with their flashing red lights and green numbers.

**Heart rate:** 79
**Body temp.:** 37.4C
**Room temp.:** 18C
**Air purity:** 98.5%

The drop in air purity is because she's in the room.

I lie down, Beth squeezes onto my bed, and we watch TV while the monitors beep and the sensors in the corners of the room flash every second, my heart rate and body temperature transmitted from sensors on my body by Bluetooth. Footsteps pass faintly by outside and I smell coffee I can't drink and food I can't eat. Me and Beth get tired of watching TV, so I flick through my iPad for books and magazines I can't have printed copies of, and she listens to music until my food comes through the hatch at five. It's my superhero power-up food, vacuum-sealed in silver foil. It doesn't taste very nice but it gives me energy. Most importantly, it keeps me alive. I open the foil and eat dried beef and rice while the sky turns from blue to gray outside.

At seven o'clock Beth gets up, kisses me on the forehead, then walks past my poster of Theo Walcott toward the door. Her white suit makes her invisible against the wall, kind of like Sue Storm from the Fantastic Four. She presses the call button and waits. I don't want her to go. The nights feel so long after she's been here. The door opens and she looks back.

"I'm not sure when I'm here again," she says. "I've got a dissertation to write."

"It's okay."

"Maybe the day after tomorrow."

She smiles again then slides between the door and the frame, as though not opening the door too wide will stop the germs from getting in. I look at the white door and imagine her on the other side, taking her suit off in the transition zone. She'll be putting her street clothes back on and pulling the elastic bands out of her hair. Then she'll talk to the nurses and check my graphs. She says she likes looking at them, not just because they're about me, but because they'll help her at med school, where she's studying to be a doctor. She's got to do a residency soon. She says she doesn't know where or exactly when she will go, only that she won't be going yet.

I walk over to the window and look down as she crosses the road between the cars and buses stuck in traffic. When she reaches the other side, she turns and looks up at me. I smile and wave, and she waves back at me, then leans against the wall and looks at her phone. Every so often she looks up, sees I'm still looking, and shakes her head, laughing. I rest my head against the glass, feel it cold on my skin.

My head starts to spin. I swallow and taste metal on my tongue as blood trickles out of my nose and over my lip. At first it spots on the window sill, then it begins to splatter. I hold my nose with my finger to stop the flow. Beth waves as a bus arrives and blocks her out. I want to stay and watch her go but my legs are wobbling, going numb. I put both hands on the sill. Blood pools in the palm of my hand and drips down onto my T-shirt, my trousers, the radiator, and then the floor. The gray building is a fog; the traffic is a blur. I need to make it to my bed . . . I need to make it

to my bed. The monitor is closer. I fall against it and press
the red button.

I'm on my bed, on my side. Greg is holding my nose with a
gloved hand.

"It's okay," he says. "You're doing okay."

I try to smile. He smiles back, then gently lets go of my
nose and presses the button to bring my bed upright.

"Here." He gives me a swab and lifts my hand up to my
nose. "Hold it, there."

My head begins to clear. I look around the room.

"Sorry about the mess."

He smiles. "It's okay, mate, just tilt your head forward."

He checks my pulse and my temperature while another
nurse I don't know checks the monitors. She clicks a button—
there's a hum of a motor, the rush of air, and I'm cold again.
Greg comes back to me.

"Let me look," he says. He lifts my hand away from my
nose, mops my blood off my face, and gives me a clean swab
so I can do it myself.

"You've been doing too much," he says.

"Too much talking?" My voice sounds funny because I'm
pinching my nose.

Greg smiles and I want to smile too, but I'm scared that
if I do the blood will come again.

"Yeah."

I look down at the red stains on my T-shirt, on my trousers, on the bed, at the spotted trail that goes back to the

window. There's a red smudge on the glass. Greg mops my forehead.

"I told you, I'm not worried about the mess, Joe. But *this* should be round your neck and not on the bed."

"Sorry." I take the panic button. The nurse asks Greg if he can manage. Greg nods and the nurse smiles at me as she leaves. I lie back a bit while Greg goes into my bathroom and comes back out with a pair of pajamas. I take my hand away from my nose.

"Yeah, it's good, mate," he says. "Change into these when you're ready." He puts my pajamas down then goes back to the bathroom. I hear the sound of running water and smell disinfectant. Greg comes back out with a bucket. I swing my legs over the bed and take off my T-shirt as he wipes my blood from the window.

"Maybe you should take it easy tonight, maybe just rest, no laptop or anything."

I put my pajama top on and look down as I do up the buttons. There's a red mark on my white body where the blood has seeped through. I don't want to shower tonight, though—I'm too wobbly. Greg shakes his head; he knows I hate showers.

"I saw nothing," he says.

I smile, and do up the last two buttons and change my bottoms while Greg mops the floor.

After he's done he comes back and checks on me again, then watches the machine for a few moments before lowering the blinds and dimming the lights.

"You want some music, mate?" he asks.

I nod and he walks over to my laptop and clicks on Spotify, but it plays so low I can hardly hear. I ask him to turn it up but he says it's loud enough, and then he walks toward the door.

"I'll check back in an hour, maybe sit with you for a bit," he says.

"You could stay now if you like."

He looks at me like he wants to, but it's like someone has gotten hold of his arm and is pulling him outside.

"In an hour, mate," he says, "if you're still awake."

I reach down by my side for the TV remote. Greg shakes his head and leaves me alone. Then I hear a buzz from my phone on the side table.

Joe, keep ☺. I'll be back tomorrow.

I smile. She said she'd be back the day after.

I turn on the TV, flick through the channels for five minutes, then turn it off. I lie back and stare at the ceiling. The hiss of the air mixes with the music and with the footsteps and the whispers as people walk the corridors, while the lights on my monitors flash like airplanes in the night. I wonder what Beth is doing and who she's with. I wish she were with me, but most of all I wish I could be with her in her apartment. We could eat potato chips, drink Coke, and watch superhero films on TV. But I can't go there. I can't even walk outside onto the street, because if I step outside of my room I could catch any disease in the world and die.

# TWO

## 11 YEARS, 2 MONTHS, AND 22 DAYS

**Greg is standing** by the monitors when I wake up the next morning.

**Heart rate:** 79
**Body temp.:** 37.3C
**Room temp.:** 18C
**Humidity:** 7%
**Air purity:** 98.0%

"All right, mate," he says. "Let's get this done." He leans over me and wraps a blood pressure cuff around my arm. "Okay?"

I nod. He presses a button and the cuff inflates like a balloon. My arm throbs like it's being blown up too.

Greg looks at the reading. "130 over 85," he says.

"That's okay."

"Well, it's not too bad," he says. "Maybe a little bit high. We'll just keep an eye on it." He types all the readings into his tablet while I check my pajamas to see if any more blood came in the night. I'm clean except for some dried blood on my fingers and a watery red stain on my sleeve. Greg slowly raises the blinds and for a moment he stands there with his head tilted like he's spotted something interesting on the street below. I ask him what he can see.

"Nothing much, mate," he says. "Just some workmen getting ready to dig up the road."

I lift my legs off my bed.

"You don't have to get up yet, mate."

"I want to," I say. "It feels like I've been lying here for ages!" I put my hand on my bed to help me keep my balance, then walk over to the window.

"There's not much to see, mate. But they're right down there." Greg points to the end of the street. I see two blue vans and four men wearing orange jackets. Two of them are setting up traffic lights; the other two are getting shovels and drills out of the van. I'd like to stay and watch for a while but my legs are beginning to ache. I turn and walk toward the bathroom, past my poster of Thor holding up a bridge with one hand. I wish I was as strong as him today, but even superheroes have to rest, Greg says. Even Spider-Man can't be out saving the world all the time.

I take off my pajamas and get in the shower. I hear Greg sliding a chair across the floor—he'll sit outside and check I'm okay. I press the water button, then another for soap.

The water is thirty-four degrees. The soap smells of nothing.
While I wash, Greg shouts to me. He tells me about his girlfriend, Katie, that she's been working late every night this
week and he's looking forward to seeing her. There's football
on TV tonight but he doesn't think he should watch it.

"But it's Man United!" I shout back.

"And she's my girlfriend." He laughs and starts talking
again as I put soap on my arms and my legs, then wash it
off. I stop the water, check my skin for new bruises but
I only find old ones—two on my left shin from where I
knocked against the radiator last week. I wish they would
wash away like dirt. Greg's still talking about football. I
lift up my arm, wash underneath and then the side of my
body. I lift up my other arm and do the same. I feel a
bump halfway down my ribs. I run my hand over it again.
It doesn't hurt but I just know that it's there. I turn the
water off, check again, shout to Greg. He comes in, opens
the shower door.

"You okay?" He hands me a towel. I wrap it around my
waist.

"I've found one," I say.

"Have you? Show me."

I lift my arm. Greg narrows his eyes, bends down, then
gently presses his fingers against my ribs.

"Must have gotten it when you fell yesterday."

"Against the monitor?"

Greg nods and presses the bruise again.

"Do you think it's okay?"

Greg makes an *umm* sound. "Yeah" he says. "Pretty sure, it's more brown than purple."

I look again, count how many ribs the bruise covers. Greg looks up at me and ruffles my hair.

"Hey, mate, it'll be fine."

I smile but I know that the doctors will want to check.

He leaves me to get dressed.

When I'm done, I find Greg standing in my room, checking the monitors and making notes. I sit in my chair with my laptop, look for messages on Facebook and Skype, and wait for the doctors to come in.

It's 9.32 a.m. when they arrive—Dr. Moore and Dr. Hussein. They say good morning, ask me how I'm feeling, and I tell them I feel okay and they check the charts. Dr. Moore points and traces the line across the graph with his finger. Dr. Hussein nods and they whisper something I can't quite hear. Dr. Moore looks over the top of his glasses.

"You sure you're okay?"

"Yes," I say. But then Greg gives me a look, so I tell them about my nosebleed and the bruise under my arm. They look at Greg's notes, then up my nose, and I wince when Dr. Hussein looks at my bruise and presses too hard.

"Sorry," he says.

"It's just a mild contusion," I say. "The type you can get from falling off a ladder, or off a curb, but not the type you get from getting hit by a car."

Dr. Moore smiles and shakes his head. "A mild contusion, Dr. Hussein?"

Dr. Hussein nods.

"Then a mild contusion it is, young man." Dr. Moore ruffles my hair. "Maybe we should all just read Wikipedia instead of studying at university for half our lives." He grins, and then he walks to the monitor and tells Greg to keep the temperature constant. Greg points to the air purity figure. It's gone down to 97.5. They talk about filters and particles, that maybe they should increase the cleaning or reduce the number of visitors.

"Maybe we should," says Dr. Moore, ". . . and maybe postpone the television people."

"Do we have to? Can't you just change the filters?"

"Just for a day or two, Joe. It's not just that. We have to work out what's going on inside of you at the moment."

"But I feel okay!"

Dr. Moore bites on his lip as he looks at my chart again.

"Joe, it's the third nosebleed in eight days."

I nod. I know that. I don't need the chart to count — yesterday, then three days ago, and four days before that. It's the third one since they started the new treatment. They're trying a new drug to keep my white blood cells up. If it works, it won't cure me, but it will stop my body getting so many infections and I won't have to have so many blood transfusions. I hate blood transfusions. It's when they give me new blood. It doesn't hurt but it makes me feel sick the day after.

Dr. Moore takes a deep breath.

"More blood tests?"

"Yes, I think so, Joe, just to be safe."

He tells Dr. Hussein to arrange a test for tomorrow

morning, and then they press some buttons on the monitor and walk back toward the door. They say good-bye and tell me they'll see me soon. I look down at my bed. Greg sits back down beside me.

"Hey, mate. It's just for a day."

"But I love it when the TV people come!"

"I know, mate. Let's see how it goes."

I look back at the monitors. I wish I could change the numbers with my mind. Make the air purity go up, make my temperature go down, keep my heartbeat constant. But I can't control them. My body does that. Not very well, though.

"Does it mean Beth can't come either?" I ask.

"Of course she can."

I lie back on my bed, hear my breath, and in the distance I can hear the low buzz of the workmen's drills outside. Greg stays with me for ten minutes until his shift ends and the new day nurse arrives.

The new nurse started yesterday. He doesn't talk to me much. All I know is that his name is Amir and that he's come to England from India. I only know that because it's what Greg told me, and he only told me that much because that was all Amir had told him.

Greg gets up and says "hello" when Amir comes in and Amir says "hello" back, but his words are muffled behind his mask. Greg shows him where stuff is, asks him if he has any questions. Amir shakes his head and mumbles that he's okay. Greg holds his arms out and shrugs behind Amir's back. I want to laugh but I can't because Amir is looking right at me. Greg slides out of the door. I wait for Amir to say something but he doesn't. He just walks around my room, slides the chair back into the corner, ties the string on the blinds, smooths his hand over the monitor, then presses his finger against the red light and for a moment it glows bright. I want to tell him that he looks like E.T., but it's hard to talk to strangers. It's easier if they talk to me first. People who come in from the outside have things they can say—they can tell me what they did last night, what time they got up, why they're unhappy, why they missed the bus. But I can't tell them what I did yesterday because it was the same as the day before and the day before that. I could tell him that I don't have anything interesting to say but you're not supposed to start conversations like that. And it's even harder to talk to people who wear a mask because I can't tell what they're thinking as easily. Some of the new people wear them when they first start. They say it's to stop me catching things, but when they leave after a few days I think it's because they are more scared of catching things off of me.

Finally Amir walks over to the window and stops. He looks across at the gray building opposite, then up at the sky. A plane flies across it and he turns his head and watches it fly over the Lucozade building toward Mercedes-Benz. Then he turns his head to look back to where the plane came from.

"We're on the flight path," I say.

Amir jumps and looks at me with his eyes bulging above his mask.

"We're on the flight path for Heathrow."

He doesn't say anything; he just looks at the planes in the sky. It's only been a day but maybe he's already wishing he was out there with them instead of being stuck in here with me.

I look up at the clock. It's nearly 11 a.m. I flip up the lid of my laptop (I've got a science lesson this morning), look at the screen, then glance over the top. Amir sighs, walks away from the window, and then stops by the door.

"You let me know if you want anything," he says.

"Okay."

He opens the door and in a second he's gone.

I wish the people didn't change so often. It's like they only stay until I've got to know them and then they move somewhere else and new people come in and I have to start all over again.

I click on my laptop and start my lesson with Sarah. Sarah is my science teacher. She has brown hair, brown eyes, and wears a blue cardigan. I don't know if she has any legs but I do know that when she says my name the *J* sounds like a *D* and the *O* sounds like an *E*, so she calls me Dew not Joe. Sarah doesn't talk to me about TV, football, or the weather. All she talks to me about is science. It's the only way I can learn without the risk of people bringing me infections. Sometimes she is there for real and we can talk, but today I think that maybe she has gone on holiday because she's left me a video of her to click on.

I have to do this lesson for two hours every week. I don't get holidays the same time as other kids because I miss school when I'm doing poorly. Today's lesson is about resonance. I click on Sarah's picture. The screen changes to a diagram of two boxes side by side with two wires inside. I close my eyes, open them again. It's only been a few seconds but I already feel like yawning. I look at my browser, think of going on YouTube, maybe Spotify. It's not like Sarah's here to check I've done it. I fast-forward. A picture comes up of sound waves beating down from a boat to the bottom of the ocean. I go to click on the boat but the Skype icon at the bottom of my screen starts flashing. I click on it.

Hi Joe                                                        11:10 AM

I smile.

Hi Henry.  What are you doing?                    11:10 AM

The pencil scribbles on the screen.

Stuck in a bubble ... You?                           11:11 AM

Stuck in a bubble.                                      11:11 AM

Ha.                                                           11:12 AM

You doing much today?                              11:12 AM

Learning physics from a cartoon. Waiting for Beth.

**You going out of your room?**                    **11:13 AM**

No ...Too hot ...The cooling system broke
yesterday.                                         11:14 AM

**Ha.**                                            **11:14 AM**

I fried!                                           11:14 AM

I smile again and feel warm inside.

**Want to go to screen?**                          **11:15 AM**

Henry feels more like my real friend when I can actually
see him.

Sure.                                              11:15 AM

**They're digging up the road outside.**           **11:15 AM**

Show me.                                           11:15 AM

We switch to video. Henry's smiling face fills the screen
and we wave. I take my laptop over to the window and tilt
it so the camera is pointing down the road. I show Henry
the roadworks, the yellow diggers, and the traffic lights, and
then I pan it across the street, show him the people walking
in the rain past the shop fronts, then the buildings up above,
the big tall windows, one stacked upon another, and then I

show him the gutters and the roofs. I stop by the building opposite and tell him that's where the man in the gray coveralls comes out and slits the pigeons' throats.

"Wait until he comes out again," he says.

"I can't see him. Maybe he's having a cup of tea."

"Show me tomorrow then."

I move the camera on, more rooftops, more shop doorways, more people walking in the rain.

"See, nothing much happens."

"Wanna see out my window?"

"Sure." The screen goes white.

"Henry!" I say. "Don't point the camera at the sun."

"Oops, sorry." He angles the camera down. I see the big redbrick buildings sticking up into the sky, and a park and a cemetery with white headstones that stretch out for miles. Henry told me it's called Clark Park—children play football and baseball there.

The cemetery is called Woodlands. Henry thinks people go there straight from the hospital morgue. The camera starts to shake.

"Henry, are you okay?"

"Yeah, I'm good. Just walking to the other window." He turns the camera. I see his blond hair and smiley face again. He's always so happy to show me around. He gets out of the way and I see more red buildings, cars and buses going down straight roads, stopping at the lights, and in the distance I see a ferry crossing a river. It's the Schuylkill River that splits the city in half. Then he sits down on his bed.

It's only taken us ten minutes to do our window tours.

He tells me he thinks London looks great today. I tell him his streets look more interesting than mine. He laughs and tells me it's boring, that I only like America because it looks so exciting in films.

I hear a door click open. Henry looks up over the top of his screen.

"Hey, Brett's here." He turns his screen. Brett is Henry's favorite nurse. He's tall and skinny and he's got spiky hair like Bart Simpson. He bends down and waves at me.

"Hey, dude," he says. "How you doing?"

"I'm okay," I say. "How are you?"

"Yeah, I'm good. Sorry, but I've got to check on this guy and give him his meds."

"It's okay. I'm going to go, Henry. Catch you later."

I close down my laptop. I like chatting with Brett, but I hate seeing the needles. Greg says it's psychological, that I'm hyper-empathetic. It's just a complicated way of saying that whenever they stick a needle in Henry, it feels like it's going into me. I don't know when it started to happen, only that it did.

Henry is my best friend. He's American and lives in a hospital in Philadelphia where his doctors think he has the same condition as me. Or maybe I have the same condition as him, because he's three years older than me so has been trapped in his bubble three years longer than I've been trapped in mine. But Henry might be going outside. Not forever, just for an hour or so. A scientist from NASA has made him a space suit with special lightweight oxygen tanks. So far he's only worn it in his room, but yesterday they let him walk to the end of the corridor. It sounds like they've still got some technical problems, but I think Henry will be going outside soon. I wish I was too. I wish I could go outside and walk with the people down the street. They might just be going to work, but I'd love to walk with them in the sun or in the rain and I'd talk to them without worrying that I might die every time I take a breath. I'd like to go a park and kick a ball and throw a Frisbee for a dog. I've never been to a park and the only time I've ever seen a dog is on TV. Henry hasn't seen one either. He saw a cat outside his window once, but I think he must have been dreaming because his window is two hundred feet up in the air.

When I was nine, I dreamt the doctors were going to fly me over to visit him. I told Henry, and we planned what we would do if we could hang out. He would bring Madden NFL 13 and I would get FIFA 13, and then we would watch old films. Henry wanted to watch *Terminator*—he would bring all four of them, and we'd stay up all night and drink our glucose drinks and play music. But the director of his hospital wouldn't let us do it in real life. He said it wasn't practical or safe for either of us to travel ten miles in a car, let alone three thousand on a plane. So we just use Skype instead.

I close down my laptop and think of him in his room. His doctors are trying something new, too. They're injecting him with something called Amphotericin B to fight off fungal infections. If it works for him then maybe it'll work me too. Last year they gave him extra vitamin D because he was sweating lots and his bones were aching. It made him hallucinate and be really thirsty. Two weeks later they tried the same with me. It made me dizzy and sick. It made me think that maybe me and Henry don't have the same thing after all; we just live in the same kind of place.

I hear a buzz by my side and pick up my phone. There's a picture of Beth on the screen and a message. She says she's sorry but she's got an assignment to finish and she won't be able to make it to me until five. I tell her it's okay, pick up the remote, and turn on the TV. The news headlines are on. There's pictures of big tanks with soldiers marching beside them somewhere in Russia, another picture of a plane and a map of the Indian Ocean, and a photograph of a boy who's raised a million pounds for cancer just by posting things on Twitter, and then there's a weather map of Britain saying it's 34C outside.

I change to the DVD remote and watch *Avengers Assemble*. It's the third time I've seen it, even though Beth only bought it for me last week. She's always buying DVDs for me. Once I asked her how she could afford them all; she just said they weren't that expensive and sometimes she just borrows them from her friends. But she never takes them back. I really love Beth. She's the only relative I have left who can visit me since Mum and Dad died.

Halfway through the film my head begins to ache and my eyelids begin to drop. I turn the sound down and close my eyes, hear people screaming, things crashing, and Thor shouting. My head feels light and I can't feel my legs or my feet.

\* \* \*

*Buildings rise up out of the dark and they're on fire. The streets are filled with cars that have crashed into one another and people are running and yelling and I'm running with them. Webs or jets? Webs or jets? Jets are quicker but web-slinging is cool. But I'm a superhero. I'm here to save people, not to have fun. I press a button on my chest and flames shoot from my feet. A car flies through the air toward me. I stop it with my hand and put it gently back down on the road. Another car, a falling lamppost, three children are standing underneath it. I flick my wrists and press two fingers into my palm, and then my webs wrap around them and pull them out of the way. I hear a rumble and look up. A building is tumbling down above me. The people are running and screaming between flying pieces of metal and concrete. I try to run with them but the asphalt is cracking and the earth's core is burning below. More metal, more concrete. I run through it all, protecting myself with Mjolnir's force field. Mjolnir is the name of Thor's hammer, but now I have it. I can protect anyone and anything. I'm Spider-Man, Thor, and Iron Man. I'm all the superheroes rolled into one. Gotta go! There's a man on a ledge whose clothes are on fire. I engage my jets and fly up into the sky. . . .*

The TV screen is blank when I wake up. There's a glass of water and a silver packet of food beside me on the table. The clock says 7:50. I turn my head. Beth is in the chair beside me. She pulls her earphones out of her ears.

"Must be tiring saving the planet."

"How did you know?"

She nods at my sheet all crumpled up at the end of my bed. "Well, it was either that or you were having a great game of football." Beth puts her hand on my arm.

"You okay?"

I nod. "Yeah, it's just too quiet today."

She rubs my arm. "And you're still tired?"

I smile even though I don't feel like it. I take a deep breath. "Another blood test tomorrow," I say.

"I know. Dr. Moore called me. Don't worry."

"The TV people might not come."

She rubs my arm again.

"Let's just wait and see. Hey, I've got something for you." She reaches down by her side and hands me a plastic bag. I pull out a new Arsenal shirt, a T-shirt with a picture of Spider-Man hanging upside down, and a pair of new pajamas.

"Thanks!" I say. "Sorry I keep getting blood on them."

"It's okay. It's not like you can help it."

I take off my T-shirt and pull the Spider-Man one over my head. Beth reaches out and fluffs up my hair.

"It looks good," she says. I brush my hand over my T-shirt. The cotton presses against my skin. Spidey has already been washed and sterilized before I get to wear him. That's what happens to all my clothes. Me and Beth usually pick them out together online or she'll send me pictures of things when she's out shopping. I like to pick my own clothes, especially my sneakers.

Beth takes a deep breath. "So, what's the new nurse like?"

I shrug. "I don't know. He doesn't say much. He just moves things around and then watches the planes."

Beth laughs. "Maybe he wishes he was on vacation."

"Maybe he's wishing he could escape the bubble."

Beth sort of smiles, then rests her head on her hand and her hair falls down the side of her face and covers the little red scar on her cheek. My laptop makes a *da-lute* sound beside me. I look at the clock. It's 8 o'clock at night in London. It's 3 o'clock in the afternoon in Philadelphia. Henry is waiting to talk to me again already.

Another beep.

Beth tells me I can talk to him if I want. I tell her I'd rather talk to her. She smiles.

"Okay," she says. "Tell me what else you've done today . . . apart from saving the planet and watching the nurse watch the planes."

I shrug. "I learned what 'resonance' means."

"Really, what is it?"

"I think you know."

"I don't; tell me."

I tell her about the two boxes with the wires in them, that if you touch one it makes a noise and then the one in the other box does the same even though it hasn't been touched. She nods like she understands.

"So you do know?"

"No," she says. "But I think that's what Paul told me happens with guitars." She bites her lip and looks back at the ground.

"It's okay. You can talk about people outside."

She smiles and stands up.

"But you're not going now, though?" I feel a bit panicky.

"No, you idiot. Slide over." She sits on my bed and puts her arm around me.

I pick up the remote, turn on the TV, and flick through the channels. I can feel Beth's body move as she breathes.

"You can bring him to visit me if you want."

"Maybe I will," she says, putting her hand on top of my head.

I flick to another channel. I don't think she will bring him, though. Jon was the last one to come here. He'd been going out with Beth for two months. I liked him and I think he liked me, but two weeks after he'd visited, Beth told me he had left. She said they had been arguing, that she couldn't finish her assignments because of it. But I wonder if it's because she spends all her time visiting me.

My laptop beeps again.

"He's getting impatient." She squeezes me. "Go on, talk to him, I don't mind."

I reach over.

Hey Joe. What are you doing?                          8:01 PM

Stuck in a bubble. You?                               8:01 PM

Stuck in a bubble.                                    8:01 PM

Beth laughs, then lies back against the pillow.

Go to screen?                                         8:02 PM

I go to screen but all I can see is blurry pink and I can hear the echo of Henry laughing. He pulls his finger away from the lens and leaves it stuck up at me. I do the same back. I turn my laptop toward Beth.

"Hello, Henry." She waves.

"Hello, Beth." Henry waves back.

Henry's room is bigger than mine. He's got a sofa and a TV area, and another table by a window where he can sit and eat. He says it's like a penthouse and that if he lives long enough he might take over the whole of the top floor and have a 360-degree view of Philadelphia. Then he'll be able to see the Comcast Center, Liberty Place, and City Hall, and on clear days he should be able to see the Philadelphia Eagles play.

Henry puts his face close up to the screen. "So what are you going to do, just stare at me?"

I smile, switch to text so I can message him and talk to Beth at the same time. It's great that he's my friend, even if it is like he lives inside a computer.

# THREE

"Joe . . . Joe!"

I feel a hand on my shoulder.

"Joe, you've been dreaming."

I open my eyes. I'm sitting at the window with Greg by my side. My pajamas are wet and stuck to my skin. I wrap my arms around my body and try to stop myself from shaking.

Greg puts his hand on my shoulder.

"You okay, mate?"

I nod. He takes hold of my left arm, leads me across the room, and sits beside me on the edge of my bed. I shiver. He hands me a T-shirt. I glance at the monitors.

**Heart rate:** 98

**Body temp.:** 37.5C

"It's okay," Greg says. "They're under control."

I feel my heart thudding through my ribs. It's still

pumping like crazy; it must have been over a hundred when I was dreaming.

"Want to tell me about it?"

I put my T-shirt on and then stare ahead. It takes a while to come back to the real world after I've had a dream. So many things can happen when I close my eyes. I can go to so many places. Last night I was running with geckos in the desert; the night before I was catching tuna fish in the sea; the night before that I was running away from an erupting volcano.

Greg leans forward. "You don't have to tell me," he says. "Just sometimes it's helped, hasn't it?"

I stare out into the darkness and shrug. My dreams can be scary—but they're exciting, too. I like being in those places. It's the waking up I don't like.

Greg taps my knee.

"Come on, mate," he says. "Maybe try and get some sleep."

I lay back on my bed. Greg sits down in the chair next to me. I look up at the ceiling, take a deep breath, and feel my heart thud in my chest. I try to sleep but my head is too busy thinking. I can't stop my legs moving and my eyelids won't stop flickering no matter how hard I try to keep them still. It's a side effect of the new drug, like it's fighting with all the other drugs in my body to keep all the infections away.

I turn my head. Greg's sitting in the dark looking at me with his chin resting on his hand. He smiles. I roll over on my side.

"Tell me about the other kids. Tell me what they've all been doing today.'

Greg laughs. "I told you before, mate. They do the same as you . . . go on their laptops and watch TV all day."

"But they must do other things, too."

Greg tells me about all the other patients he looks after, the ones in the other wards that stay in here long term. There are six of us at the moment. I'm the only one with Severe Combined Immunodeficiency. It takes a long time to say it, so the doctors call it SCID for short. It's when kids are born with no immune system to fight off disease. It can make them really ill or they can even die. Most of the time the doctors find a cure, but until they do, the kids have to stay in a bubble like me. I've got super SCID. I'm the only one who has got it in the country. It sounds exciting but it's not. It just means the doctors are still looking for a cure and I might have to stay in a bubble longer than everyone else. The other kids Greg looks after have cancer or degenerative diseases. None of them have been here as long as me—they either die or get cured and are allowed to go back home. Greg calls us all "mate." He never uses our real names. He only really tells me how old they are and the diseases that they've got. There's a kid in ward six who everyone thought was going to die. He's been here for two months and he's had two blood transfusions and a bone marrow transplant. Greg says he can't be certain but he thinks the kid might be able to go home soon. Then he tells me about a kid in ward eight who's really funny; after his hair fell out he got some paint from the day room and painted his head red and now he runs around the ward pretending he's a billiards ball.

Greg looks at me like he's waiting for me to say something, but all I can think of is the kid who's had the blood transfusions and how many I've had—so many I lose count. I'm glad they found out what was wrong with him earlier than they found out what was wrong with me. They think he's getting better now, that he'll be able to go home and see his family soon, and I wonder what he will feel like packing his bags up here and then unpacking them when he reaches his bedroom. I wonder if he will be able to sleep after all those weeks of listening to the beeps of the monitors. I wonder if I ever got to leave whether I would miss the sound, because it's been with me nearly all of my life. Beth told me that Mum thought I would only be in here for a day or two when she bought me in. I was only two months old. She thought I had a cold at first, that maybe I caught it off Beth. But then my nose wouldn't stop running and I was shaking, but no matter how many blankets she wrapped me in they couldn't seem to get me warm.

I roll over onto my back.

Thunder rumbles outside my window. Greg gets up, walks across the room, and peers out through the blinds.

Another rumble, a flash of lightning that lights Greg's face up white.

"Can I look?"

"It's late, mate."

"Please!"

Greg shakes his head, slowly. "I don't know . . ."

I keep looking at him, hoping that he will change his mind.

"Come on then, I guess you wouldn't be able to get to sleep anyway."

He pulls back the blinds and I get up out of bed and stand beside him.

Outside, the orange streetlights and green traffic lights are sparkling, and the roads look like they're steaming as cars drive through the rain.

On the far side of the street people run along the pavement, some with bags or folders over their heads. They dart through the traffic as a flash of lightning turns the buildings black, and I count to ten before I hear another rumble of thunder.

I shake my head.

"What's wrong?"

The traffic lights have now turned red and the car brake lights are blurred. Some people are still running; some are sheltering under the buildings trying to get their breath.

"I wouldn't run if I was out there."

"Then you'd get bloody wet, mate."

"I wouldn't mind."

Greg laughs. "So what would you do?"

I shrug because what I'm thinking seems stupid. But it's just rain—people see it all the time; it doesn't hurt them. If I was out there I'd stand still and let it fall on my head, let it drip off my hair, let it soak through my clothes onto my skin.

I'd stay up all night and in the morning I'd walk through the streets until I found a park with trees and a lake and I'd lie down on the grass and let my clothes dry in the sun.

No one has ever told me what the rain and sun is like. They try, but they can't describe them in a way that I can feel. I asked Henry if he thinks about it too, but he said it doesn't rain much in Philadelphia and even if it did, when he does get to go outside he won't be able to feel it through his suit.

Greg puts his hand on my shoulder.

"Come on, mate," he says. "You need to sleep."

I turn away from the window and get back into bed. Greg pulls down the blinds and sits back in the chair. I hear the rain on the window and wonder if the kids in the other wards have gotten up and watched the storm too. I imagine us all standing in a row at our windows in silence, still, with the dull yellow lights from the corridors shining behind us as the rain falls down the glass, and I wish we could talk to each other and point because outside the traffic lights have turned green and all the cars and people are moving in slow motion without making a sound.

I turn over on my side. I want to tell Greg what I've been thinking, but it's too late because the chair is empty and all I can see is his silhouette as he leaves.

# FOUR

## 11 YeaRS, 2 mOn+HS, anD 23 DaYS

**I'm sitting on my bed** trying to read *The Boy in the Striped Pajamas*. George, my English teacher, told me it's a good book; it's like studying English and history at the same time. But it's hard to concentrate on anything when Amir is standing at the window watching the planes. He's been there for half an hour now, watching them come in to land, watching them leave, turning his head from side to side, like a cat watching birds.

I reach over for my laptop, gently lift the lid. Henry has messaged me during the night.

Hi Joe                                                04:10 AM

Joe?                                                  04:11 AM

You asleep?                                           04:11 AM

You must be.                                    04:12 AM

Ah crap.                                        04:12 AM

Are you really?                                 04:13 AM

Catch you tomorrow.                             04:13 AM

Joe?                                            05:19 AM

Just want to chat. Can't sleep, my head hurts and my legs
are aching, can't keep them still. Can't concentrate, can't
play Tekken, can't read, can't watch TV. So I'd thought I'd
talk to you. But you're not there, are you?     05:20 AM

Crap. Catch you soon.                           05:21 AM

Watching Tomb Raider now.                       06:22 AM

I wish I'd been awake to talk to him. I wish we could
change the clocks so we were on the same time.

Henry, sorry I didn't reply, I was sleeping.     10:23 AM

A shadow falls across the bed. I look up. Amir stands beside
me holding a little cup of pills in one hand and a big cup in
the other.

"You sleep late." His mask puffs out as he speaks.

"I had a dream," I say. "Then the storm kept me awake."

He holds his hand up to his mask. His eyes water as he yawns.

"Did it keep you awake too?" I ask.

"Yes, it was a bad one." He turns toward the window. "But at least it didn't stop the planes."

I wonder if he's joking, but his eyes are dark and not smiling anymore. I think of telling him that the planes always stop taking off late at night, but he should know that, especially when he spends so much time looking at the sky.

He takes my cups, puts them down on the table. I slide my feet over onto the floor and walk into my bathroom and listen as he puts the chair next to the door. I get in the shower, wash, then check my body for bruises—the two on my legs have nearly gone and the one on my ribs has started to turn yellow. I smile.

"No new bruises!" I shout.

Amir doesn't answer.

I look through the gap in the door to check where he is. I can see the chair but not the back of his head. He's supposed to stay with me; he's supposed to wait by the door. I lean forward, see the monitors, see the window, see Amir's hand on the sill. Why is he so quiet? Why does he keep looking at the sky?

I'm watching TV when the doctors arrive to take my blood later in the morning. They check my temperature—37.3C. Dr. Moore pushes his lips together as he looks at my chart.

"Looks like you had an exciting night, young man."

"I had a dream."

"Who were you this time?"

"I don't know," I say. "Greg woke me up before I had time to change into a suit."

The doctors both smile, then they ask me about my bruises as Dr. Moore wraps a tourniquet around my leg. My leg begins to thud. I close my eyes and wait for the needle to go in.

"Which is better," asks Dr. Hussein. "Webs or jets?"

"I've got both," I say. "I don't have to choose—ouch!"

Dr. Moore tuts.

"Sorry, Joe, I can't find either of them here."

I try to laugh, but all I can do is squeeze my eyes tighter as he searches for another vein. Dr. Hussein looks at my picture of upside-down Spidey on the wall.

"He's my favorite," he says.

"Do you read the comics?"

"No, but I've seen all the films."

I tell him the comics are better because of the drawings and you can use your own imagination.

"I agree," he says. "I wish I had the time." Then he goes quiet like he's said something wrong. But I don't mind. I know it's true. I do have lots of time in the day. I just don't know how many days I've got left. But that's the same for everybody.

Dr. Moore taps my arm.

"All done," he says. He hands the sample to Dr. Hussein,

who puts the little bottle in his jacket pocket. Then Dr.
Moore puts his hand on my head.

"How's your throat?"

"It's okay."

"Not sore?"

"No. It's a bit dry, but I'll drink lots of water."

"Good lad," he says.

Then they leave and I'm alone again.

I send another message to Henry—if he's up we could play
FIFA, but he doesn't reply and I think that maybe it's his big
day tomorrow. Walking around the parking lot will be tiring,
so maybe his nurses gave him something to help him sleep.

Amir brings me two Warfarin tablets at lunchtime. They
stop my blood from clotting because some of the other drugs I
take make my blood too thick and that can cause heart attacks.
Amir hands me a glass of water and I swallow the pills, and
then he helps me unseal my food and walks around the room,
checking the monitors, checking the breathing machine. I turn
on the TV to fill the silence, but it's hard to concentrate when
a man with a mask is staring out of your window. I watch a
program about a man drilling for water in the middle of the
desert until Amir goes away, and then Beth comes to see me.

She sits down beside me and I tell her about my dream
on the bridge, how we were stuck in the middle of it with
all the cars crashing around us. She says it sounded crazy
and asks me if that's why I'm feeling so tired. I tell her it was
partly that, and partly because of the storm. I tell her about
Amir, that he's still not talking; she wonders if it's because

he's shy, or he's just not good at talking to strangers.

After she's left, Henry messages me. He'd just been watching *The Expendables*. We play Tekken until I get tired. Then Amir comes in and tidies my room while I get changed for bed. It was nice to see Beth and speak to Henry, but apart from that it hasn't been a very fun day.

When I come back from the bathroom, Amir's by the window, watching the sky again. I think about what Beth said about him being shy. Just because I like listening to people doesn't mean that he has to like talking, I guess. I start to walk toward my bed. He watches me for a second, then holds out his arm.

"Come here," he says.

I stop walking.

"What is it?"

He smiles. "Come and look."

I walk over to the window and stand beside him. Outside the sky is turning red and the street is full of dark shadows. Amir's looking toward the Lucozade building, where the planes fly in and out with lights flashing under their wings. He turns and looks at me, opens his eyes wide.

"Do you believe in aliens?"

"What?" Uh-oh. Amir is a bit weird.

"Do you believe in aliens?"

"I . . . I don't know."

Amir's eyes are open wide and they seem to be getting bigger the longer I look at them.

"I do," he says. "Farmers are too busy to draw crop circles."

I bite my lip. After three days of not saying anything, he's talking to me about aliens!

"I'm not sure," I say.

Amir stands up straight, scratches his head. "But I thought you did," he says. "I've seen you watching the planes outside and the ones on your television. That Malaysian one on the news."

I shake my head. "But it just crashed."

"Not crashed. It disappeared. Dark, mysterious, sinister. That could be aliens."

He stares out of the window like any moment now a plane is going to fly over. "And another thing," he says, turning back to me. "This thing in Russia, the Crimea. If this was sixty years ago, it would be war now, already. You know why it's not?"

I open my mouth to say something, but even if I did know what to say, no words would have come out. Amir nods his head slowly. "Because of aliens," he says. "We should never have meddled with Mars."

I feel my heart beating hard in my chest. I back away from the window.

"Where are you going?"

"Umm . . . toilet!"

"Toilet? But you can't," he says.

"Why not?"

"Because you'll miss them landing." He points out of the window.

I pick my laptop off of my bed and hide it behind my

back. Amir turns around. "You hurry," he says. "They travel
faster than light."

"Okay," I say. I don't mention that if they travel faster
than light I probably won't be able to see them anyway. I
back into the bathroom. "I . . . I won't be long." I close the
door. Amir is out of his mind. He's crazy. But the hospital
wouldn't let a crazy person in. They must have interviewed
him and checked his qualifications. But maybe he didn't
even meet them? Maybe he didn't even come from India.
He might have arrived on an alien spaceship and snuck in
here in the middle of the night. I put my hands on my head.
I don't know what to do, but I can't go back out there. I need
to talk to someone. Beth will be working and I can't contact
Greg. I sit down on the toilet seat and open my laptop.

| | |
|---|---|
| **Henry!** | **7:00 PM** |
| Hi Joe. What are you doing? | 7:00 PM |
| **Something's happened.** | **7:00 PM** |
| Low whites? Don't worry, they'll transfuse. | 7:01 PM |
| **No, results not back yet.** | **7:01 PM** |
| What then? | 7:02 PM |
| **My nurse is weird.** | **7:02 PM** |

How so?                                         7:02 PM

**He believes in aliens!!!!!!!!!!!!!!!!!!**      7:03 PM

Oh, cool!                                       7:04 PM

**But**                                         7:04 PM

Can he teleport?                                7:04 PM

**What?**                                       7:05 PM

Can he teleport? Maybe he could get you
over here.                                      7:05 PM

**I'm serious!**                                7:06 PM

So am I.                                        7:06 PM

**Henry, I mean it.**                           7:06 PM

Sorry. What sort of things does he say?         7:07 PM

**He doesn't talk much. He just stands at the window all
day watching planes.**                          7:07 PM

That's weird.                                   7:07 PM

That's what I said. I'm scared.                7:08 PM

Tell Beth.                                     7:08 PM

She's working,                                 7:09 PM

Tell Greg.                                     7:09 PM

I don't know where he is. He's late.           7:09 PM

Maybe the aliens got him!                      7:09 PM

That's not funny. He's outside.                7:10 PM

Outside? Where are you?                        7:11 PM

Hiding in the bathroom.                        7:12 PM

Oh crap! Ha.                                   7:12 PM

"Joe?" Amir knocks on the door and makes me jump.
"You okay?"
"I'm . . . I'm just washing."
"Okay, I wait here."

Do they have toilets on spaceships?            7:13 PM

It's not funny.                                7:14 PM

**Maybe a black hole!**                          7:14 PM

I hear a click and look up. People are talking in the transition zone. I listen, try to work out what they are saying; one of the voices sounds like it's Greg; the other is so quiet I can barely hear but it must be Amir. I wish they would stop and Greg would just hurry up and come in so I can tell him what is happening.

I go back out into my room and sit on my bed.

**Joe, you still there?**                        7:16 PM

The door clicks open. I wait for Greg's smiling face to peer round it but all I can see is a white sneaker and a brown hand on the frame of the door.

**Got to go!**                                   7:17 PM

**Why?**                                         7:17 PM

**He's just come back!**                         7:18 PM

**From another galaxy?**                         7:18 PM

I put my hand on the lid of my laptop and close it. I can't believe Henry thinks it's a joke, but maybe I didn't explain it right. Sometimes we don't always quite understand each other. Sometimes I think it's because it's hard to tell from what we write; sometimes I think it's because we're from different countries.

Amir walks in and closes the door slowly behind him. I check the clock and wonder why Greg didn't come in—the shift changes at seven, so he should have started half an hour ago. Amir stands at the end of my bed.

"Where's Greg?" I ask.

Amir shakes his head.

"He's busy. He'll be back later."

"But he always checks on me before the others!"

Amir isn't telling me the truth. Greg always comes in.

I hear a sigh. Amir is by the window with his hands on the sill. He leans forward and puts his head against the glass. Everything is quiet and still, just the rush of the air conditioner and the beep of the machines. I hear a low hum, so I glance at the monitors. They've never made a noise like this before. The hum gets louder. I look over at the window. Amir is leaning forward. The noise is coming from him! What is he doing? I lean over the side of my bed to try to see his face.

He stops when he sees me looking.

"Headache," he says. "I'm so tired. You should try this."

"Urmm . . . I'm all right."

"No, you should. It's better than pills. You take too many pills."

"They stop me from dying."

Amir smiles. "I know. I'm just saying maybe you try new things."

"Like humming."

"Yes, like humming."

I wait for him to talk more, but all he does is screw up his face like he's in pain, then turns away and starts to hum again. I lie back on my bed. Amir is right, the drugs don't always work, but there's nothing else I can do. I have to trust the doctors because they've kept me alive for eleven years. The humming gets louder as Amir rolls his head against the glass again. I rest my head against the pillow. I'll try anything to get better. I'll take any new drug, even if they make me sick sometimes. But humming? I don't think that will work. And what does a nurse who believes in aliens know anyway?

I turn my head toward the window and watch the pigeons circle outside.

I'm lying on my bed when Greg comes in. I've got a headache and even though I've drunk loads of water my throat is sore. Greg walks around checking my monitors and writing the figures down. He says he's sorry; things have gone a bit manic. A new kid with leukemia came into one of the wards today and he had to help him settle in. I ask him if he can stay for just one minute; I've got something important to tell him and it won't take long.

"You should speak to one of the doctors," Greg says.

"No, I can't. I can't talk to them about things like this."

Greg looks at his watch.

"Maybe in a couple of hours, mate. Can you wait? Things might have slowed down by then."

I open my mouth. I want to tell him now, but he really is too busy because he's already halfway out the door before I can say his name.

I'll text Beth. She'll know what to do. I start typing my message, then put my phone down again. She worries about me too much already. And I'm not sure she'd believe me anyway. She'd probably say it was my imagination playing tricks on me.

I open my laptop—four messages from Henry.

| | |
|---|---|
| Where are you? | 7:51 pm |
| Joe! | 7:53 pm |
| Have you been abducted by aliens? | 8:01 pm |
| Joke! | 8:23 pm |

It's nearly midnight when Greg comes back. He stands at the end of my bed and whispers to see if I'm awake. I tell him that I am, that even if I wanted to sleep, I couldn't. He says he's got a few minutes now but I think that it'll take longer than that to tell him everything.

Greg sits down in the chair by the side of my bed. I roll over and look at him. He yawns, then pushes his hair out of his eyes.

"I'm sorry, mate," he says. "I'm exhausted, things went a bit crazy."

"Is he okay?"

"Who, mate?"

"The new kid."

"Yeah, he's good now. His mum and dad are with him. They're going to stay the night."

"What about the billiard-ball kid?"

"Yeah, mate, he's fine too. He's just had a bit of a reaction to a drug like you do sometimes."

"But he's all right?"

"Yeah, it just made him run around twice as fast for a while. Hey, you're nosey!"

I laugh but I'm not sure I should. I know what it feels like when the drugs go wrong. It's happened loads of times when the world moves in slow motion but inside my heart is beating double fast.

I look down at my bed.

"Hey, mate." Greg taps my arm. "I said he was okay. . . . And you had something to tell me. What is it?"

"It's okay."

"No, come on, tell me."

I smile. It doesn't feel right to talk about it now. Not when I hear about all the other kids and their problems. Maybe I've been worried about nothing, and Greg seems really tired. But then I look at the window and imagine Amir standing there waiting for the aliens. I've got to tell Greg now or I'll never get to sleep.

"It's the new nurse," I say.

"Amir?"

I nod.

"What's up? Don't you like him?"

"He's okay."

"So what is it then?"

". . . I think he might be crazy."

Greg leans forward and ruffles my hair. "We all are, mate. We've got to be to work here."

"No, this is different. He believes in aliens. . . ."

"But that's okay, isn't it? Lots of people do."

"Maybe, but they don't spend all day looking out of the window, waiting for them to land!"

Greg laughs. "Hey, Joe . . . think you've been watching too many films."

I sit up on my bed. "No, I think he's really crazy-mad. He gets really bad headaches too."

"Hey, relax." Greg puts his hand on my shoulder.

I take a deep breath.

"It'll be okay, mate. Don't worry about it. I'll talk to him. Maybe he's messing around. Or it could be he doesn't know how to talk to kids your age."

I nod and take another deep breath. Thinking about Amir being a secretly insane person is making my heart rate go up.

Greg glances at the clock.

"Do you have to go?"

He shakes his head.

"No, we've got another five minutes. Have you told anyone else?"

"Only Henry. He thinks I've been abducted."

Greg laughs and rubs my head.

"Everything's going to be fine, mate, I promise. He seems like a good guy. If there really are aliens then they wouldn't need an airport to land and I doubt they'd be coming to see Amir."

I laugh.

"Feel better?"

"Yes."

"Good man." Greg stands up. "Hey, listen, I won't see you tomorrow. It's my turn for a three-day shift this week, but I'll see you when I get back."

I nod. I already knew his shift was ending; I'd counted the days just like I always do.

I ask him what he's going to do on his days off and he tells me he's going to go with his girlfriend to see her parents. They live in a small house in Margate with old windows that rattle at night and keep him awake. I ask him if he likes going there and he tells me it's okay, that him and Katie sleep in the attic room, where if he stands on tiptoe he can look out of the window and catch a glimpse of the sea.

"Can Katie see it too?"

"Yes, but only if I pick her up."

He smiles and I smile too.

"Is she little?"

"Yeah, mate. She's not much taller than you."

"Is she nice?"

"Of course."

"Do you love her?"

"Yes."

"Are you going to marry her?"

"Might."

"Even if she doesn't like football?"

Greg laughs. "Hey, mate. I'm telling you too much."

I smile. "It's okay; I'm not going to tell anyone."

I think he's going to say something else, but he just looks at me for a long time, and then he looks down at his wrist and slowly pulls back his sleeve.

"I know," I say. "You've really got to go."

"Afraid so, mate. But it's only for three days." He puts his hand on my head. "And hey, make sure you're looking good for the TV documentary."

"Am I allowed to do it?!" I forget about the aliens for a second and am just filled with excitement instead.

"If you're feeling okay. Dr. Moore's going to check again on you tomorrow." He notices the giant smile on my face. "Ha, that cheered you up! So you're good now?"

I nod, then slide down into my bed. I listen to Greg's footsteps as he walks to the door; it clicks open and closes after he has gone. I lie in the dark and think of him talking to Amir in the morning. Everything will be fine after he does, especially now that the TV people are coming. Then I think of Greg leaving the hospital—maybe if I'm awake I'll get up and watch him cycle out onto the road. I wish I'd told him I'd do that so that he would stop at the bus stop and wave up at me. I wish I could text him, but it's too late. I pick up my laptop. Henry might have been annoying earlier but I want to wish him luck for his walk tomorrow.

**Hi Henry**                                                    **00:06 AM**

Hi Joe.                                    00:06 AM

What are you doing?                        00:07 AM

**Stuck in a bubble. You?**                **00:07 AM**

Stuck in a bubble.                         00:07 AM

Not for much longer.                       00:07 AM

**You looking forward to going out?**      **00:08 AM**

Yeah ... bit nervous.                      00:08 AM

**You'll be all right.**                   **00:08 AM**

You think?                                 00:08 AM

**Yeah. Today the parking lot, tomorrow the
world!!!**                                 **00:08 AM**

Ha. Are you OK?                            00:08 AM

**Yeah, bit tired. Going to sleep now.**   **00:09 AM**

We'll chat after I've been out. I'll be too busy getting in
the space suit to message in the morning.   00:09 AM

| OK. | 00:09 AM |
| Hey Joe! | 00:09 AM |
| What? | 00:10 AM |
| How's the alien? | 00:10 AM |
| I spoke to Greg. | 00:10 AM |
| So you're cool? | 00:10 AM |
| Yep! Really tired now. | 00:11 AM |
| OK. | 00:11 AM |
| Good night | 00:11 AM |
| Good night | 00:11 AM |

# FIVE

## 11 Years, 2 Months, and 24 Days

**Amir comes into my room** at seven. I watch him through half-closed eyes as he walks over to the window and raises the blinds. I wait for him to look to the right, over toward where the planes fly, but he just stands there looking at his shoes. Something is itching my foot. I want to scratch it but I don't want to move or he'll know I'm awake. I hope Greg spoke to Amir to tell him to be less crazy around me.

The air conditioner clicks. Amir looks up at the unit as the blades swivel, blowing clean air around the room. I scratch the bottom of my foot with my heel. Amir turns his head and looks at me. He knows I'm awake now. I don't know if I should speak or stay still. He walks past the end of my bed, opens my wardrobe, takes out a clean set of clothes, and puts them on the chair beside me. I close my eyes tight, lie still, and wait for him to leave, but his shadow is hanging over me.

"You tell him."

I look up. Amir's eyes are circles of water.

"You tell Greg about the aliens."

I push myself up onto my elbows.

"I'm sorry," I say. "I was scared."

"You shouldn't be scared of aliens."

"I'm not."

"Then you afraid of me?"

". . . A little."

Amir holds his hand against his chest and suddenly looks really sad and worried.

"I'm sorry," he says. "I not mean to make you afraid. I just thought maybe we could be friends. Anyway, superheroes shouldn't be afraid of aliens!" He looks at me, then at all the posters on the wall.

I smile. Maybe he's only a little bit crazy.

"So we can be friends?"

"Of course."

He holds out his hand. "It's okay," he says. "They clean."

I shake his hand. He looks around the room like he's lost something.

"What's wrong?"

"I thinking . . . You've got nothing to do in here." He glances at the electrical sockets in the corners, at the TV, at the window, then back at me.

"Tell you what. Now you my friend, I get us Sky TV!"

"Sorry?"

"You need Sky TV? You can get lots of channels, lots of films. You only got 47 channels, I get you 607."

"But I can't pay, and people will notice."

"It's okay," he says. "It's not a big dish and I bring my card from home. We can watch football. Who you support?"

"Arsenal."

"Snap!" he says.

I sit up. My head spins. I lean back on my pillow and wait for it to stop. Amir doesn't seem to have noticed. The worry has gone from his eyes; now they're sparkling bright. I don't understand how someone can look so sad one minute and then look so happy the next. He jumps out of the chair, walks to the end of my bed, and checks the wires on the back of the TV. I think of all the new channels I could watch. I'd have so many that I wouldn't have to go to sleep early just because there was nothing on! I could stay up all night, watch the same films as Henry, and Beth wouldn't have to spend all her money on DVDs anymore.

Amir shouts something.

"Sorry?"

He looks over the top of the TV.

"How long you been in here?"

"All my life," I say.

"All of it?"

"Nearly. Didn't they tell you?"

"That's terrible. You've been in here all your life and they don't give you Sky TV?"

I laugh. Amir is smiling at me. After being scared for so long I suddenly want to laugh. Amir is so confusing. Maybe he's not a real person. I look around the room for hidden cameras, waiting for him to take off his disguise to reveal himself as a celebrity.

Amir walks over to the window, bumping his head against it as he tries to look up at the hospital roof.

"We could put the dish up here," he says, putting his hand on the wall.

I swing my legs over the side of my bed.

"But what about the aliens?"

"They don't need dishes."

"No," I say. "I mean if you're watching TV, you won't be watching the aliens."

"That's okay. We can look out for them at the same time."

I was wrong. He's definitely still really crazy.

I check the time. The doctors will be here in half an hour and I've not even showered. I put my feet on the floor. My head spins but not as much as yesterday. I need to feel better before the doctors arrive. I don't want to miss the documentary team. I pick up my clothes and walk into the bathroom. Amir pulls his chair to the door and all the time I'm washing I can hear him talking outside. He tells me that his brother will install the dish, that he'll put wire around the edge so the pigeons won't sit on it and ruin the signal. He says his brother knows all the things like that.

I check my body again—no new bumps, no new bruises. Then I realize the TV plan won't work.

"Amir!" I shout. "It won't work, they won't let him in."

He doesn't answer so I shout again, but there's still

nothing. I dry myself off and put on my clothes.

"Amir—"

I stop. The room is quiet and still. Amir is back at the window. Dr. Moore and Dr. Hussein have arrived and are standing by the monitors. Dr. Moore has his notes clutched to his chest. Dr. Hussein is smiling without opening his mouth. I know what that smile means. I sit down on the edge of my bed.

"It's okay," I say. "Low whites?"

Dr. Moore nods.

"Yes, low whites."

"Do I have to have a transfusion?"

"No, we're going to hold off on that for a while. Just to see how you do. You're not feeling too tired, or have a sore throat?"

"No." I stare ahead and hope they can't tell that I'm lying.

The mattress sinks as Dr. Moore sits down beside me.

"Joe," he says. "There's something else, something in the platelets that's causing your anemia."

I look up. Amir's eyes are still bright. I wonder if he knows I am lying about my throat. He turns and looks out the window.

Dr. Moore puts his hand on my knee as he gets up. "Don't worry, Joe," he says. "It's just a case of working things through."

I watch the doctors leave the room. I'm glad I don't have to have a transfusion. I hate the achy dizzy feeling I get as they take the old blood out and put the new blood in. It makes my white blood cells increase, helps me fight infection, makes me stronger—but I have to lie down for the whole day afterward. The documentary people would definitely have left by then. But what about the anemia? That's when I don't have enough iron in my blood. Is it really serious? Maybe they're letting me do the documentary because it could be the last thing I do. Maybe they think I'm going to die. I think about dying a lot. It's hard not to when a monitor beeps every time my heart beats. I never, never want the beeps to stop. I might not be able to do much in here or go outside, but I've got Beth and I've got Greg. I'd miss them and I know they'd miss me. I'd rather live all my life in a bubble than die. It's cool to even be born. That's what me and Henry say.

Amir turns away from the window. The room is so quiet it's like all I can hear is the sound of us breathing and the men drilling outside. I wonder if he knew about the anemia. Maybe he did and that's why he's trying to get me Sky. Maybe it's his plan to help me watch all the programs and films in the whole world before I die. He smiles at me nervously and picks up the TV remote. The TV flickers on.

"Oh, great. *Countdown*! Do you like it?"

"No," I say. "It's for old people."

Amir looks pretend-angry. "My wife records it and we watch every night when I get home!"

I sigh. Amir walks around to my side.

"What's wrong? I upset you, Joe?"

I don't want to tell him what I've been thinking.

"It's nothing. I'm just tired of TV. Is it okay if we talk instead?"

"Talk? We going to get 607 channels and you want to talk?" He pokes me gently on the top of my arm, but not enough to bruise it. "I joking." He turns the sound down. "I like to talk too. What you want to talk about?" He sits down beside me. I look at the TV. A pretty woman picks letters off the board. I quickly glance at Amir. I've said I want to talk but I don't know how to start. I look around the room, at the monitors, the window, my laptop. The minute hand on a big clock counts away the seconds on the TV. It ticks past five seconds on toward ten. Amir slams his hand down on my bed.

"Blindworm!" he shouts.

I jump. Oh no. The craziness is coming out again. I edge to the other side of the bed.

"Sorry, I no mean to frighten you." He nods at the TV. "Blindworm, I'm right, just you see."

Oh yes, the program. Phew.

I look back at the TV. The *Countdown* clock is still ticking. Amir turns the sound up and tilts his head like he's thinking.

"Born wild," says a man with gray hair and glasses.

Amir laughs. "You can't have that! It two words."

Another man with dark hair opens a dictionary and shakes his head. The man with glasses looks down at his pad. A lady smirks beside him.

"I've got 'owl,'" she says.

"Owl,' says Amir. "Three letters. My children do that."

"The longest word is 'blindworm,'" says the man with the dictionary.

"Ha! You see!!"

Perhaps Amir is insane but also a genius. Cool.

"Wow, can you do that every time?"

"Yes," he says. "As long as there not more than six consonants. Then it gets hard. It's harder than a Rubik's Cube. I do that in twenty-three seconds. I show you. Have you got one?"

"No. I don't think they're hygienic."

"Never mind, we watch the planes instead." He turns the TV off and walks over to the window. I blink and shake my head. Amir's talking so quickly he's making me dizzy.

"Come on," he beckons.

I get up and walk across to the window. For a while we don't say anything. I look at the people walking and the traffic while Amir watches the planes. Down the road the men in orange coats are still drilling. They're getting closer every day but they're as slow as snails. I look up at the roof opposite me. The man in the coveralls is walking between the silver vents and the poles. The pigeons flap their wings, jump up and down, and bash against the cage. The man bends down, opens a cage. The pigeons flutter as he puts his hand inside. I wish they could squeeze past his arm out of the cage door. I wish they could escape his hand and fly away.

The man grabs a pigeon and slits its throat. I look away.

Beth's right. It's not nice. It's not fair that they die like that.

Amir leans forward and starts rolling his forehead against the glass. He stops, looks at me out of the corner of his eyes.

"You really should try this." He starts to hum.

"Why?"

"Just try. It's like whistling. It takes bad things away."

The man in the coveralls walks back across the roof toward the door. I put my hands on the windowsill, slowly lean forward until my forehead touches the glass. The cold of the outside comes through and cools my skin. I hum, very quietly. I don't know if it takes my bad things away, but it makes my head feel like it's lifting off.

"It nice?" Amir asks.

I close my eyes and it's as if I can feel my blood slowing down, moving in slow motion through my arms and legs, getting slower and slower until it stops and the only place I can feel it is in my head.

"Yes, it's nice."

"And don't worry." Amir stops rolling his head, looks down to the street, then back at me. He stares at me for so long it's like he's looking into my mind. "I know what you worry about," he whispers.

"Do you?" I wonder if he's an insane genius who also has psychic powers.

He taps the side of his head. "Everything will be okay."

"Will it?" It sounds true when he says it. Not like when the doctors say it.

Amir nods his head slowly. "Of course. My brother got long enough ladders to reach up here."

His head has flicked us back to talking about the TV. He's really weird but I'm starting to like him.

Amir smiles.

I smile.

We start to hum.

# SIX

## 11 Years, 2 Months, and 25 Days

**My eyes are blurry** and my head is aching when I wake up
the next morning. The sound of the drills is getting closer
but I don't think it's that. It feels like someone has taken off
the top of my head and poured hot porridge inside. Sarah
has been beeping on my laptop but I don't feel like learning
about sound waves today, especially when I know the TV
people are outside. I can hear the sound of laughter and I
recognize Graham's voice as he gets changed in the transition zone. He's the one who makes the documentary. He
made the first one when I was two and we've done another
nine since then. I can't wait to see him—not because I want
to be on TV, but because for once something different gets
to happen in my day.

I go to the bathroom and splash cold water on my face.
I still feel dizzy. I shake my head and try and clear the porridge, but it doesn't work. On the other side of the door the

voices are quieter. I stop by the door. Charlotte R. is talking.

"I don't know," she says. "I'm not sure. I was told you had to reschedule."

I hear the sound of running water and a squirt of disinfectant. I press my ear up against the door.

"Reschedule?" says Graham. "No, we've not heard anything about that. It's our last day. We want to spend it with Joe."

"But — Dr. Moore said—"

"Did you want to check, then?"

The door to the corridor clicks open. I hear footsteps. The door closes. Graham and someone I don't recognize talk in the transition zone.

"Spray everything," says Graham. "Camera, tripod, microphone."

"Everything?"

I hear the sound of metal scraping the floor, the hiss of the antibacterial fluid being sprayed.

"What is she talking about, postponing? The whole point is that these programs are about life and death."

"I know. I guess she's just doing her job."

"David, they should know it's not all about survival and recovery. We can't stop filming just because somebody dies."

They stop talking.

Die? They can't mean me. Can they? Am I about to die? It's so hard to tell, sometimes. My whites are back up. I might have a headache and I know I feel dizzy, but I'm feeling better than I did three days ago, and I haven't had a nosebleed since then. No, I don't think it's me. It could be anyone because kids die in here all the time. They might mean the boy with the billiard-ball head. But I thought he was getting better. Maybe it's the girl who chases him, pretending to be a horse, or it could be the boy who reads the *Hunger Games* all day. It could be any of them and I feel bad for whoever it is.

The corridor door clicks open.

"Sorry," Charlotte R. says, "he's not answering his pager."

"How about we get started and see how we go?"

"Okay, but I'll sit in. Then if things get too much—"

"We stop. Of course."

"Okay."

"All set, David?"

I walk back to my bed.

My door slides open. Charlotte R. walks in, followed by a young guy wearing white overalls. He's got a camera in one hand, and a silver box hangs from the other. He nods at me, puts the box gently on the ground, and then looks slowly around the room like he's landed on Mars. Charlotte R. walks over to me.

"I've told them I'll sit in for a while. Okay?"

I smile.

"But you tell me as soon as it gets to be too much."

"It won't," I say.

Charlotte R. shakes her head. "I know you want to do this, but you just tell me if you feel bad."

"I will." (I won't.)

She walks toward my bathroom and sits down in the chair outside it. I hear a knock, and then Graham walks in with a tripod in his hand and a big smile on his face.

"Hey, there he is! How are you doing, young man?"

I smile and feel warm inside. Graham makes me feel special. Just hearing his voice makes me feel like I'm the most important boy on Earth. I push myself up on my bed.

"I didn't think you were coming!" I say.

Graham leans the tripod against the wall. "Wouldn't miss it. It's not every day we get to catch a real live superhero on film." He walks over to me and rubs my head like he's my best friend. He's not my best friend, but he is the person that I've known the longest. Last year he thought it would be the last time he would be able to do the program. The BBC told him they were going to cut his money and they were only going to allow him an hour instead of a whole series, but when four million people watched me on their TVs, they decided to let Graham film again. Graham tells me I'm famous, that there isn't a day that goes by without someone asking him how I am. I don't feel famous, though. After each episode goes out, Graham forwards me emails from people who watched it, but they only last for a few weeks.

Graham sits down on the edge of my bed.

"So how are you, Joe?"

My head begins to throb. I tilt my head down and hope that it will clear. Graham gently squeezes my shoulder.

"Hey," he says. "Where's the lively lad I met last year, eh?"

"Refueling his jets and webs." I point at my Spider-Man T-shirt.

Graham laughs. "And maybe getting a bigger suit," he says. "You've grown."

"Not as big as the Incredible Hulk."

"No, not that big, yet."

My head spins again. I close my eyes.

Charlotte R. stands up and walks over to my side. "You shouldn't be doing this if you're not feeling right."

"No, I want to! I'm just a bit tired."

"You're like my kids when they were your age," Graham says. "Too tired to get up in the mornings and even when they did, they spent all day in their pajamas on their phones."

I grin. "I do that all the time."

Graham laughs. "Yes, I bet you do. You're all the same. Look," he says to Charlotte R. "I think Joe's old enough to make up his own mind."

Charlotte R. bites on her lip. I don't want to get her into trouble; she's nice.

"I'll tell you if I feel bad. I've been looking forward to this for ages. I can't stop just because I'm tired."

"Do you promise you'll say?"

"Yes."

Charlotte nods at me, then at Graham.

"Okay," she says. "Let's see how it goes." She walks back to her chair.

Graham grins at me. "Good lad." He rubs my head again and I don't know if it's because he makes me happy

or because we're getting ready to film, but suddenly I feel
better. Graham sees me looking at the camera guy.

"Ah, introductions, new cameraman—David, this is Joe.
Joe this is David." New-cameraman-David takes his eye
away from the viewfinder and waves. I wave back. New-
cameraman-David looks back through the lens and pans
around the room.

"See they've given you a sofa, Joe," Graham says, ". . . and
a new TV."

"I'm getting Sky TV, too."

"What? We can't have you watching the competition."
Graham's face goes straight, then cracks into a smile again.
He looks different from the last time I saw him. He's still
as friendly as I remember, but his hair is much grayer than
last year and his face is brown like he's just come back from
vacation. He makes me feel like my white face is practically
see-through! He looks at me for a long time like he's waiting
for me to talk but I can't think of anything to say. Graham
nods at my Theo Walcott poster.

"So, you won a trophy at last."

"Yes. But he didn't play. He was injured."

"He's always injured."

I want to say more, but I can't. I only get to meet Graham
once a year, so it's like I have to get to know him all over again.

"Tell you what, why don't we just watch the DVD to
remind us where we are." He gets up, takes a DVD out of
the silver box, and puts it in the player. New-cameraman-
David moves toward the window.

"Here we go." Graham hands me the remote and sits down beside me.

I press play.

**The Bubble Boy. Highlights.**

We watch a montage of my life: me wearing a Spider-Man suit and sitting with Mum and Dad on my birthday. Mum and Dad talking to Graham, Mum smiling, Dad looking worried, me pretending to ride an ATV around my bed. Me sitting in bed with a bald head from chemo when I had the bone-marrow transplant. Beth crying, me crying, me and Beth hugging each other after the transplant didn't work. A picture of Mum and Dad on the front of a newspaper. Doctors looking at my charts, Graham talking to the doctors. Then the camera zooms in on Graham asking me the same question every year.

"*What's it like to live in a bubble?*"

"It's great. I don't really notice."

"*What's it like to live in a bubble?*"

"It's okay. I get to be on TV."

"*What's it like to live in a bubble?*"

"It's horrible. I want to escape."

More images flash in front of me, and I feel my heart rate pick up. I glance at the monitor, and that makes it pick up even more.

Graham smiling, Graham still smiling, Graham talking into the camera—

*"And that's the extraordinary story of an extraordinary boy. A real-life superhero."*

Graham presses the eject button. David is pointing the camera right at me. The lens whirrs as it zooms in. I look at the ground, then out the window. I'm supposed to speak now but my throat closes up from the pressure and I don't know what to say. What can I say when my life highlights only last ten minutes? For other kids in the hospital it must take ages—their parents film them riding around the park, playing on swings, sliding on zip-lines, jumping on trampolines—and that's probably just one day. They've got loads to talk about. All I've got is what happens in this room and in my dreams. And no mum or dad to make the videos.

When I look up Graham gives me a smile that I think means "it's okay."

"It must be difficult," he says. "Don't think I'm ever standing here thinking it's easy." Graham clears his throat. "So," he says. "Let's talk about what's happened in the last year."

I shrug. "Not much."

"We'll pack up then, shall we, David?"

New-cameraman-David grins behind the camera, and then it goes quiet again.

"Tell you what, I'll tell you what I've been doing, and we'll see how we go from there. Okay?" I nod. I know the program is supposed to be about me, but I like to hear what's happened in Graham's life. Every year he learns more about me and I learn more about him.

"Had Libby gone to university, last time I saw you?"

"No, she was taking her A-levels."

Graham smiles. "Of course, well she's at Exeter now."

I lean back on my pillow and Graham tells me about what his family have been up to. He has a wife and two children. They live in a three-story house in Manchester but they're thinking of moving because the children have grown up and they don't have any space to park their cars. He's got a daughter called Libby who's really good at English and a son called George who's studying biology at university. He shows me pictures of them all. I tell him they've grown and that his wife looks pretty and he says he'll tell her. Then he shows me a picture of them all walking their dog on the beach. I take it and hold it really close to my face, like I'm there too. Graham is standing with his arms around his wife and Libby's shoulders. George has got his arm ready to throw a ball and the dog is getting ready to chase.

"Do you still think about going to the beach a lot?" asks Graham.

I nod. "Yes. When I see pictures like this, or ads for vacation on TV. I'd like to jump over the waves."

"Or surf, even."

"Yes, I'd like to surf, but I don't even know if I could swim."

I look at the picture again: Graham's family, the other children playing behind them, the shiny sand, the waves, frozen in time. New-cameraman-David leans against the wall by the monitors and points the camera over Graham's shoulder.

Graham leans closer to me. "Tell me what you're thinking, Joe."

My stomach goes tight. Graham glances at the monitors—95. My heart rate has increased 5 beats.

"Don't worry. It just does that. Greg says it goes nuts when I dream."

Graham chuckles, glances at the camera, then back at me. "So what were you thinking?"

"I was thinking about what it's like to walk on sand."

Graham puffs out his cheeks. "Wow," he says. "That's a hard one; it's hard to describe. Sometimes it's as hard as this floor and your feet stay firm; sometimes it's soft and your feet sink in."

"But what does it *feel* like?"

Graham turns his head. His eyes search the room. "I don't know, Joe. Maybe it feels like walking on your bed."

"But with water filling my footprints."

"Yeah, something like that."

I look back at the picture. "I like talking about your family," I say.

"Why?"

"I like seeing where you've been."

"Even though you can't go there?"

"Yes. I'm not the only one who hasn't been to the beach. Henry hasn't been either, but lots of kids that don't live in bubbles don't get to see the world, either."

"True." Graham nods. "True . . . How is Henry?"

"He's okay. We're hoping we might get to see each other soon. NASA has made him a space suit so he can go outside."

"That's great."

"Not really. He only went to the end of the corridor. But he thinks he's going farther tomorrow, and then next month he's going to the mall."

Graham smiles. "Brilliant," he says. "Tell him good luck from me. What about you?"

"I can't get a suit; I wrote to the prime minister to see if he could get me one."

"What did he say?"

"He sent me a letter. He said he'd seen me on TV. He couldn't promise anything but he'd talk to some scientists."

"Great!"

"I know. But that was three months ago."

I reach over and get the letter from my drawer. Graham reads it and shows it to the camera.

"I sent one to the European Space Agency too, but they haven't replied. Henry told me to write to Stark Industries. It's where all the Avengers work. Stark has loads of money, more than the NHS, more than NASA."

"Yes, they probably have." Graham hands me back my letter. "But what would you do . . . if you could go outside the hospital?"

"Even if they had the money I don't think the doctors would let me go outside."

"But if they did."

"I'd go and live with Beth."

"And where does she live?"

"Islington, but she's got to go away soon. It's her residency."

"Where's she going?"

"I don't know. But I hope it's not far."

Graham waits for me to say something else but my throat is aching and I can feel my eyes watering. I look down at my bed.

Graham taps his hand on my leg.

"Joe," he says. "Would you rather talk about something else?"

I swallow, shake my head, and stop the tears from coming out. "No, it's okay. I know she has to go. She wants to be a doctor. I want her to be one too."

"She'll be great," says Graham. "And what about you? What would you like to do for work?"

I look down at my hands. He always asks me that but he knows that kids with SCID die before they're old enough to get a job, if they don't get fixed.

Graham leans forward.

"Joe?"

"You always ask me that."

"I know. It's just this year the answer might be different. People change their minds as they get older."

"I won't."

"Still want to be a superhero?"

"I am a superhero. That's what everyone says."

New-cameraman-David makes a circle with his index finger and thumb and the red light goes out.

"That's brilliant, Joe."

"Have we finished already?"

"No, but you need to take a break," Charlotte R. says as she walks over.

"But I'm okay!"

David sets the camera up on the tripod.

"It's all right," says Graham. "We'll go to lunch and leave the camera running. You know what to do. Just forget it's there. Like it's a fly on the wall."

"There has never been a fly in here," I say. "There's never even been an ant."

"Ha! It's funny," he says, "but I hadn't thought of that."

"But I saw a wasp once!"

"Did you?"

"Over here." I walk over to the window. "It was down there, on the other side of the window." I point to the corner where the frame meets the wall. "It flew around all day. I couldn't hear it but I could feel the buzz through the glass with my finger. It just kept buzzing around like it was looking for a hole. I thought it would get in. I saw it on TV: wasps can eat their way through stone and concrete. Greg told me not to worry, but I did, I dreamt the room was full of wasps. They were buzzing all around me. They were in my hair, in my ears, up my nose, in my mouth, and they were flying into the air conditioner, blocking the vents, jamming the blades. They were everywhere, in the plug sockets, in the machines. I thought—"

Charlotte R. puts her hand on my shoulder. "Hey, Joe, it's okay. They're not here now."

I step away from the window. My heart is thudding and my arms are sweating. It was scary when the wasp nearly came in. Charlotte guides me back to my bed. Graham stands beside me.

"Take it easy, Joe. Just relax and we'll be back soon." He walks toward the door with New-cameraman-David.

Charlotte rubs my arm. "You just stay still and I'll check that Dr. Moore is on his way."

I nod and they leave me alone with the fly on the wall. I'm not sure what to do. I can't just stay still. People will want me to do something. It'll be boring if all they see is me lying on my bed. I look at my laptop, my TV, but that isn't actually doing anything; it's me just staying still, looking at screens. But what else can I do? I don't do anything else all day. Once, the doctors gave me an exercise bike with a DVD that I had to watch at the same time. They said it would be good for my blood supply and it would help my heart and my lungs. I pedaled for an hour. The wheels spun around but I didn't move an inch, and it felt like I was a hamster in a ball. I didn't go on it again. It's boring watching a simulator on a DVD when everyone else gets to cycle by fields. The running machine was worse. They put electrodes on my chest and wired me to the monitors. I only ran for two minutes. My heart rate went up to 142 and then I stopped. The doctors thought it was because I was tired but it was because I was scared to see my heart rate so high.

I look around the room. The red light is still flashing on the camera. I lie back and go to sleep. I have a dream, but I don't remember what it is about, only that it has wasps in it.

* * *

Rain is running down the window when I wake up. Graham and New-cameraman-David are whispering in the corner. They both turn and look at me when I sit up.

"Sorry," I say. "Don't think I did anything interesting."

"Don't worry about it," Graham says. "You were brilliant. How are you feeling? Charlotte told me Dr. Moore came by and said you're doing fine."

"I'm okay, but still tired."

"Dr. Moore said it's best that we shoot in half-hour slots and you rest in between."

I nod. "Okay." New-cameraman-David stands in the middle of the room and holds up a gadget that checks the light. Then he goes back to his camera and takes it off the tripod.

I sit with Graham on the sofa. I like talking to him but when the time goes past 3 o'clock, all I can think about is how empty the room will be when he and New-cameraman-David leave. I want to say something that will make them want to stay longer. I wish they would come more often, but I don't think I do anything interesting enough to be on TV more than I already am.

At four o'clock Amir comes in. He checks I'm okay, checks the monitors, looks out the window, hands me a cup, and gives me my pills. Graham asks him how long he's worked here, but Amir doesn't hear him. He can be so funny and noisy when he's with me but so quiet when he meets new people. He's nervous and some people don't like that. You have to wait a while for him to turn into a friend.

Amir goes into the bathroom, then turns and waves his hands behind Graham to get my attention, but I don't understand what he wants.

He opens his mouth wide and points at the sky like he's playing charades.

HAVE YOU SEEN ANY?

I shrug, and try to mouth: PLANES?

Amir shakes his head.

NO. A-LI-ENS!

Graham turns around.

Amir scratches his head.

"Are you okay?" asks Graham.

Amir nods. "I'm good. You good?"

"I'm fine . . . ," says Graham. I can tell he thinks Amir is a total loony.

"Then we all good, aren't we, Joe?" Amir winks at me and I grin back, trying to concentrate on not laughing, in case Graham thinks I'm laughing at him.

"Right," says Graham. "Where were we?"

Amir points at the window. KEEP WATCHING, he mouths dramatically.

I'm still smiling as he walks out of the door.

Graham glances up at me.

"He's . . ."

"Weird?"

"Yes."

"He is, but he's brilliant at *Countdown*."

Graham laughs. "Perfect, Joe," he says. "We're going to wrap it up there."

"Already?"

"Afraid so."

New-cameraman-David takes the tripod down and puts the camera in the silver case, then holds out his hand.

"It's been nice to meet you, Joe."

"You too." I shake his hand and then follow him and Graham toward the door.

"When will I be on TV?" I ask.

"Next Monday," he says. "Oh, and don't forget to answer your fan mail."

"I never do. I answer every one of them. It's the fans that go away."

Graham looks at me like he wants to hug me. I get this look a lot. "Don't worry," he says. "Maybe you'll get some good friends this time."

"Hope so."

Then he does hug me. Not too tight but just enough for me to feel his hands in the middle of my back. Then he's gone.

Sometimes he leaves me with a present. He brought me a microphone once, another time he brought me a copy of a script from *Doctor Who*, signed by David Tennant. He didn't leave anything this time. I think maybe he forgot, that when he gets in his car he'll find something in his pocket and he'll run back in and leave it in reception. I wish I saw him more often or at least got a text from him once a week or maybe a month. But he doesn't send me texts. He just goes out of the door and I don't hear from him again for another year.

# SEVEN

**The diggers** are getting closer. I can feel the drills vibrating through my hand on the window pane. And I can hear them too, a distant buzz. I've been watching them since Graham left—two yellow generators, eight men with fluorescent jackets wearing white hats—two of them talking, two of them drilling, two of them in diggers, scooping up the road and filling yellow trucks with rubble. Another two men stand by the traffic lights talking, one of them pressing buttons, changing the lights next to a van with red letters on the side: *If you smell gas, ring this number—0845 500200—anytime.*

The door clicks open. Amir walks in.

"You see they start laying the landing strip," he says.

I scrunch my face in confusion.

"The workmen. They digging up the road to lay huge magnets to create a magnetic field—electric charges and elementary particles with quantum properties."

"I think they're just laying a new pipe for the gas," I say. "It says "London Gas" on the vans."

Amir taps the side of his head. "That's what they *want* you to think. They not stupid. They get humans to do all the work for them."

I smile in what I hope is a convincing way. It's not true—I've seen the road being dug up, but I've not seen any massive magnets.

Amir turns away from the window and yawns. "Sorry, I was up all night," he says.

"Looking for aliens?"

"No. Just couldn't sleep."

His eyes are dark but there's a watery sparkle that makes me thinks he was up all night watching the stars. He sits down beside me.

"How the documentary go?"

"It was good," I say. "But I'm a bit tired."

"Yes," he says. "It must be tiring being on TV. I wish I on TV. I could be in Bollywood."

"Hollywood?"

"No, Bollywood. Indian films. You no see them. Like *Slumdog Millionaire*, but much better. They very different, lots more singing and dancing. I could have been in that film."

"Really?"

"Of course. I do many things. I not always a nurse. When I was in India I used to be a train dispatcher."

"What's that?"

"I dispatched trains."

"You got rid of trains? Why?"

"No, I no get rid of them. I dispatch them. I check the doors and blow a whistle. Then they leave."

"Oh." Amir is talking so quickly that he's confusing me. He doesn't seem to mind. He just keeps talking.

"I prefer my job before," he says. "I used to be graphic designer for newspaper in Delhi. It was good job, but rubbish money. That's why I come to England . . . to get a better job for me and my family. But we no talk about the past. We talk about the future."

His eyes dart from side to side and I wonder what he's going to say next. Sometimes I don't think he knows either. He stares at me like he's waiting for the next thought to zap into his head, but finally it looks like he's going to stop saying stuff.

I rest my head on my pillow.

"You okay?"

"I feel really tired now."

"Okay. I just sit here a while."

"Haven't you got to see the others?"

"No. I stay with you."

I lay back and think about the TV crew. They'll be in another ward now, talking to someone just like me. Graham might be talking to the billiard-ball kid. I hope he is, because when the program is shown next week, I'll get to see him on TV. I wish I could see him for real but I know he can't. He's too sick to leave his bed and come and see me, Greg says.

I look at Amir. After talking so much he's suddenly quiet, twisting a gold ring on his finger.

He sees me looking. "Ten years," he says.

"Sorry?"

"Me and my wife. We are married ten years tomorrow."

That's nearly my whole life. "Do you have any children?" I ask.

Amir's face lights up. "Yes. Do I not tell you?" He holds up three fingers and taps the tips of each one. "Ajala, Shukra, Guru."

"I like their names."

He touches his fingertips again. "Earth, Venus, and Jupiter. Nine, seven, and three. I love them." His eyes shine like his children are standing in front of him.

I smile at how happy his kids make him. He must be a really fun dad. I bet he chases them around his house like my dad used to chase me around this room. I don't remember it, but Beth says he did. She said he used to put me on his shoulders and pretend he was going to bump into my bed, and then he'd make an engine noise and swerve around it like we were in a car. Then he'd slow down and put me gently back onto my bed. Sometimes I think I can remember it. That I can smell the shampoo in his hair and his aftershave as we ducked to miss the lights. It feels so real when I think about it. I look up at the ceiling—the lights are too high—I wouldn't need to duck. It's like I've blocked it all out, or maybe it was just another dream.

I swallow. Amir does the same.

"I sorry," he says.

"It's okay. Do you have a picture of them?"

"No. I don't need one. It's like the letters in *Countdown*. I see them all in here." He taps the side of his head. "But maybe I'll bring you one to show you one day."

I nod and look at the TV. I don't see the picture or hear the sound. I wish I had pictures of my family in my head but all I have is a pain in my chest and tummy. I've seen a few documentaries where people talk about losing someone, but they're all older than me. They say things like "it's hard," that "the pain never goes away completely, but it does get easier in time." But I'm eleven now, and it doesn't get easier for me. I wish when I hear the word "orphan" that my ribs didn't squeeze my heart. I wish I was like Amir. I wish I had a family. All I have is me and Beth. I'll always want Beth here with me. I just wish Mum and Dad could be too.

I lean over, open a drawer, and take out a photo to show Amir. "It's me, Mum and Dad, and Beth."

Amir holds the edge of the photograph between his fingers and smiles. "Everyone looks so happy. How old were you?"

"Six."

Amir nods and looks at the picture again. I'm sitting up on the middle of my bed. Mum and Dad are sitting on either side and Beth is kneeling behind me. I don't really remember the day, only what Beth's told me. She says it wasn't a special day like Christmas or any of our birthdays. It was just a day of the week when they all came to see me. The photo was taken in the same room as I'm in now. I've never been moved out of this room, because it was built specially for me. I had posters of Transformers on the walls then, and my bed was smaller, and the monitors were bigger and gray, not white. Sometimes when I look at the photograph I can hear my family talking. Mum looks and sounds like Beth, only older, and Dad looks and talks like Frank Lampard. Beth talks to Mum about school and what subjects she needs to take her last two years of high school. I talk to Dad about football. I tell him I'm sorry, but even though he does look like Frank, I support Arsenal. Dad says he doesn't mind; he likes José Mourinho. I look at Dad smiling in the picture. I wonder if he knows that José Mourinho left Chelsea and then came back again, that when he came back he let Lampard go and now Frank's scoring goals for Man City. I'll tell him out loud one day, when Amir isn't here.

Amir hands me the picture and I put it back in the drawer. When I turn around he's looking at his watch.

"I know," I say. "You have to go."

"Sorry."

I get up and walk over to the window. The traffic lights change from red to green. The drilling has stopped and the workmen have gone home. I look across the rooftops and watch the planes come and go into Heathrow. Hundreds of them fly every day and night. Sometimes they fly so close that I think they'll crash into each other and explode. But the planes never touch each other. The people in the control towers make sure they don't do that. I wonder if there's a person in a control tower somewhere controlling my life. Maybe he sits there watching me on a screen deciding what will happen to me next. Maybe that's what God does. He watches me from a control tower. I don't know if God is real, but if he is, why does he make me live in a bubble? And why wasn't he in the control tower directing the traffic the day Mum and Dad had their accident?

My laptop beeps behind me. I smile. I know it'll be Henry. I feel really tired, but so much has happened in both our lives today that we have to talk.

I pick up my laptop and sit down on my bed.

| | |
|---|---|
| Hey Joe | 8:08 PM |
| Hi Henry | 8:08 PM |
| How's the alien? | 8:08 PM |
| He's not an alien. He just believes in them. And I like him. | 8:08 PM |
| So you're not scared then? | 8:09 PM |
| No. He's funny. He's getting me Sky TV. | 8:09 PM |
| Sky? | 8:10 PM |
| Satellite. | 8:10 PM |
| Oh, what about the TV crew? | 8:10 PM |

**They were great. Miss them already. But why are we**
**talking about them?**                              8:10 PM


**What?**                                            8:11 PM


**Your walk!**                                       8:11 PM


Oh, my walk. Ha! It was OK. Not great       8:11 PM


**What happened?**                                   8:11 PM


It was weird. I got to the end of the corridor
and wanted to turn back.                     8:12 PM


**Germs?**                                           8:12 PM


No. Saw this before I went:
http://www.myfoxphilly.com/story/24951458/9-shot-3-
dead-during-violent-night-in-philadelphia
Happened yesterday.
Didn't think my suit would keep out bullets.   8:12 PM


**You were only going to the car park.**             8:12 pm


Shootings happen in parking lots. It was just around the
corner.                                      8:15 PM


**But you went though?**                             8:15 PM

Yeah, Brett checked the whole area like SWAT.
Drainpipes, stairwells, everything.
NASA said it I didn't go now the schedule
would have to go back by a month.              8:15 PM


**A month?**                                    8:16 PM


Lots of men in suits here telling me what to do.
Not space suits. Suit suits. I had to go. No choice.
Nearly peed myself when they opened the door.
It was bright outside. I think the sun was out
but all I could see was gray asphalt and green walls,
because of the helmet, and they taped the whole parking lot off so no one could get in. Big fence, couldn't see
over, couldn't see under. And my helmet was so heavy
I couldn't lift my head to see the sky.         8:17 PM


I wait for Henry to write more but all I can see is the
pencil, still, on the screen like he doesn't know what to
say next and I don't know what to write either. I sigh.
After waiting for so long to go out, all he got to see was
asphalt and walls. And I guess nothing much is different
out there, really. Just more dangerous. But I wish I could
breathe some dangerous fresh air. Just one time.


**Henry.**                                      8:20 PM


Yeah.                                           8:20 PM

Do you want to switch to screen?          8:21 PM

No. I'm OK here.                           8:21 PM

Sure?                                      8:21 PM

Yeah ... But thanks ...
I'm fried. Just want to sit here.          8:21 PM

Me too. Not feeling great.
Got a bit of a sore throat.                8:22 PM

Be careful.                                8:22 PM

I know.                                    8:23 PM

I reach over for a cup of water. I drink it but with every gulp it feels like I've got a hedgehog stuck in my throat. I swallow again. It's still there. I look back at the screen. I really want to go to sleep but Henry is typing at a hundred miles an hour, now.

---

Got to go again tomorrow. Don't want to.   8:23 PM

It's freakier than I thought it would be.
But the mall will be better. Going to be on
Philly news. Wish you could see it.         8:24 PM

I'll ask Amir if he thinks we can get it.
It's going to be great.                     8:24 PM

You think so?                              8:24 PM

**Burgers and hot dogs!**                  8:24 PM

Not so sure.                               8:25 PM

**Why not?**                               8:25 PM

Ms. Rambo!!!                               8:25 PM

**Who?**                                   8:25 PM

http://www.nydailynews.com/news/
justice-story/ms-rambokilling-spree-article-1.1211691

**Henry.**                                 8:28 PM

Yeah.                                      8:28 PM

**I think you worry about getting shot too much.**   8:28 PM

You worry about car crashes, I worry about guns.
                                           8:29 PM

My stomach aches; the pain moves up toward my heart. My fingers hover over the keyboard, shaking. I wish he hadn't written that.

Joe? You there?                            8:31 PM

**Yeah.**                                          **8:31 PM**

**Sorry. Just a joke about the difference
between England and America.**          **8:32 PM**

**It's OK. I'm just really tired.**          **8:32 PM**

**Want to go?**                              **8:32 PM**

I look at the clock. I know I should go to sleep. But I love
talking to Henry.

I feel really tired and funny—like all the blood has gone
from my face. I look at the clock.

**Henry.**                                     **8:39 PM**

**Yeah.**                                       **8:40 PM**

**Wish you could come here.**          **8:40 PM**

Wish you could come here, too.
Maybe the transition zone is really a
teleportation machine. Zoop! Zoop!      **8:41 PM**

**Haha.**                                      **8:42 PM**

Or you could just jump on one of your planes. **8:42 PM**

**Wouldn't get past airport security.**     **8:43 PM**

Cut a hole in the fence. Just Jump on.          8:44 PM

Kid did it over here. Hang on ... Here you go.
http://edition.cnn.com/2014/04/
21/us/hawaii-
plane-stowaway/                                 8:44 PM

I click on the link.

## Teen hitches ride in the wheel of a plane

I scroll down and read how a boy climbed an airfield
perimeter fence, ran across the asphalt, climbed up a wheel,
and hid in the hold of the plane. I smile. I can't believe it.
The boy flew all the way from San Jose to Hawaii. He was
sixteen. It doesn't say what his name is.

See.                                            8:48 PM

What do you think?                              8:49 PM

Don't know. Can't catch a bus, so no chance
of a plane.                                     8:49 PM

But you could, if you got a suit.               8:50 PM

I smile and keep reading. The boy flew for five hours
curled up in a ball. He had no reason to go to Hawaii; it's
like he did it for a dare. Scientists said he's lucky to be

alive because it was minus eighty degrees. He said being in the wheel was the same as being without much oxygen at the top of Mount Everest.

Want to do that?                                          8:53 PM

I don't know. Bit cold.                                   8:54 PM

Yeah. Need a blanket!                                     8:54 PM

I look out of the window. The planes are only sixteen miles away. The Internet says it takes thirty-one minutes to get to Heathrow in a car, forty-two minutes on the Tube. If I was Thor I could get there quicker. But if I was Thor I wouldn't need to go to an airport; I could fly all the way to Philadelphia on my own. I'd only have to sneak up onto the roof, stand on the ledge, point my hammer at the sky. If I can reach the stratosphere and come back down without taking a breath, it would only take me a few minutes to get to America. I'd be faster than a plane, faster than a rocket even. I'd be there so quickly that I wouldn't even have to stop for lunch. My laptop beeps. I look back at the screen.

Hey Joe. Next plane leaves at 2:10 PM.
Terminal 3.                                               8:57 PM

I chuckle.

| | |
|---|---|
| **Henry.** | **8:58 PM** |

| | |
|---|---|
| What? | 8:58 PM |

| | |
|---|---|
| **They said the stowaway boy might get brain** | |
| **damage.** | **8:59 PM** |

| | |
|---|---|
| Oh crap. I didn't read all of it. Sorry. | 8:59 PM |

My head begins to swirl. Sweat drips off my face and trickles down my neck.

| | |
|---|---|
| **Henry!** | **9:00 PM** |

| | |
|---|---|
| What? | 9:00 PM |

| | |
|---|---|
| **I really don't feel good.** | **9:01 PM** |

The monitors beep.

**Heart rate:** 111
**Body temp.:** 40.1C

The numbers start to blur. I blink.

**Heart rate:** 119
**Body temp.:** 40.2C

| | |
|---|---|
| **Henry** | **9:02 PM** |

Press—                                            9:02 pm


My head falls against my pillow. My laptop crashes to the floor.

I try to shout but all that comes out is a croak.


This is a crash.

This is when the blood goes from my head to my feet, pours out into the room, and drains through a hole in the middle of the floor. This is when the walls start spinning and the pictures blur. Then the ceiling turns black and the floor turns black and I don't know which way I'm facing anymore. My body is cold and wet. My sheets are messed up and falling off my bed. This is a crash when all I can hear are footsteps and voices around my bed.

"I feel sick . . . and my head aches."

"We know, Joe," says Dr. Moore. *Increase saline, take the atropine to 50 ml.*

*Charlotte shouldn't have let them stay so long.*

*It's not her fault. We all share responsibility. This could have happened whether they came or not.* "Easy, Joe. Easy."

I roll over on my side. A nurse puts her hand on my forehead. My stomach cramps and I retch over a bowl. The room spins again—Dr. Moore, Dr. Singh, two nurses—*we can't stop filming because someone's going to die, we can't stop filming because someone's going to die.* I retch again.

"Am I going to die?"

*Temp 40. BP 70 over 35.*

"Am I going to die?"

*100 over 55. . . .*

"Am I going to—?"

"Steady, steady. No, Joe, you're not going to die." *Increase the atropine to 60 ml. Let's leave it there.*

Needle in my hand, cold fluid in my veins, I feel it surge up my arm, through my shoulder, and into my chest.

"Relax, Joe. Deep breaths. Nice deep breaths."

I try to breathe. I try to breathe deep and not too fast. I try to imagine my feet sinking into soft sand.

"I want to walk on the beach."

"Easy, Joe. Easy."

"Watch the waves."

"Don't talk, Joe. Just breathe. It's okay, we can talk later."

I blink, see Dr. Moore standing over me. Feel so tired. Feel so—

"I want to watch . . ."

This is a crash.

# EIGHT

## 11 YEARS, 2 MONTHS, AND 26 DAYS

**There's an IV drip** by the side of my bed—a plastic bag full of blood hangs from it and there's a white container marked *BLOOD* on the floor.

A nurse I've not seen before smiles at me. My eyes are too blurry to read her name tag.

"Okay?" she whispers. "Joe, are you okay?"

My head is so heavy it's like it's stuck to the pillow.

She puts her hand on my shoulder. "It's all right, Joe. It's done now."

I look at the dark blood flowing from the bag, down the tube and into my arm. My eyelids are heavy. They drop down. I open them again. Dr. Moore is leaning over me. "Okay, Joe?"

I try to nod.

"It's all right." He puts his hand gently on my head. "We've got you back now."

He walks to the end of my bed.

"Look after him, nurse," he says. "He's a gooner."

The nurse looks at me, puts her hand up to her mouth, like she can't believe what Dr. Moore has just said.

"A gooner." He nods at my poster of Theo Walcott on the wall. "He supports Arsenal."

"Oh, I see. I thought—"

Dr. Moore shakes his head. We both know what she thought he'd said.

My eyelids fall down.

Dr. Moore's footsteps fade away.

Am I a goner? Maybe I am. I hope not. These new drugs were supposed to make me better, not kill me. The nurse sits down next to me.

"I'll be right here," she says.

"Okay."

The new blood goes into my body as the old blood drains away.

I wish Beth was here. She used to come for all my transfusions but I know she can't be here all the time. They always make me tired and weak. Sometimes it can make it feel like the room spins around. I've only ever had that happen twice; Henry has had it happen twice too. He told me it happens because the blood has been in storage for too long and has got too much potassium in it. But I already knew; I'd looked it up like he had. That's when I read about graft versus host disease: it's when the immune cells attack the white cells and the body goes to war with itself. That's what happened when they tried a bone-marrow transplant when I was four.

They took the marrow from Beth; at first they thought it was working but even with the antirejection meds, my body wouldn't take it. That's when I got a massive fever and my body went to war. I don't want a war in my body.

I hear a click and look up at the ceiling. The lights are bright and my ears are full of silence.

"It's okay," says the nurse. "I'm changing the bags."

I take a deep breath, then another. My arms and legs feel heavy, like they are made of metal. I've always wondered what it's like to be Iron Man, to be able to pick up cars and bash my way through walls and then press a button and shoot up high into the sky.

The nurse sits back down beside me. More aches, more pain, more blood in the tubes. I take another deep breath as tears bulge behind my eyes. I want to cry. Iron Man never cries. But I bet he would if he felt as bad as this.

# NINE

## 11 years, 2 months, and 27 days

*Beep. Beep. Beep.*

**Heart rate:** 87
**Body temp.:** 39.6C
**Room temp.:** 19C
**Humidity:** 9%
**Air purity:** 98.5%

*Beep. Beep. Beep.*

I roll over onto my side. The sky is bright white, whiter than I've ever seen it. The light pours through the window, across the floor and into my skull. I hear the sound of someone whispering but can't see who it is. Out of the bottom of my eyes, I see Amir standing by the window. He's waving his hands around above his head like he's guiding the planes.

"Amir?"

He doesn't hear me. I try to call again but my voice is too weak and my lips are dry.

Is Amir really there or am I dreaming?

I close my eyes and open them again.

He's still there, waving his hands at the window. What's he doing? Maybe the aliens have flown in and landed in the road while I was sleeping.

Amir glances back at me, then back out of the window.

"No, no, not like that, Rashid," he whispers. "Rashid, not like that!" He taps his finger gently on the glass. "No." He turns and looks at the wall opposite my bed.

Theo Walcott has been moved to the wall opposite the window. There are twelve blank TV screens in his place, four across the top by three down the sides. Wires trail out of the back of them onto the ground. The screens are on, but there are no pictures on them—only white fuzz and white noise.

Amir holds up a finger. "Rashid," he whispers loudly. "Point it at the sky, not at the ground!"

A man wearing a hard hat stands in a window cleaner's cradle holding a wrench in his hand. He holds onto the cradle with one hand and reaches up with the other. He knocks the wrench against a satellite dish until, gradually, it moves and points toward the sky.

Amir tuts and scratches his head. Rashid touches the satellite again.

THAT OKAY? he mouths.

Amir shakes his head. "I no understand," he says. "Why it not work here when it work at home?" He walks over to the screens and looks at them one by one like he's in an art gallery. Something makes a clicking sound; something else tumbles over.

"Ah!" says Amir. He holds up a plug. "I got it. I forget to plug the receiver in!"

Outside, Rashid opens his eyes wide. "Amir, what the hell?!"

"Stay there," says Amir, laughing. "I'll switch it on now."

Rashid sees me looking. He looks down at the ground far below, makes a funny face, then holds his hands out by his side. *WHERE DOES HE THINK I GO?* he mouths, still attached to the window.

I'm still so sleepy. So sleepy. My eyelids start to drop but I don't want them to close in case I can't open them again. I feel a shadow standing over me. I open my eyes. Amir's standing by my side. I try to speak.

"Shush." He puts a finger up to his lips.

I take a deep breath.

"You going to be fine," Amir whispers. He takes a deep breath too. "With me," he says. "You breathe with me." He slows his breath and waits for me until our chests go up and down at the same time. "Better?"

My head feels like it's lifting off the pillow; my arms are lifting into the air and my body too. The monitors beep, slower and slower. The ceiling lights start to flicker.

*Beep. Beep. Beep.*

I close my eyes and everything is dark again.

# TEN

## 11 YeaRS, 2 mON+HS, anD 28 DaYS

**This afternoon** I think a bird flew into my window. I heard the thud. But when I opened my eyes it was gone.

A bird can fly at 60 miles per hour.

A falcon can fly at 100 miles per hour.

A bullet flies at 761 miles per hour.

Nobody knows how fast Superman can fly, but it's faster than that.

Everything goes black again.

# ELEVEN

## 11 years, 2 months, and 28 days

The ceiling lights are dimmed. Music is playing; a piano with a lady singing so quietly that I can't hear what the song is. I breathe but it's hard because my chest aches like someone is sitting on it. The monitors flash and beep. The bag of blood has gone. Now there's another bag full of saline that drips through the tube into my arm. That's water mixed with salt. They give it to me to rehydrate my cells. It's supposed to stop me feeling giddy but from the sick feeling in my stomach it doesn't seem to be working yet.

I feel a warm hand on top of mine. I turn my head. Beth smiles at me.

"Hey, there you are," she whispers. "You've been fighting a war."

"Yeah." There's a lump in my throat.

Beth bites down on her lip. Her eyes are red and dark around the edges; there's a smudge of black on her cheek.

Sometimes when I'm ill it looks like she is hurting as much as me. She squeezes my hand tighter and I don't want her to let go.

I try to speak again. Beth pours me a cup of water and holds it to my lips. My throat is so sore it's like I'm swallowing glass. I take a deep breath and try again. It's easier this time. Beth puts the cup on the table beside me.

"So, who were you? Spider-Man or Superman?"

"I don't know . . . but I thought both of them were going to get beat up."

Beth smiles. She's not supposed to be here this week, but I'm glad she is. She rubs my hand again. I swallow hard but it doesn't stop the tears from falling out of my eyes.

"I'm sorry," I say. "I couldn't help it. Sorry you had to come."

"Joe, it's okay. I had to see you." She looks down at my bed, then back at me. "But why didn't you tell the nurses you weren't feeling well?"

"I just wanted to be on the TV again."

Tears fall down the side of my face onto the pillow.

"Hey," she says. "It's okay." Beth holds me tight until my body stops shaking.

"Sorry."

"If you say you're sorry one more time, I'm going to get up and leave!"

We both laugh. Neither of us believes what she says.

I tell her I'm tired but I don't want to sleep because she's here and she'll have to go soon. She tells me that's where I'm wrong, because her university has said she can stay for the weekend. I lie back and try to relax. I want to tell her what I heard Graham say in the transition zone about kids dying but I don't want her to worry. I can't tell her I think they were talking about me. I turn my head and look at her. She smiles and rubs my hand. She's always here when I need her.

Beth rubs my arm again. Sometimes it's like she knows what I'm thinking. I try to speak but my lips are cracked and my mouth is dry.

She smiles at me. "Hey, just go to sleep," she says. "We'll catch up tomorrow."

I close my eyes and drift off to sleep.

My legs are twitching like snakes under my sheets. Greg's walking around the room. He has to have a vacation but I'm so happy he's back. He checks the monitors, checks my chart, then looks at me.

"You should sleep, mate," he says. "You know that's what makes it better."

"But I can't stop them." I sit up and clamp my hands on my knees. I need to sleep to stop my legs twitching but it's because my legs are twitching that I can't sleep. Greg puts the chart down and walks over to me.

"Don't worry about it, mate. At least it's a sign you're coming back to life."

I press my knees down into my bed again.

"But it's worse than I've ever had it before."

"I'm not surprised it's bad. You've been out for hours."

He glances at my monitor. "Your temperature's 39C. It's still high but it's moving the right way. Let's try and walk that ache off."

I get up and see the empty chair by my bed.

"When did Beth leave?"

Greg looks at his watch.

"About two hours ago. She's sleeping upstairs, in one of the guest rooms. I told her she'd be more help to you if she got some sleep. . . . So, are you ready to try a walk, mate?"

I nod. Greg helps me sit up. I slide my feet over the bed and onto the floor. Blood rushes from my head and the lights turn fuzzy.

After a minute or two my head begins to clear. I nod to Greg and he puts one hand on my wrist and the other on my elbow. I take a deep breath and stand up. We walk to the end of the bed and stop. Greg looks at the wall.

"So, where did those come from?"

The TV screens hang on the wall like black holes.

"I thought . . . I thought I was dreaming."

"Amir?"

I scratch my head. "I remember something. A man floating outside the window."

"Why does Amir think you need twelve TVs?"

I shrug and look at the screens.

Amir only said he was getting me Sky; he didn't say anything about getting more than one TV. I don't know why he's done that. It doesn't matter how many screens we have, we'd only ever be able to watch one program at a time.

Greg pulls me up. "We'll have to ask him. Come on, mate. Let's get these legs sorted."

We walk up and down the room three times and he tells what he did on his days off. He went bowling with his friends and to the cinema with Katie. They saw *The Maze Runner*.

"I'd like to see that," I say, "but I'll have to wait for the DVD."

Greg looks over his shoulder at the screens. "Maybe that's what Amir's trying to do," he says, "build you a cinema. Now all you need is popcorn and Coke."

"That would be great," I say. "I just need him to tell me how to turn them on."

"Well, that would help. . . . Come on then, mate. Let's keep going."

Me and Greg walk to the window and back toward the door. On the fourth turn we stop for a rest and look out. The planes are flying between the buildings. Down on the streets the roadwork have reached the phone shop. We watch the lights change and the traffic moves on.

"Amir says they're building a magnetic field for aliens to land."

Greg smiles. "Mate, you shouldn't believe everything Amir says. He might just be playing."

"No, I don't think he is. I think he really believes it."

Greg nods down at the traffic. "Well, if they do land here, I hope someone tells that lot to get out of the way." He puts his hand under my arm again. "Come on," he says. "Let's keep moving. Another half hour and the Pramipexole will kick in. You should be able to settle down then."

I rest my head against the glass.

"Hey, mate, I said you'll be okay."

"I'm just tired."

"If you're sure?"

I roll my head from side to side and feel the cold glass on my forehead. I close my eyes. What if Graham and New-cameraman-David were talking about me dying? I look up at Greg. "Tell me about the others?"

"What, now? It's late, mate."

"Tell me."

"They're fine, mate."

"The boy with the billiard-ball head?"

Greg smiles. "Yes, he's good."

"Is he still running round?"

"Was the last time I saw him."

"What about the girl who chases him pretending she's a horse?"

"What about her?"

"Is she okay?"

"Yes, mate, she's fine."

"And the boy who reads *The Hunger Games*?"

"Yes, he's still . . . Mate, what's this about?"

I turn away from the window. "Is he okay?"

Greg puts his hands on my shoulders. "Yes, mate, he's okay. Now tell me, what's up?"

I shrug. "Something I heard Graham say."

"What?"

"He said he couldn't stop filming just because people die."

Greg puts one hand around the back of my neck.

"Mate, you're okay. Everyone else is okay, and anyway, Graham might not have been talking about anyone in particular. It's a hospital. Unfortunately people die all the time."

He glances at the time and we walk back to my bed. The light is flashing on my laptop. I stop. Henry. His walk! I've been so ill for so long that I'd forgotten about him.

I flip the lid. Greg nods at my bed.

"Mate, not now, it's going to be time to get up before you even get to sleep."

"But it's Henry. He did his second walk today!"

Greg sighs. "Okay, just the one message. Let's not push it."

I sit on my bed. Greg hands me my laptop.

Joe          7:08 PM

Joe?          7:45 PM

Guess you're busy. Been out again.
It wasn't great. More asphalt and green fences.
Couldn't see anything.

But they're thinking of letting me go out
earlier.        8:12 PM

**BTW the new assistant from NASA is nice.**

**Arianne. She's French!**                                   8:15 PM

**Umm ... not sure where you are.**                          8:19 PM

**Maybe Beth's with you. Hope so. Tell her
I say hi.**                                                   8:21 PM

**Need to sleep. Try you again later.**                      9:14 PM

I start typing.

**Hey Henry. Sorry your walk was boring.**                   9:15 PM

**Great you might get to go out earlier.
Sorry I haven't replied. Had a crash.**                      9:16 PM

I press enter.
"Mate," Greg reaches for my laptop. "I said one message."
"I know, but you didn't say how long."
Greg shakes his head.

**Anyway, guess what Amir did? He got me 12 TVs! 9:17 PM**

"Finished?" He closes the lid down.
I rest my head back on my pillow. Greg closes the blinds and dims the lights until all I can see are shadows again.

I take a deep breath, then another. I can relax now. Greg is back and Beth is here and I get to see her again tomorrow. And soon Amir will be back to switch the TVs on. I close my eyes and listen to the machines beep. The beeps are good. They mean I've made it.

# TWELVE

## 11 YeaRS, 2 mOn+HS, anD 29 DaYS

**It's early in the morning.** Dr. Moore and Dr. Hussein are standing by my bed. Three interns are with them. They are people who are training to be doctors. I've met loads of them. Sometimes they stay here after they've qualified; sometimes they go and work somewhere else. Dr. Moore asks Beth if it's okay that they're here. Beth tells him I enjoy it, that I like the attention. I smile because I know she's right. It's nice to have attention, but not all the time, especially not if I'm really ill. But this morning I'm feeling better.

"So," says Dr. Moore. "How are things with you, young man?"

"I'm okay," I say. "But my head still hurts."

He leans over the bed and looks into my eyes.

"Increase fluids?" I say.

Dr. Moore smiles. "Increase fluids, indeed, and we need to run some more blood tests."

"Do you think it has something to do with the new drugs?" I ask.

"Quite likely."

I look down at my arms, at the little red marks and bruises where they've taken blood before. I always bruise more when I'm sicker, because my platelets are low and my blood doesn't clot very well.

"Do you think it could be secondary hemolytic anemia?"

"Well, you've certainly reacted to something." Dr. Moore smiles and turns to the interns. "So everybody, this is Dr. Joe Grant. Doctor of Medicine and Pediatrics."

". . . And expert in superhcrocs," says Dr. Hussein.

The three interns laugh. Dr. Moore smiles at Beth, then looks back at the interns. "So everyone, what are we thinking?"

One of the interns bites his top lip, one scratches the side of her head, and the last one raises an eyebrow then he stares down at the ground. Dr. Moore grins at me.

"Well, Joe," he says. "Looks like you've stumped the brightest brains of Cambridge." He looks to the interns. "Discuss it among yourselves."

They gather in a circle and start to whisper.

I look at the monitors, then up at the ceiling. I wish I didn't stump them. I wish I didn't stump the proper doctors too. I wish the things they do to fix other kids had worked on me. I've read about other SCID kids who have injections that cost lots of money. It doesn't cure them, but it does mean they can go home and they can go to school. They have to wear a mask and stay at home if other kids have

colds. They tell me the clock is ticking; that the older I get
the harder it will be to find a cure. But every year they try
something new and say that maybe I'll make it outside. Last
month they talked about giving me gene therapy. It's really
new. It's when they grow a new gene and then they'd put it
in my body and give me a new immune system to fight disease. But nothing seems to get rid of my super SCID. I hope
they find something soon. I know I'm safer in my bubble,
but one day I'd love to go to school and learn my lessons
from a real teacher and not a cartoon or a satellite feed.

"So," Dr. Moore says. "Now you've had your chat, tell me
your conclusions. Miss Hunter?"

"Decrease temperature?"

"Exactly, Miss Hunter. Check for foreign objects in the
filters and let's decrease the temperature to . . . what do we
think?"

"Nineteen," I say.

Dr. Hussein smiles and nods at one of the interns. "Mr.
Henderson, I think this chap might know more than you.
Maybe you need to hand over your coat."

They all laugh, and then Dr. Moore asks me to roll up
my sleeves.

"And what about the bruises?"

"They're nearly gone," I say.

"You haven't got any on your body?"

"Only a few, but they're disappearing."

"Maybe we should take a look."

I lift up my sweatshirt and pull it up over my head.

"Contusions, and . . . Mr. Henderson?"

"Malnutrition—vitamins C, K, and B12. Sepsis?"

"I think what's more relevant here." Dr. Moore presses his fingers gently on my back. "Anything else? Mr. Francis? Can you help us out?"

"Reaction to drugs—aspirin, the corticosteroids prednisone and prednisolone, anticoagulants, antibiotics, and blood thinners."

"Excellent . . . and?"

"Liver disease."

The room goes quiet. There's so many things that could go wrong with me but I'm used to talking about them now.

Dr. Moore taps my back. "Good lad," he says.

I put my sweatshirt back on. The door slides open. I sigh. Charlotte R. walks in carrying a silver dish with a needle and swab. She puts the dish down on the table next to my laptop. Dr. Moore looks at Beth in a way that says: *We need to talk somewhere where Joe can't hear us.* She tells me she'll be back in a minute and follows Dr. Moore toward the door.

"We'll check in again later, Joe."

I nod. They all walk out into the transition zone. I listen and try to hear what Dr. Moore's saying to Beth but all I can hear is them spraying disinfectant and running the taps. Charlotte R. taps me on the shoulder.

"Sorry," she says. "But we have to do this now."

"It's okay."

I hold out my arm. Charlotte R. looks for a space where the bruises have faded. She finds a white bit of skin halfway between my wrist and my elbow, squirts the numbing spray, then picks up the needle. I turn away. I've had hundreds of injections but I still can't look.

"There, all done."

Charlotte R. presses a bandage onto my arm. I turn back and she shows me my blood in the syringe.

Sometimes when I'm ill I think it will come out a different color, but it doesn't matter if my whites are up or down, it always looks the same. Dark red, so dark it's almost brown. They've taken loads of it before. They must have taken so much out of me they could fill another body.

I hold a swab down on my arm while Charlotte R. screws the top down on the tube of blood and puts it in the dish.

"I know," I say. "You've got to go."

"Yes, I'm sorry. I've got to get this back."

"It's okay."

She smiles and goes out the door.

It seems like everyone is busy, rushing round looking after everyone else. They're buzzing around like bees. Busy. Busy. Running down the corridors in and out of wards. It's like there's not enough of them to look after us. The sick kids.

I'm trying to catch up on my algebra when Beth comes back in. I thought of telling Vic, my math teacher, about my crash, but I think the only thing he wants to talk about is math. I ask Beth what the doctors had said to her. She tells me that they didn't say much more, only that they think the worst is over and that neither of us should worry. I look at her and try to work out if there's anything else but she just gives me a tired smile. She looks like my picture of Mum when she's tired. Her eyes turn dark and her cheeks look red and sore. Beth says it's the wind blowing in her face as she walks down the street, but I know it's because she got up so early to see me.

I shut Vic inside my laptop and we watch a program about badgers on TV. When the commercials come on I look at Beth. She usually talks during the breaks. But today she's staring into space, twirling her hair around her finger. She sees me looking.

"You okay?" she asks.

"I am. But you're quiet."

"Sorry," she says. "I didn't really sleep last night."

"Because of me?"

"Yes . . . and the noise of the traffic."

"I'm sorry."

"It's not your fault London's so busy."

We smile at each other, and then she looks down and picks the skin on her fingers. I swing my legs over the side of my bed.

"But there is something wrong."

She takes a deep breath. "Not wrong, just something I need to tell you. Don't worry, it's not anything the doctors said."

"It's okay," I say. "I think I know what it is. You've got to go away."

She nods.

"I don't mind," I say. "You said it was going to happen sometime. I don't mind."

She smiles, then laughs. "You're brilliant," she says. Then
she stands up and I stand up too and she hugs me so tight I
don't think she'll ever let go. "It's only for a year," she whispers. I close my eyes. I don't want to leave her but I know
she must. Just because I'm in a bubble it doesn't mean she
has to be stuck in one too.

She lets go of me. I look at the TV.

"Want to play *Tomb Raider*?"

"Okay. Anything's better than watching that badger drink
from a saucer."

I pick up the controls. My heart beats hard in my chest.
Beth puts her arm around my shoulders and rests her head
against mine.

"It'll be fine," she says. "I won't be able to come so often
but when I do I can stay for longer."

I hand her a controller and nod at the screens on the wall.
"We'll have to play on normal TV. Amir hasn't shown me
how to turn them on."

Beth looks weirded out. "Why did he get so many?"

"I don't know, but I can't wait for him to come back and
show me how to work them!"

I press play and we play *Tomb Raider* for the rest of the
morning. I get to the amulet in a record thirty-five seconds,
but Beth is trapped in a cave and every time Lara falls off a
ledge onto spines Beth lets out a little scream and we laugh.
I tell her I can get her out if she wants. I found a website
that tells you how to do it. She tells me she doesn't want
to cheat, and then she makes Lara climb a rock face, but a

piece of rock gives way and I laugh as Lara falls back onto the spikes again.

After an hour Beth gives up and puts the controls down on my bed and we eat vacuum-packed ham sandwiches for lunch. I tell her about Henry and his walk, that he's got to get used to going outside before he's ready for his big trip to the mall, and I tell her about Amir and the aliens' landing strip. She tells me to wish Henry good luck, then tells me that maybe Amir is nuts after all.

In the afternoon we look up Edinburgh on my laptop. We look at a map and I trace the red line out of London, through Cambridge, Nottingham, and Sheffield and stop. I'm at 161 miles and it's still not halfway. I keep going through Leeds and Newcastle until I get there—403 miles. Beth sighs when she sees it will take seven hours and fifteen minutes by car.

"It only takes four hours twenty minutes on a train," I say.

"Well that's better," she says.

I look back at the map. I've looked at it loads of times, to check the places where Greg goes on his holidays, or places where other nurses go to work when they leave me. But no one's ever gone to Edinburgh. I never realized it was that far. I close my eyes.

"Shall we see what it looks like?"

"Okay," she says.

I type in Edinburgh. We look at pictures of the castle, and the university, and a big square in the middle of the city surrounded by tall black buildings.

"It looks nice," I say.

"The streets are really wide and straight," she says. "And it's windy. . . . Look up the hospital."

I search it, and we look at a picture of a big black house with spires at the ends. Beth points at another picture of a white glass building.

"That's the old part," she says. "I'll be working in the research lab."

"Good," I say. "That other place looked creepy."

She laughs and we look at a few more, and then we watch *Taken* on DVD. We've seen it three times, but I still jump when the man pulls the girl out from under the bed and Beth still gets tears in her eyes at the end.

When the screen goes blank, Beth yawns and looks at me. My stomach cramps. We don't have to say anything. We both know it's time for her to go. I get up and go to the bathroom. She's standing by the window when I come back out. I go and stand beside her and we watch the roadwork's traffic lights change from red to green and back again three times. My chest is tight and my throat aches. I want to talk to her, but we've been quiet for so long that if I say something now I think it might make us both jump. She presses her finger against the glass like she's going to draw.

"It's only for three weeks at first," she says.

"It's okay."

She turns and wraps her arms around me. Three weeks is a long time, but I'll have to get used to her going.

"It's okay," she says. "We can Skype!" I feel her breath

on my ear as she squeezes me a little tighter. I'm glad we can Skype like I do with Henry. I must write to the person who invented Skype one day. Everything would be so much worse without it.

The streetlights are flickering as I watch her walk out onto the pavement and cross the road. She looks up and waves to me when she gets to the other side. I send her a text.

See you in three weeks.

She looks down. My phone buzzes.

Love you, lots.

**Love you a bit.**

She walks along the road with her head down. Nearly bumps into a man who's walking toward her. She looks up and waves. Then the bus comes.

Didn't mean it. Love you lots too.

I know.

I must write to the person who invented text too.

# THIRTEEN

## 11 years, 3 months, and 1 day

The screens hang like black pictures on the wall. They've been
blank for several days and Amir hasn't been back to switch
them on. I walk over to the window. It rained yesterday but
today it must be hot because all the men digging the road
have taken off their shirts. Across the road the people in the
glass building are sitting at their desks, waving pieces of paper
in front of their faces like fans. I lean forward to see if I can see
Amir walking up the pavement. My head bumps against the
glass. I can't see him anywhere. All I can see are people crossing the road to walk in the shade. I glance at the monitors.

Heart rate: 86
Body temp.: 37.5C
Room temp.: 18C
Humidity: 7%
Air purity: 98.5%

It's like everyone is melting except me.

I go over to my bed and turn on my laptop. Sarah smiles at me. It's another video, so she must still be on vacation.

"Hi, Dew. Today we're going to learn Archimedes' Principle." She points at a picture of a watering can. I shake my head. I'm too tired to learn anything today. I go back to the window. A white van pulls up outside the glass building. Two men get out, open up the doors, and carry fans and portable air conditioners inside.

I type a message to Henry.

| | |
|---|---|
| **Hey Henry** | **11:03 AM** |
| **Hey Joe** | 11:03 AM |
| **What are you doing?** | **11:03 AM** |
| Macbeth. It's boring. You? | 11:04 AM |
| **Archimedes' principle. If I get in a full bath and collect the water, it will weigh the same as me.** | **11:05 AM** |
| Have you got a bath? | 11:05 AM |
| **No** | **11:05 AM** |
| ☹ ... Macbeth killed four people. | |

Wish he'd killed Shakespeare, too. Ha. Got to go. 11:06 AM


**Really? I'm bored.**                                    **11:06 AM**


I'm sorry. Breakfast and more NASA stuff.
I'll catch you later.                                      11:07 AM


**Okay.**                                                **11:07 AM**


I want to ask Henry more about his trip but his Skype icon has gone off.

I look back at the screens. I wish Amir would hurry up. The people in the glass building plug in their air conditioners and fans. Pieces of paper blow off the tables onto the floor. The workmen stop digging up the road, put their drills down, and drink bottles of water in the shade.

I go back to my bed and turn on the TV. People are dying in West Africa from a new disease. The reporter says three and a half thousand have died already in Sierra Leone and then he points at red dots on a map. The disease is spreading across Mali, Nigeria, and into Chad. A doctor has flown back to America. She didn't know she had the disease but she's taken it back to Houston with her. She's in quarantine and the police have closed off all of the hospital.

I turn off the TV and lie back down on my bed.

It's hot outside and there's a new disease that going to spread all over the world.

I look around the room. I feel trapped in it today. Sometimes I wish it was bigger. Sometimes I wish I could get up and push the walls and they would slide back until the room became the size of a tennis court. But I wouldn't stop. I'd keep pushing until the room grew as big as a football pitch. Then I could put a goal net up, paint a penalty spot, kick the ball, score a goal, and run around with my hands above my head. I'd run toward the crowd and they'd shout my name, *Joe Grant! Joe Grant!* and I'd pump my fist, take off my shirt with number 10 on the back, and throw it to them. And they'd cheer louder and I'd jump into them. They'd carry me above their heads, pass me from one person to the next, and I'd feel their hands pressing on my back but I wouldn't care about that, because I'd be big and full of muscles and all my bruises would be gone.

I wish my real world was as big as the one in my head. But the walls are where they've always been. They haven't moved, only the posters have. Theo Walcott is still there smiling at me. I wrote him a letter once asking if I could have his autograph, and if perhaps he could send me a ball. He sent me the picture that hangs on the wall. Sometimes I wish he would come and see me and I think I can hear his football studs on the floor in the transition zone. I think I hear him talking and another person replies and he speaks in Spanish and for a moment he's brought Cesc Fàbregas with him, but it can't be, because he plays for Chelsea now, but he might have come back because every time I see them on TV Theo Walcott smiles at Cesc Fàbregas and I think they might be good friends.

I look at the screens. If they were working I could watch every football match in the Premier League at the same time. I take a deep breath and blow out my cheeks. More than three days they've been blank but it feels like three weeks. I lie back, stare at the ceiling, and wish it was the sky.

It's late in the afternoon when I hear voices in the transition zone. I don't recognize one of them, but the other is Amir's.

"I'm okay," he says. "False alarm."

"But you know the rules."

"Yes," says Amir. "I took the three days and an extra one to be sure."

"Okay."

I hear the sound of running water, then the spray. The door slides open and Amir walks in. I stand up.

"Amir, where have you been?"

Amir smiles. "It's okay," he says. "Don't worry. I thought I had a sore throat but I remembered I swallowed a chicken bone."

"Was it serious?"

"Yes," he says. "It got stuck for a while but I'm okay now." He grins. I know him better now but I still can't tell if he's joking or not.

He walks over to the window and looks out, first across the buildings, then to the side of the window, then down the street. He whispers, "Yes, yes, yes."

"What is it?" I ask.

Amir rubs his hands together quickly like they're cold. "It's all good," he says. "The planes still come, the satellite dish is on the wall, and the landing strip is halfway up the road."

It's only been a few days but I'd begun to forget what it was like to have Amir around. I love Greg but Amir is the best at making me forget where I am.

He turns away from the window. "You not been well?"

"No."

"But you better now?"

"I think so. Just a bit bored. It would have been better if they were working." I nod at the screens.

"Oh, the TVs!" He opens his arms wide. "12 x 1920 x 1080 HDMI DVI full HD. My brother get them from his work. They're upgrading to Hitachi. Do you like them?"

"Yes, I like them, but Amir—"

"What? They the wrong color? We could get some paint and spray them silver."

"No, it's not that."

"What then?"

I hold out my hands. "Amir, why did you get so many?"

"Oh." He puts his hand on his head like he's only just noticed. "That how many he get. I know you had room. You saw me measure the wall. Have you switched them on yet?"

"No, I couldn't find the remote."

"Oh, sorry. I take it home." He taps his pockets. "Here." He hands me the remote. It's got more buttons on it than I've ever seen. Amir leans over and points. "You press the red button first, then the green."

I press the red button. I hear the click of speakers then the sound of static. Three of the screens flicker on. There's a picture of cars and trucks going down a street, another of a dark empty alley, then another alley with a black stairwell, full of boxes and bins.

I look at Amir. "I thought you said we were getting Sky."

"Press the button again."

I do as he says and four more screens flicker on. There's a delivery truck parked on a curb, a security guard standing by a door, a man walking with a briefcase, and a lady typing on a laptop behind a glass screen. I don't know what I'm watching but it isn't Sky.

"Amir, what are you doing? Are you going to rob a bank?"

"Ha, no, come here."

I follow him over to the window. He looks down onto the street, then back at the screens. The delivery van stops in the road. The delivery van stops on the screen. I scratch my head.

"Amir, what have you done?"

"Me and Rashid. We get you hospital CCTV."

I shake my head. I didn't want CCTV. I only wanted Sky. I walk along the screens and look at them one by one. The security guard throws his cigarette on the ground and walks back around the corner. He disappears from one screen and then appears on another. He nods at the people who walk past him through the hospital doors. I follow them inside; they form a line in front of the lady typing behind the screen. On the next screen the bus has stopped and people are getting off; some wear coats, some carry backpacks, some carry plastic bags.

I shake my head.

"You no like it?"

I don't know what to say to him. He's gone to all this trouble but I didn't want this. All I wanted was to watch football and films; I didn't want to see traffic and people walking without sound. I can do that every day when I look out the window.

Amir stands in front of me. "I thought I show you real people, not film stars."

"But real people don't do anything interesting."

"They do. They walk, they talk. Not everyone run around shouting and firing guns." He takes the remote from me. "Look," he says, "there's thirty-two cameras. Two in reception, sixteen in the corridors, four on the roof and . . ." He stops talking and turns his head like a dog.

"What's wrong?" I ask.

"It's okay . . . I think I hear someone coming. If they do, just press this button or we get into trouble." He presses a red button and the TVs change to color—a woman is reading the news from a studio in Moscow; a reporter is standing in front of the Empire State Building in New York; ten people are playing ice hockey live from Ontario and women are playing volleyball on a beach in Brazil.

"Wow!" I put my hands on my head.

"Haha. You think I not get you Sky too?"

"I was worried."

"Of course we got Sky. I get you the other satellites too. Now we watch TV all day and all night. Rashid get us extra 847 channels, 36 countries."

"Do you think we'll be able to see Henry when he goes to the mall? He'll be on Philly news."

"Umm . . . I not know. Sound like it might be cable. I ask Rashid." Amir presses another button. "Hey, we got *MasterChef* in Italian."

I shake my head.

"What? No *MasterChef*?"

"No, it's not that. It's just . . . Amir, I can't believe what you've done."

"It great," he says. "Which one we watch? This one?" He points at the first screen on the second row. A shark swims across an ocean. Amir presses another button. All the screens go blank, then bits of the shark appear on all the screens: its head in the top left, its tail in the bottom right. It swims toward a man in a cage with a harpoon. "Oops," says Amir. "Maybe we watch something not so scary."

I turn and walk back to my bed. Amir gives me the remote and sits down in the chair by my side. I press another button and we watch a program about how skyscrapers are built to survive earthquakes in San Francisco. Amir's eyes are shining so brightly that the skyscrapers reflect in his eyes. We both smile. Greg was right. He was building me a cinema. I might not watch hospital CCTV very much but I didn't think Sky would be as good as this.

Amir has to go and look after the others so he leaves me to watch TV on my own all afternoon. I watch a woman white-water rafting down a river and a man snowboarding down a mountain, and then I try out some of my DVDs—*The Amazing Spider-Man*, *Avengers Assemble*, *Batman Returns*. I loved them on normal TV. I love them even more on my massive screens.

I take a picture on my phone and send it to Henry.

**Thor never looked so big!**                              **3:06 pm**

I wait for a few minutes but Henry doesn't reply. I find the scene where Thor smashes a truck into a burning building. I wish Henry could see this. We could sit here all afternoon and flick through the sports and movie channels, and MTV. We could connect my X-Box too. I check my messages again. Maybe he's preparing for another walk. What if his walk in the mall goes well? They probably still won't let him come over here but he'll be out all the time. He won't have time to message me or play Tekken. He'll be busy like everyone else. Even Beth is too busy now. I look up at my screens. I love what Amir has done but it's not so much fun watching them on my own. There's no one to point out things to, or to laugh with or cheer with when someone scores a goal. But I shouldn't be grumpy. I should be grateful. It must be the drugs. Maybe it's because I'm tired. I pick up the remote and turn the screens off.

Amir turns them back on when he brings me my tea. He asks me if I'm fed up with them already. I tell him I love them but I've been thinking about Henry and that he seems busy.

"But he won't be all the time. Anyway," he says, "maybe you get busy too."

"In here?"

"No, but if the suits works for him maybe you can wear it too."

"I don't think so. It's too expensive and Henry's way bigger than me. They wouldn't do it and the European Space Agency still hasn't replied."

"We don't need them. I could make you one. We can't go to Philadelphia, but there's a shopping center near Enfield."

"Amir, I'm serious. They've got scientists."

"I serious too. I got my brother. He go to university."

"Is he a scientist?"

"No, he get a degree in geography."

"But—"

"We a great team. I design the suit, he tell us how to get there—wow, ninety minutes."

"What?"

Amir nods at the screens. "Ninety minutes. The sperm whale can hold its breath for ninety minutes. I held mine for four when I got stuck in the elevator last week."

I lay back on my bed. The TVs have been on too long. My head is aching and I feel really tired and Amir is talking about things that can't happen.

"I think we should turn them off now," I say.

Amir looks at me. "Turn the TVs off? We only just got them. You need to watch them, watch everyone in the hospital, the doctors, the nurses, the security guard."

"The security guard?"

"Jim, he funny. He come in when everyone go. Haven't you seen him yet?"

"No."

"You should. Watch him tonight. He funnier than Ricky Gervais."

"Who?"

"No matter. Just watch."

"But I need to turn them off sometime. Won't they get warm and make the room warmer?"

Amir shakes his head. "No, the thermostat will adjust and keep the room temperature constant. Anyway, we can't turn them off, there's another program I want you to watch at eight. It's about orangutans."

"Why do I want to watch that?"

"Don't you like orangutans?"

"Yes, I suppose so, but I might fall asleep before it starts."

"I set the alarm on your laptop."

"Can't I watch it in reruns?"

"I get you hundreds of channels and you want reruns?"

"Sorry."

"It's okay. I only joking."

He points the remote. The screens go blank and then he gets up and walks toward the door. "See you later."

"Okay." I smile and close my eyes. My head begins to thud. I'm supposed to be taking it easy. Amir should know I'm not supposed to get as tired as this. He's talked so much he's made me confused. He can't build me a suit; it costs millions. He can't really mean it, and even if he did, how would he get me out without being spotted? I love Amir and I love my TVs but I can't help think he's bought them for himself and not for me.

*The sun is shining and so are the car roofs. I'm in the back of our car, Beth is next to me playing on her Nintendo DS. Mum and Dad are in the front seats talking and listening to music.*

*"Can I put the window down?"*

*"It's hotter outside."*

*"But can I put it down?"*

*"Yes, okay."*

*I wind down the window and look out. A little girl in the car next to me is asleep with her head against the glass.*

*A man gets out of the car behind. "It's an accident," he shouts. "Just heard it on the radio. Twenty-seven-car pileup."*

*"Yeah, heard it too," shouts another man.*

*He looks up at the sky. I hear the thud of rotor blades. I lean out of the window and three helicopters fly over my head.*

*Dad is smiling at me in the side-view mirror and I reach out and touch his arm.*

*"How're you doing, Spidey?" Dad says.*

*"I'm okay, but the man just said there's a bad accident up ahead. Twenty-seven cars."*

*"I know." He smiles again, then rests his head on his hand.*

*Beth is laid out flat on the seat. Her hair is hanging down over her face and her Nintendo DS is smashed on the floor.*

*"Hey, Beth," I say. "It's an accident, twenty-seven cars . . . and you missed the helicopters."*

*I lean over. My seat belt pulls me back. I move it down onto my belly and reach out farther. "Beth, the helicopters, there were three of them."*

*Beth's hand falls off the seat. I pull her hair back off her face. There's a cut across her cheek. A line of blood trickles from her nose.*

"Mum! Dad! There's something wrong with Beth!' I tap Mum on the shoulder. Her head falls forward onto her chest. Dad turns around.

"Get out, Joe," he says. "The gasoline is coming in."

I look down. Gasoline is seeping under the door and covering my feet. The smell burns up my nose and makes me feel sick.

"Joe, now."

"But—" I pull at my seat belt and reach down for the button. "Dad, I'm stuck!"

"Press the button, Joe. The red button."

"I am, Dad. I am!"

I look up through the windshield. Four firemen run toward me, hoses and axes in their hands. Behind them I see ambulances and police cars and blue flashing lights. I press the button. It clicks but my belt doesn't release. Dad reaches back, pushes my hand out of the way. My belt goes slack.

"Now go, Joe."

I look around the car.

"But what about Beth, Dad? What about Mum?"

He shakes his head. A fireman reaches in through my window. He grabs my hand, wraps his arm around my chest.

"Come on, son. Let's go." He drags me out.

"What about my mum and dad . . . and my sister?"

He looks in the car, then back at me.

"Son, there's no one else here."

I look back at the car. Mum and Dad and Beth have gone. All the traffic has gone; it's just white lines and asphalt for miles and miles. I look back for the fireman. He's gone too.

# FOURTEEN

**I open my eyes.** My hair is wet and my pajama shirt is stuck to my skin. I shiver and wrap my arms around my body. The room temperature is constant but I still feel cold. I take off my top and pull my sheets up. They're wetter and colder than I am. My phone buzzes and makes me jump. The screen's all blurry. I blink. It's a text from Amir.

Hey Joe, you wake?

**Yes.**

Good. Is the TV on?

**No.**

Why not?

**I've just had a nightmare.**

Are you okay? Is Greg there?

**No.**

Charlotte?

**No. I just need to go to the bathroom.**

Okay.

I put my feet on the floor and walk to the end of my bed
and stop. My heart still thuds in my chest and my hands are
shaking. I walk to the bathroom and take off my pajamas.
My body is skinny and white under the light and my eyes
look big for my face. I turn on the taps and wash my face.
This nightmare is the worst one I have, and the one I've had
most. I used to call Beth after I had it. She says I still should
but I know it upsets her to talk about it, and it upsets me too.
It's hard to talk about a nightmare when most of it is true.

In my nightmare I am always there in the back of the
car, but I wasn't there at all. It was just Beth and Mum and
Dad. They were on the way back home to St. Albans after
visiting me. I can't remember saying good-bye to them; all
I can remember is both my nans and grandads coming in
to see me the next day. They never told me what happened,
only that there had been a crash—I don't remember much

about the day, everything was a blur. I think I was playing with soldiers on my bed. People were walking around and talking to me. They kept telling me Beth was injured and that Mum and Dad were dead. It was like my brain had been switched off, because all I can remember are the soldiers and the tanks and then looking up at the transition room door, waiting for them to come in. Beth says maybe it's better that way. Sometimes I wish she would talk about it so I know what happened. I didn't find out for ages until I got my laptop and searched it. A truck was in front of Dad. It swerved to miss another car and jackknifed across the road. Four other people died as well. Sometimes I wish I hadn't looked it up. But if I didn't have this nightmare it would only be replaced by something else. I screw my eyes up tight and bury my head in the towel. I'm always a super-hero in my dreams. I wish I could have been one that day.

I go back into my room, get some clean pajamas from my wardrobe. My phone buzzes. It's Amir again. I should be grateful that he's chatting to me, but after my nightmare all I want to do now is lie down and go to sleep.

Joe, are you sure you're okay?

**Yes, I'm better.**

Maybe this is no good idea. It wait.

**No, it sounds important.**

You sure?

**Yes. Watching orangutans might help me forget about things.**

There no orangutans.

**What?**

It no matter. Just don't touch nothing else. Not the satellite.

I pick up the remote and turn the TV on.

Turn on all the screens and put your headphones on.

**Amir, what are you doing?**

All done that? Joe?

I sigh and walk over to my PlayStation and put my head-phones on.
My phone buzzes again.

**Now turn on all the screens.**

I press the button. All the screens flicker on. It's dark, just shadows, and then a light flashes on and lights a path that leads to a door. I hear a voice in my headphones.

"Can you hear me?"

"Amir?"

Amir laughs. "Well, at least I know you hear me. But can you see too?"

"Yes, I can see. But Amir, what are you doing?"

The camera moves up the path toward the door. It's painted green with little bits of red and there's a bronze number 8. Amir's hand appears and lifts a knocker.

"Amir, where are you?"

A light switches on above the door. I hear a lock turn. Amir chuckles.

"Joe, you say you wish you meet my family."

"Um, yes, but . . ."

The door opens and the light shines out. A woman stands in the doorway. She wears an orange sari with a bright blue sash across her shoulder. She's got a bindi mark on her head.

Amir steps over the doormat and gives her a kiss. "Joe, this is Abha, my wife. Abha, this is Joe."

"Hello, Joe."

"Say hello, Joe."

I kneel up on my bed. "Hello, Abba," I say.

"No, Ab*ha*," says Amir. "Abha—beautiful glow, lustrous beauty."

Abha puts her hand over her mouth. "Amir, stop."

"But it true," says Amir. "Don't you think, Joe?"

"Yes." I think she's one of the most beautiful people I've ever seen.

Abha smiles and looks at the ground. I hear screaming and shouting. Three children run through the hall and disappear through a doorway. I swing my legs over the side of my bed and look at the screen. My heart is beating fast and my face is aching. I can't stop smiling. It's like I'm unwrapping the biggest present I ever had. I can't believe it's happening. I put my hand up to the side of my face and pull the microphone close to my mouth.

"Amir, how did you do this?"

He laughs. "It's easy, Joe. I connect laptop to camera and put camera on my head." He looks down and opens the buttons on his shirt. I see the hairs on his chest, below that his laptop is strapped to his belly with black tape. He shows me the camera wire that comes out of a port on the laptop and tracks it up his body until it disappears into the hairs under his arm. Then he closes the door, walks into the hall, and stops by a mirror. I laugh. The camera shakes. Amir is laughing too. A camera is strapped to his head with a sweatband and above it is a picture of me smiling.

"Where did you get that?" I ask.

Amir puts his finger to his lips. "Took it when you weren't looking. Want my children to see what you look like. But don't tell anyone."

"Amir," I say. "You know I'm good at keeping secrets."

"Yes, you are." He does the buttons up on his shirt. "Now what we do? Ah yes, I show you around."

We turn into a room. A huge TV is on in the corner. The three children are climbing on top of each other in a pile on the sofa. Amir taps one of them on the shoulder.

A little girl turns around. She's got big round eyes and a gap between her teeth.

"Say hello to Joe."

Her smile grows wider and she waves at me. "Hello, Joe."

"Joe, this is Ajala."

"Hi, Ajala."

She smiles and waves again. I lift up my hand.

"Amir, can she see me?"

"No," says Amir. "She just see picture. We connect camera for you next time."

"Great," I say.

Amir turns his head. Two boys jump in front of him. They both have dark hair and brown eyes. One has a mole on his cheek; the other is wearing glasses. Amir introduces me to his sons, Shukra and Guru. They say hello and jump up and down again.

"Do you want to watch TV with us?" Shukra points. *Blue Peter* is on the TV.

"No," says Amir. "Joe's got his own TV; he watches it all the time. Let's show him around the house instead."

Shukra reaches up and holds Amir's hand and they walk out of the room. Amir glances back. Ajala and Guru follow behind. They all walk into the dining room. There's a big table in the middle with six chairs. There are boxes piled high in the corner containing washing powder and disinfectant and smaller boxes of Mars Bars and Snickers. I ask Amir why he's got so much stuff. He tells me it was cheap to buy loads;

it's not usually in the dining room but he's decorating the kitchen. He walks back through the hall and into the kitchen. Wallpaper hangs off the walls. Abha is standing next to the oven with a saucepan of water boiling on top. The picture goes misty. Amir reaches up with a cloth and wipes the lens.

Abha picks up a wooden spoon.

"I think we come back later," he says.

Abha smiles. "No, Amir. Come here." She walks toward the camera and puts her hand on Amir's arm. "I think you need to calm down."

"We just having fun."

Abha turns her head to one side. "I know," she says. "I'm just saying." She reaches up and strokes the side of Amir's face and looks at him for a long time.

"I okay," whispers Amir.

Abha smiles. Amir leans forward and kisses her forehead.

"Oops, sorry Joe, forgot you were there!"

Amir is so funny.

"Now, where was I going? Ah yes. Upstairs."

Abha laughs and tuts at him. Amir turns back into the hallway and starts to climb the stairs. There are pictures on the walls. Amir points to them as he walks.

"This is my father, and this is my mother . . . and my grandfather and my grandmother, and this is all of us outside the Taj Mahal." He presses his finger against the picture and tells me it was taken three years ago before his grandmother died. The camera stays still for a while, and then Ajala tugs on his arm and says she wants to show me her room. She runs across a landing. The floors are wood and the walls are painted purple. We go through a doorway into a room. Ajala is standing in the middle. She turns in a circle and points at her bed and her wardrobe, then at a red rug on the floor that's covered with dolls. She picks one up, tells me its name is Simba. Then she opens her wardrobe. It's full of bright dresses and DVDs. She asks me if I want to borrow any. I laugh.

"I don't think your dresses would fit me!"

"I meant the DVDs, silly."

Amir laughs and tells her I've got loads of DVDs already. She holds up a blue pen. "Can he have this, then?"

Amir takes the pen, and then he leads me out onto the landing and into another room where the walls are painted blue. Shukra and Guru are laughing as they bounce up and down on their beds.

The camera shakes from side to side.

"Nothing much to see in here," says Amir. "Just a mess." He turns in a slow circle. I see Amir's reflection in a window and posters of Transformers all over the walls. Shukra picks up Ultra Magnus, fires his guns at the camera, and then turns him into a truck. I tell him I used to have one. I don't think he heard me.

"Crazy," says Amir. "They drive me crazy." He turns and we go back onto the landing. Amir takes a deep breath, then another. The *Blue Peter* tune is playing downstairs. Amir shows me a closed door and tells me it's his BED-ROOM and he shows me another door with bathroom written on a sign and a picture of bluebells underneath.

"The bathroom," he says. "You want to see in there?"

"It's okay."

"Then that's it," says Amir. "I show you everything, Joe!" He walks along the landing and stops by a mirror at the top of the stairs. His hair is wet and his skin is shiny. He wipes his forehead on his arm.

"Oops, sorry."

"It's okay," I say. "I'm still here."

"So, you meet my family."

"I really like them. They're nice. Not as crazy as you!"

"That's good!" Amir smiles so wide that it fills my room. I wait for him to say something, but he just looks down at his feet then back up to the mirror. When he's here with me he doesn't stop talking but now it's like he doesn't know what to say, and after everything he's shown me I don't know what to say either.

Abha shouts something I don't understand. The children push past Amir and run down the stairs.

"Have to go," he says.

"Okay."

"Did you enjoy it? Better than orangutans?"

"Yeah! It was great. I like your family. I'd like to meet them for real one day."

"Maybe you will. Maybe you get a special suit like your friend."

"I don't think so. I told you the ESA hasn't replied."

"The ESA? They no good. They fly a satellite all the way to Mars and crash into a mountain."

I laugh.

"It's true. We find something else."

"I'm okay."

"What do you mean you're okay? Don't you want to go outside?"

"Yes, but I like what you did."

Amir smiles. "Me too," he says. "I think they all like you."

Abha shouts again.

"Coming!" Amir lifts his hands up to his head. "I'm sorry. Really have to go."

He takes the camera off his head and the screens go blurry.

"Amir?"

"Yes?"

"Thank you."

"That's okay. . . . Oh, Joe . . . I nearly forget."

"What?"

"Don't forget to watch Jim."

"Who?"

"The night security guard."

"But, Amir. I'm tired."

"But you try? He worth it."

"Okay."

"Good night Joe."

"Good night."

I press the remote and the screens come back on. Jim the security guard is reading a book in reception. He turns a page and takes a bite out of a sandwich. Another security guard walks toward him and they talk for a while. Jim circles his finger in the air. The other security guard nods, then walks down the corridor and gets in the elevator. A minute later he appears on screen nine. He walks up and down the corridors checking the doors, then gets back into the elevator and does the same on the second floor. I look back at screen one. Jim's still reading and eating. On all the other screens the corridors are quiet and empty, except for two porters talking outside the operating theater door. I look back at screen one. The reception is empty. Jim is walking down the corridor with his book in his hand. He stops and pushes the toilet door open. I don't know why Amir told me to watch him. He hasn't done anything funny yet.

I yawn and rest my head on my pillow. My room is empty, dark, and cold. I think of Amir and his family. For a while it was like they were all in here with me, laughing and talking. I close my eyes. I imagine Amir sitting at the table. I can see Shukra, Ajala, and Guru smiling with their knives and forks in their hands. Abha holds out her hand and tells me to pass her my plate. Ajala asks me if she can get me some water. I nod. Abha passes my plate back. It's piled high with chicken and potatoes. She smiles. "It's nice to have you here, Joe."

Amir picks up a glass and holds it in the air. "Friends," he says.

I nod. My headphones slip down onto my neck. I open my eyes. They've all disappeared like ghosts.

# FIFTEEN

## 11 YEARS, 3 MONTHS, AND 7 DAYS

**It's nine o'clock** in the morning and the doctors have already come and gone. They think I'm getting better; my whites are back up over 3,000 and my temperature is going down. I feel better too. I can walk around the room without holding on to my bed and they're letting me go to the toilet without a nurse having to wait outside. Dr. Moore said he thinks the worst is over. He smiled and ruffled my hair when he said that. Then he looked at my screens and shook his head.

"Young man," he said. "You might be feeling better, but I think you should give your eyes a rest."

"I will," I said. (I won't.)

I've been watching the screens all week. First I watched all my favorite films one after the other. I watched Thor beat up Loki and throw him off a cliff; I watched Captain America, the Falcon, and Black Widow take down Hydra, and Greg came and sat with me to watch Spidey stop the Lizard. The next day I searched through all the channels but all I could find was the news from all the countries in the world and talk shows with people shouting at each other in languages I couldn't understand.

I've been watching the CCTV too. The men digging the road outside have passed the hospital doors and are on their way to Starbucks. It's gotten so hot that they've brought in huge floodlights so they can work at night. Two days ago a truck delivered three massive rolls of copper. Amir said it's to increase the magnetic field so the alien ship can hover and not actually touch the ground. He said it's called maglev. I looked it up on my laptop. It didn't say anything about aliens or spaceships, but there's a railway being built with magnets to propel trains in Japan.

The door clicks open. I pick up the remote.

Greg walks in and glances at the screens. An excavator jerks along the road, lowers its claw, and digs at the ground.

"Mate, come on, you've got to get dressed sometime." He puts clean clothes on the back of my chair.

"But I like it."

"I know, but do you have to watch this?"

"No." I press screen eight.

Greg laughs. The picture changes to the hospital door. The woman at reception is outside talking to the security guard.

"I think he's going to ask her out," I say. "He walked her to the end of the road last night."

"Mate, Keith's been walking Julie to the end of the road

for months. He's not going to ask her out. It's just an excuse for him to have another cigarette."

"But he bought her a kebab!"

"Ha, well, she's bound to say yes, then."

On the screen, Keith says something I can't hear. Julie laughs. I can't hear that either but she's still smiling when I switch to screen three and see her sit back down at her desk.

Greg wasn't supposed to know about the CCTV but one night I fell asleep and he came in and saw Jim reading his book. I thought my screens would be taken away but Greg says he won't tell anyone. I still have to turn the screens over if anyone else comes in. Amir is trying to find some sensors that will turn them off when my eyelids drop. His brother is working on it. He thinks he can get me one of the eye sensors that soldiers use to fire guns on war-zone simulators.

I press channel twelve. A laundry van arrives and backs up to the back of the building. Two men get out and slide back two big doors.

"Mate."

I look up. Greg's standing by the door.

"I said, I'll be back in to watch the football later, and don't forget your documentary will be on."

The two men load bags of dirty laundry into the back of the van. I think the young one has a girlfriend because he's in the back of the van texting on his phone, or maybe he has a best friend and sends him texts all the time. The older man throws a bag down and says something. The young one shakes his head and puts his phone in his pocket.

My laptop beeps. It's Henry. He's been quiet. His doctors and the people from NASA have been building up his energy levels and he's been walking around in his room getting used to his suit.

| | |
|---|---|
| Hey Joe, what are you doing? | 2:06 PM |
| **Watching people in the street.** | 2:06 PM |
| You're crazy | 2:07 PM |
| **It's good. Better than real TV.** | 2:07 PM |
| Better than Avengers Assemble? | 2:08 PM |
| **No. Not that good. How are you?** | 2:08 PM |
| I'm OK. Boots are OK, too. Helmet's a bit small. Face looks like a watermelon. | 2:08 PM |
| **Ha** | 2:09 PM |
| My folks are coming today. Last time Dad can see me before I go to the mall. Have you got your suit yet? | 2:10 PM |
| **No. I don't think Amir meant it.** | 2:10 PM |

Hasn't he done anything?                    2:11 PM

**Not really. Just checked my trainer size
and the label inside my pajamas.**          2:11 PM

NASA measured me up with lasers and stuff,
but if your sneakers and pajamas fit
it's kind of the same thing.                2:12 PM

**I'm not sure.**                           2:12 PM

Maybe it's a joke.                          2:12 PM

**No, Amir's not mean.**                    2:12 PM

Exactly. So it's true. Where'd'ya like to go?   2:13 PM

**Empire State Building! Hang out with Spidey.**   2:13 PM

Ha. Be great. Shame it's in New York.       2:13 PM

**Yeah**                                    2:13 PM

Hey, it's only in the next state.
You could pop over and see me.              2:14 PM

**Ha!**                                     2:14 PM

You told anyone you're going out?           2:15 PM

No. Don't want to worry Beth, and Amir said if
anyone found out he could lose his job.                2:15 PM


True. Did he say where you're going?                   2:16 PM


Not really. He said there's a mall in Enfield.
Most of the time he just watches the planes.           2:16 PM


Weird.                                                 2:16 PM


Do hope it's true.                                     2:16 PM


Me too.                                                2:17 PM


*Hey, my folks just arrived.*                          2:17 PM


I'll get off.                                          2:17 PM


No. It's OK. Go to screen.                             2:17 PM


We turn our cameras on.

I see Henry smiling and hear the sound of people talking.
Henry turns his laptop around. His mum and dad are standing by the door wearing white overalls. They wave at me and
smile. Henry's mum's got blonde hair like Henry and his dad
is going bald. Henry says it's because he worries about pay-
ing for the hospital treatment so much. Henry's room and
treatment aren't free like mine. To begin with his parents had
some insurance but it wasn't enough. So now his dad has to

work away from home for months on an oil rig near Nova Scotia in Canada. It's a long way from Philadelphia—it takes five hours on a plane. His dad looks so tired that I think he might just have gotten off it. They smile and wave and I wave back. Then they walk over to Henry, tell him they've missed him and they love him. Henry opens his arms, says he loves them too and they hug one another for a long time. It's like they've forgotten I'm here but I don't care because if my mum and dad could come and visit me I would hug them for a long time too. Eventually they pull away.

"Where's Matt?" I ask.

"Don't think he's here, Joe," says Henry.

I hear someone giggling. Henry turns the camera toward the ground. His brother is crouched down at the end of his bed.

"*Pow!*" He points his fingers at me, pretending he's got a gun in his hand.

I clutch my hand to my chest and fall back on my bed. "You got me," I say.

Henry laughs. "You can't shoot Joe. He's a superhero. He can catch bullets between his fingers even if they travel at the speed of light."

Matt and I laugh.

I haven't seen Henry's brother for three months. He's half Henry's age and half as big, but his face is so chubby it almost fills the screen. I turn my laptop around.

"Hey, Matt, I've got something to show you."

I flick the TV monitors on.

"Wow, how did you get all of those?"

"My nurse," I say. "He brought them in while I was sleeping."

Matt's face breaks into a grin. "It's cool. . . . Hey, Mom, Joe's got twelve TVs!"

Henry's mum's smiling face creeps in at the edge of my screen. "That's nice."

"Can I get more in my bedroom?"

"No, Matt," she says. "I think one TV is enough."

Matt sticks out his lip and I laugh. I wish I had a brother. I love Beth but it'd be great if I had a brother too. I wonder if he would look like me. We could play together in our backyard and run down the road and buy candy from the corner store. We could eat them and then play pretend war on the way home. He could be the Green Goblin and I would chase after him as he zigzagged across the road on his hoverboard and I'd catch him in my webs and we'd both nearly die laughing as we rolled on the ground. But Mum and Dad thought it was too risky to have another kid, just in case it had the same disease as me. There was a fifty percent chance that it would. I wish they had, though. Henry's mum and dad were told the same too. Sometimes when he annoys Henry, Henry tells me Matt was a mistake. I think he's a good mistake.

The camera wobbles as Henry carries the laptop across the room and puts it down on a table. He sits down on a chair. His mum and dad sit down on the sofa. Henry's dad leans forward and moves the screen.

"That okay, Joe?"

The picture moves to the left. Matt's sitting on the arm of

the sofa, picking his nose. I laugh. They all look at the camera and smile. It's like I'm in the middle of a circle. I love it that when they come to visit Henry they come to visit me as well. Sometimes Henry talks to Beth when she visits. It's good, but it's not the same as if I had a bigger family to share.

Henry's mum is the first one to speak. She is wearing bright red lipstick and when she talks she looks around at everyone, just to check they're listening.

"I've got a new job," she says, "at a new accounting firm that just opened in town. They seem good people, but I don't know how I got it. I thought I was too old, but I guess I make good coffee and can type 120 words a minute."

"Yeah, and unfortunately she talks that fast too," says Henry's dad.

We all laugh. Henry's mum tries to be quiet but it's not long before she starts talking again. She tells us her car broke down last week out on the highway, which is American for motorway, but she didn't mind too much because the tow-truck guy looked like Tom Cruise. Henry's dad says he's not sure we all want to hear that, but all she does is smile and then start talking again about the tow-truck driver and then about a cat on her street that died after climbing into a tumble dryer. Eventually she stops and looks around the room. "Okay," she says. "I guess it's someone else's turn." She looks at Matt. He reaches into his pocket and pulls out a piece of paper and holds it up to the camera.

*Things I did.*

He turns the list around and reads it out. "My boat sank

in the lake. I lost my bike. I found ten dollars. I bought a hamster. I fell over in the mall—did this—" He rolls up his trousers and shows us the scabs on his knees. "Went to the movies, got a new Transformer, spoke to Dad on Skype, spoke to Henry on Skype, lost my hamster, late for school, got a lock for the cage, got a new hamster, drew a T. rex, packed stuff to go to see Henry and Joe. The end."

His dad smiles and puts his arm around Matt's shoulder. I wait for someone to ask Matt questions about his list, but they don't and I think that they've already spoken to him about it and the list was just written for me. I hear a door slide open. Henry's mum walks in front of the camera, then comes back a few moments later and puts two cups of coffee down on the table. She looks at Henry. He smiles at her, then looks in my direction like he wants to say something but all he does is shrug. I do the same. It's weird how we can talk to each other all night and all day but can't think of anything to say when other people are around.

Henry's dad leans forward and picks up his cup of coffee. "Hey, Joe," he says, "Henry says you might be going outside too."

"Sorry, Joe. It just slipped out."

"Oops, sorry, Joe. Didn't know it was a secret. This guy's going to the mall." He puts his arm around Henry's shoulders. "Where are you off to?"

I shrug. It seems silly to talk about where I'm going. Amir hasn't told me anything; we don't have any plans. Henry knows exactly what he's doing. He's had a timetable mapped out for months.

"I don't know. I could tell you where I go in my head, though."

"Yeah, Joe," says Henry. "Tell us one of your dreams, the superhero things. Start with the soccer guy."

I smile and look up at Theo Walcott. I'd love to play football with him, and after the game at Wembley he'd shake my hand and give me one of his shirts and show me around the dressing rooms and I'd meet the rest of the team. On the screen, everyone is waiting for me to speak, but I feel nervous that I won't say anything interesting.

"My dream is to go into London and meet Beth at Covent Garden. She likes a café there. I don't know the name, but she says it's inside the market, by the clock. I'd get Greg to text her, say he needs to talk to her about me. But he wouldn't be there; it'd be me. I'd walk up behind her while she's drinking coffee and reading her book. I'd tap her on the shoulder and make her jump. Then she'd give me a massive hug."

I stop talking. Henry's mum smiles at me.

"Go on, Joe. What happens next?"

"I don't know, but she always says she'd like to go on the London Eye."

"Do you know the route?" She says it like "rowt."

"Sorry?"

"The route . . . Do you know the way?"

"Oh, yes, I've done it on Google Earth loads of times. It's in my head."

"But don't take the subway," says Henry. "You don't want to go underground after being stuck in a room all your life." We all laugh.

"Maybe you could all meet her," I say. "We could go to her house."

"Is it near your hospital?"

"Not now, she's gone to Edinburgh. It's miles away."

Henry's mum rests her head against her husband's shoulder. I wait for Henry or Matt to say something, but they all just sit there looking at me. I look down at the floor. I didn't get to go to Beth's house before she moved. It was only two miles away. I've seen pictures of it when she's there with her friends, but that's just pictures of people sitting on the sofa watching TV or drinking in the kitchen. If I visited her I wouldn't want anyone else there. I'd just like to sit on the sofa by her side, eat dinner, and watch TV. But I can't do that. It's silly to think I could.

I hear a sniff and look up. Henry's mum is smiling but wiping a tear from her eye at the same time.

"I'm sorry," I say.

Henry's mum wipes her nose on her sleeve.

"You good, Joe?" says Henry's dad.

"Yes, I'm just a bit tired now."

"Not surprised," says Henry. "You've been all the way to Trafalgar Square and back again."

I smile. "Think I might get some rest."

"Okay."

They all wave and shout good-bye. I pick up my phone and text Beth.

Miss you.

A minute later she replies.

**What made you send that?**

No reason. Just felt like it.

**I'm on my way to work.**

I'm lying on my bed.

☺

**Been talking to Henry**

Bet he's excited about the mall.

He is . . .

My fingers hover over the keypad. I want to tell her that Amir is taking me out too, but she'd tell me not to go. She might even tell the nurses. But she'd want what I wanted, wouldn't she? I press the keys.

I've got something to tell you. Don't worry about me, but I'm going outside too.

My thumb is over the send key.

**Got to go.**

I shake my head. I don't want her to worry. I take a deep breath and press delete.

OK

**I'll text again after work.**

X

X

I sigh and hold my phone down by my side.

On my screens the workmen are still digging the trench. The traffic lights are changing from red to green. On the bottom screen I see someone on the roof of my building. It's the man in the coveralls. He slides his bag off his shoulder, reaches in, and pulls out a knife. I didn't think that we had pigeons on our roof too. They damage buildings and carry disease. They could get trapped in the cooling towers and the disease would come through the tubes and out through the vents. But the vents have got filters and my machines have got sensors. I look up at the air-conditioning unit. The blades turn down toward me and the air blows in. The germs could be coming in right now. I close my eyes and take a deep breath. How can I even think of going outside when I'm so scared of catching a disease in here? I take another deep breath and open my eyes. The man walks between the cooling towers. I pick up my remote and turn the screens off.

# SIXTEEN

## 11 YeaRS, 3 MON+HS, anD 8 DaYS

**The light on my laptop** has been flashing all morning. The documentary was on TV last night and already the messages have started to arrive. It's like this every year. At first they didn't let me see them all. They censored them by blocking all the rude ones or the ones they thought would upset me. But now I'm older they let them all through, except the ones with the f-word.

Greg sat and watched the documentary with me. I was on for fourteen minutes and forty-five seconds. They cut out the bit about the wasp, all the times I went to the toilet, and the hour the fly was on the wall was cut to fifteen seconds. But they left in the bit about me being a superhero. Greg laughed when he heard me say that. The rest of the program was interviews with doctors and some of the kids in the rest of the wards. I saw the girl who pretends she's a horse trotting between the beds and I saw the boy

who reads *The Hunger Games* on his own in a corner with
his book. He didn't really say much, except that his favorite film was *The Amazing Spider-Man*. I thought the boy
was quite cool and wished we could watch it together. But
the billiard-ball kid was my favorite. He never sat still.
Graham was trying to talk to him while New-cameraman-
David chased after them with the camera and when he
caught up with them the billiard-ball kid was out of breath
and talked really fast.

"ThedoctorsandthenursesarereallykindlikeandIlikethe
otherkidstooeveniftheydon'tsupportNewcastle."

Me and Greg laughed. Then we laughed even more when
he got a sheet from his bed and ran around the ward pretending he was a ghost. But even though he laughed a lot
I could tell he wasn't very well. I could see his veins underneath the red paint on his head and his legs were the same
thickness as my arms. I'd like to meet him, but if I did I
think I'd be too tired to keep up with him.

I pick up my laptop. I've got six messages and I've already
had conversations with some of them. I click on the first
one.

**BBC Bubble Boy Forum**
**Tue August 24, 10:01 PM**
*Dear Bubble Boy,*
   *I just saw you on TV. Sorry you're stuck in a bubble. Are there*
*any things you can do to help you forget about it?*
   *Amy Hobbs. Dumfries.*

**BBC Bubble Boy Forum**

**Wed August 25, 07:23 AM**

*Dear Amy. Yes, I dream.*

What do you dream about?

Lots of things.

Does it work?

Yes.

Great!

But when I wake up I'm still here.

*Oh*

Sorry. Got to go to school. Bye.

Bye.

**BBC Bubble Boy Forum**

**Wed August 25, 09:23 AM**

Dear Bubble Boy, would you like to come to my birthday party? It's on August 28th. You can bring Henry too and my mum said Greg can come as well if he likes.

Georgia D. Brighton

**BBC Bubble Boy Forum**

**Wed August 25, 10:25 AM**

*Dear Georgia, I would love to.*

But I can't.

Happy Birthday.

Most of the messages I receive are like these. I think they think they are the only ones who ask the same questions, but I don't mind. It must be what it's like for film stars when they get interviewed for newspapers and on TV. Greg said it's a good thing because at least it shows people were watching me and thinking about me. A new message beeps on my screen.

**BBC Bubble Boy Forum**
**Wed August 25, 10:21 AM**

*Dear Bubble Boy, my dad thinks that you're not really in a bubble, that there's nothing wrong with you and it's all a publicity stunt to get people to donate more money for the hospital. He says when the cameras go off you walk outside and go around the corner to KFC. I told him that can't be true because you would die outside, and anyway you can only eat food wrapped in foil. He said that's garbage, that you were in there last week eating a whole bargain bucket and drinking Coke. He knew it was you because you had an Arsenal shirt on. And he got your autograph on the box. I hope this isn't true, but I also hope it is too. It can't be nice living in a bubble.*

*Tom Huntingdon*

*Basildon*

I wish it were true. I wish I were faking. I wish when they stopped filming I could just put my coat on and go outside. I would love to go to KFC. I've only ever seen it on TV or sometimes I've seen the red boxes blowing down the street. I don't know what it tastes like. Greg told me it's greasy and smells of sawdust, but that doesn't help because I don't know what sawdust smells like.

My phone buzzes. My mornings are never as busy as this. I pick it up. It's a message from Beth.

Joe, are you up yet?

**Yes**

My phone rings. I look at the screen. Beth? She never calls. Maybe she wants to talk about last night. I hold my phone up to my ear.

"Joe."

"Yes."

She says my name again but then all I can hear is a muffled sound and the roar of traffic.

"Beth," I say. "I can't hear you." I look at my phone. I've got three bars. "Beth."

The noise of the traffic has gone, all I can hear is Beth crying. My heart beats fast. I get off my bed and walk around the room.

"Beth, what's wrong?"

She tries to speak but all she does is cry more.

"Beth, where are you?"

The phone goes dead. I look at my screen. She's gone. I walk over to the window and dial her number. My phone buzzes in my hand before I get through.

Joe, I'm sorry. Shouldn't have called.

My hands are shaking I can hardly type.

**What's wrong?**

I'm not going to stay in Edinburgh.

**Why not?**

I saw you on TV. You didn't want me to come up here.

**What?**

You cried when they asked you.

Oh no! I forgot I did that. I look around the room, up at the air conditioner. I could tell her it had switched on when Graham asked me the question. I could say it was blowing really hard, so hard that the air stung my eyes, but she'll know that's not true.

Joe? Are you still there?

**Yes. I'm sorry. It was the drugs. These ones make me cry.**

I look at my phone and wait for another message. The screen goes blank. I hate it when Beth goes quiet.

**Wish I hadn't gone on TV.**

But you like it. And you were great.

**Not really.**

You were. The bit when you said you were a super-hero was lovely.

**But I am.**

Ha

I smile and close my eyes and try to think of something else that will make her laugh but my phone buzzes again before I can.

Joe, I know it wasn't the drugs. I'll come back. I'm going to look closer to London.

**You said you had to go there.**

I'll see if I can change.

She has to stay there. If Mum and Dad were alive, she would. I want her to do what she wants to do and get the best job, and be happy. I don't want her to be thinking about me all the time.

**I want you to stay there. Just because I'm stuck in a bubble doesn't mean you have to be too. It'll be boring if you**

**don't. You won't have anything to talk to me about.**

OK. OK! You can stop now.

**But I mean it.**

I know you do.

**You're just panicking like I do. Take deep breaths.**

Ha! The expert!

**We'll Skype every night.**

You're too busy chatting to Henry!

**When he's having dinner.**

Squeezing me in?

**I'm joking.**
**So you'll stay up there?**

☹

I smile. I'm winning. I need to get off the phone before she changes her mind.

**My battery is dying.**

It can't be.

**It is.**

You've got a charger.

**It's broken.**

I know what you're doing!

**You're staying. OK.**

But only if you call when you need me.

**I will**

Promise?

**Battery going . . . battery going!**

Joe! Promise?

**OK**

Is your battery really going?

**No. I want to pee. Ha!**

X

X

I turn my phone off and put it down by my side. My chest is aching and my head is too. I wish I hadn't cried on TV. I wish Graham hadn't asked that question, or they had cut it out.

# SEVENTEEN

## 11 YeaRS, 3 MON+HS, anD 9 DaYS

There's a line twenty people long at reception. Julie has been busy taking presents all morning. They're stacked up against the wall behind her desk. I can't see what they all are, but if it's the same as last year they'll be mostly teddies, dolls, and remote-control cars. Some of them are old toys that people don't want anymore, but some are newly wrapped with labels with kids' names written on them. They cut most of them off but I don't mind. It's not fair that just those of us who were on TV get to have everything, and my room isn't big enough for them all anyway. But I would like the FIFA 15 game that a man and his little boy brought in an hour ago.

The line grows even longer after midday as people take their lunch hour and go to the shops and bring more presents in for us. Then after two o'clock the reception area is quiet again and the pile goes down as Keith takes them down the corridor and locks them in a room. I switch cameras and watch the workmen for an hour until I spot Amir walking along the sidewalk with his backpack. He nods to Keith. Then when he's in the reception area he turns, glances up at the camera, and gives me a thumbs-up. He's so silly.

It usually takes him twenty-two minutes to get to my room from the reception area, but today nearly two hours have gone before I hear him in the transition zone. He smiles as he walks into my room.

"You okay?" he asks.

"Yes, I'm okay, but where have you been?"

"Sorry, things are a bit busy."

"With the others?"

Amir nods his head quickly. "Yes, but I was looking for this, too."

He holds up his hand and shows me a tiny square chip between his finger and thumb.

"What is it?"

He grins. "My brother got us a decoder upgrade—Quantax 635i with tri-media processor," he says. "It scans through all networks at the same time—every country, every city, terrestrial, satellite, and cable."

"But I don't watch all the ones I've got."

"You can't have enough," he says. "Everyone wants more channels; you can't have too many channels. The world is so big you might miss something somewhere." He kneels down by the receiver.

I get off my bed and kneel beside him. "Amir, where does all this come from? It must cost a lot of money."

He takes the cover off the receiver and looks at me. "No, it free. My brother gets it from backs of trucks."

"It's stolen?"

"No, we just borrow." Amir grins at me as he clicks the new parts into place.

"There," he says. "Now all we've got to do is find the channel."

"Which one?"

"The one your friend will be on."

"Henry?"

"Who else? No point in sending a man to the moon if no one turns on the TV and watches him."

I smile. Henry isn't going to the moon, but I know what Amir means. It wouldn't be the same if Henry just told me what it was like to walk around the mall; he'd leave things out that he thought weren't important and he might make things up that didn't happen, which he sometimes does when he's excited. It would be much better to see him.

I stand up. Amir points the remote at the TV as we walk backward toward my bed. The monitors flicker but all we see are fuzzy pictures and all we hear is white noise.

Amir looks confused. "It's not on Galaxy," he says. "But it must be on here somewhere."

The channels change again—cars on a racing track, a girl on a motorbike, camels walking across a desert—Amir taps the remote against the side of his head.

"I call him," he whispers.

"Henry?"

"No, my brother." He takes his phone out of his pocket and walks over to the window. As he presses the keys I try more channels but all I find are silly commercials about cornflakes and detergent. Amir holds his finger in the air. I stop scanning.

"Rashid, we can't find it!" Amir listens, then starts talking faster. "'Kay . . . 'kay." He turns off the phone.

"What did he say?"

He walks over and takes the remote from me. "My fault," he says. "We on Astra when we should be on Echo Star." He glances at his watch. "But we haven't got time now. We've only got two days."

"Until the aliens come?"

"No," he says. "Until you go outside."

"What? Am I really going?" My breath starts coming out in quick little bursts and my heart rate speeds up straightaway. Outside. Outside!!

"Am I really going?!"

"Of course, it short notice, but it the only day my brother can lend us his car."

We've only got two days but he hasn't told me anything! Henry had a plan mapped out for three months. He's been on a special diet and been out for trial runs. All I've done is watch TV on my bed!

"What's wrong? Are you nervous? It okay. Everybody gets nerves, even him." He nods at Theo Walcott.

I bite my lip.

"Come on," says Amir. "What is it?"

"I'm a bit scared. I don't know what I'm wearing or where I'm . . . going."

Amir leans toward me. "Don't worry." He taps the side of his head. "It's all up here. I know everything."

"But I need to know, too."

Amir looks at his watch, then back toward the door.

"Yes, of course you do. Sorry. Quick, pass me that."

I reach over to my table and hand him my laptop. Amir looks angry, suddenly.

"What's this?"

He reads the post about me being in KFC.

"That garbage," he says.

"I know."

Amir types:

*Your dad is wrong. It wasn't KFC, it was Burger King.*

He presses send and then grins at me. "So," he says. "I tell you what we going to do."

He opens a blank document, then starts to blink quickly like there's something in his eye.

"Are you okay?"

"Of course, I just thinking." He blinks again and starts to type.

"This is a checklist," he says. "Things you have to do, things I have to do. Don't save the document, just remember what I type and then delete."

I look at the screen and try to follow what he's writing

but his fingers move so quickly the page scrolls up before I
can read.

"There." He turns the screen toward me.

**ETD 03:06 a.m.**
**Compressed Air 19.5%**
**Oxygen 80.5%**
**Nitrogen.**
**Volume 1 liter. Air flow 3 cubic feet per minute.**
**Duration 2 hrs 52 mins 26 seconds.**
**ETA 06:58 a.m.**

"Ha," he says. "Did I tell you I used to work on the
trains?"

"So this is all we need?"

Amir nods quickly. "Yes," he says. "I worked it all out.
I give you an extra twenty-six seconds of air in case we get
stuck in the elevator."

I read the rest of the list. Some of it makes sense; some of
it is numbers and words I don't understand. There are things
on it like cubic capacity, internal and external temperature
variability, light pollution, and density of traffic. Amir then
opens his e-mail account. "And here," he says, "I do this at
home." He shows me a picture of a person with my name
above its head.

**Height 150 cm.**
**Weight 54 kg.**

Body Mass 12.2.

Lung capacity 4.5 ltr.

Resting breath 23 per minute—variance 100% increase for PA.

I look up. Amir grins at me.

"Some I got from your records, the rest from *wikiHow*."

I scratch my head.

Amir laughs. "I joke," he says. "Trust me. I consult the best doctors. I no ask anyone here but I know some of the top people in India. Oh, I nearly forgot. Seven-eleven." He takes a deep breath.

"What's seven-eleven?"

Amir lets his breath go.

"Increases lung capacity," he says, "and it keep you calm, too. Breathe in for seven seconds and out for eleven. Try it. Like this."

I watch him and breathe in for as long as he does, then let my breath out.

"Good," he says. "And again. Does it make you feel good?"

"No, it makes me feel sick."

Amir laughs a lot. "Me too, but it goes after a while. Practice tonight."

I tell him I will, and then I read the list again. There are so many numbers. He's done so much research, but I don't know whether to trust him or not. This is a really, really important thing. If he'd installed the TVs wrong, all that would have happened was the channels would have been mixed up or maybe they wouldn't have switched on. If he's got this wrong, I could go outside and die.

Amir's pager beeps. "I've got to go," he says. "Keep watching the screens. Especially Jim."

"But he doesn't do anything!"

"You no find him and Phil funny? They like them Chuckle Brothers. Or Ant and Dec. Maybe you take notes, Joe. They so funny you should watch them all night."

"Why?"

"I like to know what happens when I not here. Have you got any more messages on here from the people?" He turns my laptop around before I can answer.

**BBC Bubble Boy Forum**
**Thu August 26, 12:17 PM**
*Dear Bubble Boy,*

> *You were so cute when you were eight.*
> *What happened?*
> *Stephen H. Bristol*

Amir tuts. "Some people," he says. "They no understand."

*He grew up, and so should you.*

"Brilliant!" I laugh.

Amir's pager beeps again.

"Must go," he says. "Somebody else need me. I might see you later, but I'm not in tomorrow."

"But Amir . . ." I look back at the screen.

"Yes?"

"Why are we going out at night?"

"It's too risky during the day. And this way you get to see what the aliens come here for."

"What's that?"

"The greatest show on Earth."

"What's—"

Amir grins and slides out the door.

I turn the screens off and lie back on my bed. I really am going outside. I really am. I really, really am! I pick up my phone. I want to tell Beth. I want to ask her if she thinks I'm being stupid believing that it could really happen, or even for going at all. But I can't tell her. She's already worried about being so far away from me. I don't want to add another thing. I know she would think it was too risky and I can't tell Greg because he would think that too. I want to go outside, even though it might be dangerous. No one can understand how much. Only Henry knows what it feels like to be stuck in a bubble. But my legs start to twitch and my chest feels tight.

Deep breaths. Deep breaths.

I get up and walk up and down the room. My laptop beeps again. A new message.

**BBC Bubble Boy Forum**

**Thu August 26, 3:08 PM**

*Dear Bubble Boy, I saw you on TV last night and you were watching Source Code. It's one of my favorite films. I think Jake*

*Gyllenhaal was great in it. He was brilliant in Donnie Darko, too. Have you seen that? Anyway, when you were talking to the interviewer, he asked you what you would do if you had eight minutes to live and you said you would look out the window. I thought that was a bit sad. But ever since, I've been thinking what I would do in eight minutes. At first I thought I would like to do exciting things like go to Disneyland Paris or climb Mount Everest, or maybe I would go to New York, but then I realized that eight minutes isn't very long and I would freeze in time before I got anywhere. So in the end I thought I would just stay at home and watch TV with my mum and dad.*

*I hope you get better soon.*

*You can write back if you like.*

*Dan Essex*

I walk over to the window. The workmen are digging the trench, the people in the offices are staring at their computer screens, and the planes are flying over the Lucozade building into Heathrow. If I really only had eight minutes, what would I do? I couldn't do anything. I couldn't go anywhere. I might make it through the transition zone and the corridors and the elevators. I might be able to make it to reception, but by the time I got there it would be time to go back. But now I've got more than eight minutes. Amir said I've got nearly three hours. Three whole hours outside. I walk back to my laptop and open a new tab.

*What can I do in London in three hours?*

323,000,000 results—I can buy a tourist card and get on a bus. I can visit Buckingham Palace, the Houses of Parliament, and the Tower of London. If the line isn't too long, I can go to Madame Tussauds. I can walk in Hyde Park. I can get on a barge and float down the Thames. I can have tea at the Ritz; I can see a play. I can do nearly seventy million things, but they'll all be closed or it'll be too dark to see anything at four a.m. Amir, what are we going to do when we have to get up so early?

My chest cramps again. I'm not sure I want to go. What if I die? Deep breaths. I won't be able to go anywhere if I can't breathe. I lie down beside my laptop and look at the question again. Dan hasn't got three hours. He's only got eight minutes. I close my eyes, think for a moment, and open them again.

*Dear Dan, I haven't seen Donnie Darko but I love Source Code and I'd love to do all those things you said you'd like to do. But I think if I had eight minutes, I would stay at home too.*

I turn my laptop off and look at the screens. Nothing much seems to be happening. I'm watching the same thing over and over again. It's like when the robbers override the security system and play the film on the CCTV while they steal money from a bank. I yawn and think of trying to find some football to watch. But Amir told me to make notes. I make them on my laptop.

4:10 PM Man arrives to repair photocopier

5:05 PM Messenger delivers blood.

5:30 PM Julie says good-bye to Keith and walks down the road.

6:22 PM Keith is talking on phone.

7:55 PM Jim arrives.

8:00 PM Julie meets Keith outside. They kiss in the service alley.

8:30 PM Jim takes his book to the toilet.

8:46 PM Jim comes out of the toilet.

9:15 PM Phil checks the first floor.

10:00 PM Jim goes to the toilet again.

I close my laptop down. This is so boring. How can Amir say I should watch them all night? I don't think the Chuckle Brothers are very funny, but they're funnier than this. Ant and Dec definitely are. I looked them up.

# EIGHTEEN

## 11 YEARS, 3 MONTHS, AND 10 DAYS

I'm practicing my breathing exercises when Greg comes in the next morning. His eyes are red and his face is white; he looks like he's been up all night. He sits down beside me and leans forward with his elbows on his knees.

"Much happening, mate?" He nods at the screens.

"Nothing much. Keith kissed Julie, and I saw you fall off your bike when you turned the corner this morning."

Greg tuts. "It was the bloody cones, mate. Somebody moved them during the night."

"That was Terry." I point to screen four. "He's in charge of traffic lights and cones."

"Ha, have you given everyone names?"

"Of course."

"Go on then. Let's hear them."

I get off my bed and stand by screen five. "Mike, Andy, Dave, and . . . hang on . . . I wish he would stop doing that!"

"Who, mate?"

"The guy in security. He keeps moving the cameras."

Greg laughs. "Mate, I think they're more bothered about stopping crime than they are about you watching TV."

The camera pans back and I show him Dave and Mike.

"They're from Brighton," I say.

"How do you know that's where they live?"

"It says so on their van."

"Ha, you know everything."

I walk back to my bed. Greg yawns and puts his head in his hands. I want to tell him that I might not have to make it all up soon, that I might be able to go out and meet them all for real. But I can't. He might stop me going and I don't want Amir to get fired.

Greg's pager beeps. He takes his hands down from his face and looks down at his belt.

"Mate—"

"It's okay. I know."

"It's just been a little crazy lately."

I want to tell him things have been a bit crazy for me too.

Greg stands up.

"Is everyone all right?"

"Yeah, mate, why?"

"It's just that Amir was busy last night too."

"Everyone's fine, honest." He pretends to limp toward the door. "You just stay there and tell Terry he better not move those darn cones again tonight."

* * *

Greg doesn't come back all morning. I watch the screens and do my breathing exercises until a nurse I've never seen before comes in and gives me lunch. She doesn't tell me her name but she knows mine. I decide to talk to her but she's gone before I think of what to say.

After lunch I click on the BBC website. I've got a new message.

**BBC Bubble Boy Forum**
**Fri August 26, 10:01 PM**
*Dear Bubble Boy,*

*I hope you don't mind but I saw you on TV and just wanted to write to you. I wrote to you last year but I changed my mind before I sent it. My name is Hannah and I'm fourteen years old. I live in Wells and I go to school at St. Mary's High. I'm not that good at talking to people. I just like sitting in my room reading and playing music. I love reading The Little Prince (I've read it a hundred times. Have you?). And I like watching Lord of the Rings. I stay in most of the time. Sorry, that must sound bad, when I could go out but don't and you haven't got a choice. Sorry again. I just wanted to tell you that your room looks great and I loved it when you went to the window and showed us the planes. I've never been on one but I often think of all the places they go. I'm not sure if I've said anything sensible in this letter but I just wanted to write something to you. Hope you don't think it's silly. Maybe I should delete it like the last one.*

*Hannah*

I smile and start to type.

> *Dear Hannah,*
> *Thank you for writing. It's OK, I don't mind what you said*
> *about me being stuck in a bubble. People do it all the time. Even*
> *my sister does. I haven't read The Little Prince and I prefer super-*
> *heroes to hobbits. I read Marvel Comics and DC too but I prefer*
> *Marvel because the superheroes are brave and they have more*
> *fun. Spider-Man is my favorite and I really like Wolverine, too.*

The door opens. Greg walks in. "All right, mate? What
are you doing?"

"Just replying to a message." I turn my screen toward him.

"Hey, great." He walks over to my bed and starts to read
the messages. "Hey, you got one from a girl."

Greg looks at the screen and starts to laugh.

"What's wrong?" I ask.

He points at my reply. "Mate, I don't have time to read it
all, but she's a girl; they don't want to talk about superheroes
all the time."

"Beth does." I also don't think Greg is right, but maybe
Katie doesn't like superheroes, so he doesn't know that not
all girls are like that.

Greg laughs again.

I look back at my screen. Now that Greg has said that,
I don't know what else to write. I hold my finger over the
keyboard and think of pressing the delete key. Greg checks
the readings on the monitors.

**Room temp.:** 19
**Air purity:** 98.2%
**Heart rate:** 77

"Ask her something," he says. "Sounds like she's stuck in a room too."
"Like what?"
"Anything, mate."

*I'm glad you like my room and the planes. What can you see out your window?*

Greg glances at my screen. "Yeah, that's good." He walks toward the door.
"Are you going already?"
"Yeah, mate, I'm sorry. I've got to get back."
"Back where?"
"What's that?" He puts his hand on the door.
"Where have you got to go back to?"
"Just the other wards. That's all."
"Is it the norovirus again?"
"What?"
"The reason everyone's so busy. Is it the norovirus?"
"No, mate, where did that come from?"
"It's just you're busy, and so was Amir."
"We all are, but don't worry. Hey"—he nods at my laptop—"maybe ask her what music she likes too . . . I'll try and get back to you later."

I look back at my laptop.

*What music do you like?*

I press send and lie down. The last time Greg was this busy was when the norovirus was here two years ago. He didn't tell me what was happening then, but every day all the nurses were running around looking after people and cleaning and there were TV crews and reporters outside. I watched it on the news. Loads of people were sick—patients, nurses, and the doctors. Four hundred people caught it. It was so bad they sent some patients home while they closed down six wards for two weeks and sprayed them with disinfectant. I thought I was going to have to move too, but they told me that would never happen because I was in the safest place in the whole hospital. I haven't seen any TV crews outside but maybe this time it's so dangerous everybody thinks they will catch it.

I open a new tab and type in *norovirus*.

**938,400 results**
**Symptoms: vomiting and diarrhea**

I can't see anything about the norovirus here.
My laptop beeps. I glance at the corner of the screen.

**Hey Joe, what are you doing?**                      2:00 PM

**Looking up norovirus.**                             2:00 PM

Crap! Have you got it there?                     2:01 PM

No.                                              2:01 PM

I scroll down.

But 300 people have got it in South Wales.       2:02 PM

How far's that?                                  2:02 PM

Hang on . . . 220 miles                          2:02 PM

That's close!                                    2:02 PM

Is it?!                                          2:03 PM

Well, it is over here.                           2:03 PM

It's got to go over a bridge to get here.
Would that stop it?                              2:03 PM

Think it travels in the air not by road. Ha.     2:03 PM

Pigeons!                                         2:04 PM

No, don't think so. What does it say?            2:04 PM

It spreads from person to person

by the fecal-oral route.                      2:04 PM

Sounds like a toothpaste.                     2:04 PM

This is serious.
I don't want to go outside if it's here.      2:05 PM

Sorry. I'm sure it's not.
So you're definitely going?                   2:05 PM

Yes, I think so. Tomorrow.
Amir left me loads of instructions.
I've got to memorize them.                    2:06 PM

Cool. What time are you going?                2:06 PM

4 o'clock.                                    2:07 PM

Same time as me.                              2:07 PM

Really?!                                      2:07 PM

Yeah, NASA just told me. Countdown to 4 PM!!!
                                              2:07 PM

No, I'm going at 4 in the morning!            2:08 PM

What! That means you get to go before me!     2:08 PM

| | |
|---|---|
| **I know.** | **2:08 PM** |
| You can tell me about it before I go … | 2:08 PM |
| No, don't tell me. | 2:08 PM |
| **Might spoil it?** | **2:09 PM** |
| Yeah, you won't be able to get me anyway. | 2:09 PM |
| I'm on news black-out, like it's top secret. Only people who can get me will be Mum and Dad. | 2:09 PM |
| **OK. Chat after. Can't wait.** | **2:10 PM** |
| Me neither. | 2:10 PM |

I smile. After worrying about everything, I can't wait to go. I tell Henry what's written in Amir's notes, how much air I've got, and that he's worked out I can take 4,576 breaths in three hours and still have some air left. Henry tells me NASA worked that out for him too but he hasn't seen the data because all the scientists have it protected on their laptops and they all need to scan their fingerprints to access it. I tell him that I still don't know where I'm going, only that I won't be able to see much at first but it will get light while I'm out.

Hey, Joe.                                           2:12 PM

Maybe he's taking you out for breakfast at McDonalds.
                                                    2:12 PM

Ha.                                                 2:12 PM

That's what I'm looking forward to most.
Burgers and chips at McDonald's.
NASA told me they're getting special
sterilizing units in to cook it.                    2:12 PM

Really?                                             2:13 PM

No. I made that bit up. Ha.                          2:13 PM

What are you taking with you?                        2:13 PM

I don't know. Thinking.                              2:14 PM

I look around my room. When people go on a trip they
usually know where they are going. They take sandwiches
and drinks and eat them in the car or get out and sit on a
blanket in a field. Greg told me that whenever he goes away
with Katie he always takes a backpack with important things
like a flashlight, a penknife, and a coat in case it gets cold
or rains. I don't know if I'm going to a beach, to a river, or
a park, or if it's going to be cold or hot, but even if I did, I

don't have anything to take with me. I don't have any walking boots. I don't have a coat. I don't even have a backpack for drinks or food. All I've got are my sneakers and clothes.

| | |
|---|---|
| **Henry** | **2:20 PM** |
| Yeah | 2:20 PM |
| **I haven't got anything to take.** | **2:21 PM** |
| Yeah, I was just looking too. | 2:21 PM |
| Least we don't have to carry anything. | 2:22 PM |
| **True.** | **2:22 PM** |
| I'm gonna have to go. Big NASA meeting soon. | 2:23 PM |
| **OK.** | **2:23 PM** |
| People pointing at charts and stuff. Like a military mission. | 2:23 PM |
| **The Expendables** | **2:24 PM** |
| Ha. Yeah. Catch you soon. | 2:25 PM |

The Skype light goes out. I think of messaging Hannah again but she hasn't replied yet. I pick up my controllers and play FIFA. I'm Arsenal and we're playing Barcelona. I play all afternoon, ten games. Lionel Messi is too good. He scores twenty-two goals. I keep trying but I still can't get Arsenal to win.

The sky begins to turn black outside and the lights in the glass building are dim. I turn on Spotify and listen to music while I'm in the shower. I close my eyes and let the water fall on my head. It soaks my hair and drips down my body. Is this what rain feels like? I screw my eyes tight and try to imagine what it would be like, but all I can see are purple circles on the inside of my eyelids. I take a deep breath. I can't see the rain. I can't see my and Beth's house—it's like all the pictures in my head have gone. I open my eyes and smile. It doesn't matter that the pictures have gone because tomorrow I'm going outside and I'll see the world for real.

I hear the door slide open. Greg shouts out and asks me if I'm okay. I tell him I am. I want to tell him what's going to happen. I want him to feel as excited as me, but I know if I do he won't let me go.

"Mate, you okay? You're taking a while."

"Sorry, I'm fine. Just checking for bruises."

I dry myself and check my skin. There's a small bruise on my elbow where I leaned on the windowsill, but it's more red than brown. I don't think it's worth telling Greg about. I don't want the doctors coming around and getting in the way.

When I go back into the room, Greg is sitting in the chair by the side of my bed. His head is back and his eyes are half closed. I put my dirty clothes in the basket by the door and get into bed.

"Everything okay, mate?" Greg asks softly.

I nod.

"Did you send the message?"

"Message?"

"You forgotten already? The girl."

"Oh, yes. Sorry."

I pull my sheet up over me. Greg puts his hand on my shoulder.

"Mate, you sure you're all right? You look a bit worried."

"I'm fine. I'm just a bit tired."

Greg looks at me for a long time like he's trying to work out what I'm thinking.

I reach over for my laptop. "I'll just check my messages," I say.

"You just said you were tired!"

"It's not just hers."

"I know, mate. She's probably asleep anyway. Like you should be." I look at my laptop. Greg shakes his head. "Go on then, but just make it the one."

I look at the screen. My last conversation with Henry is still there. I click off it and look at Greg. I don't think he saw. He's got his head rested against the chair like he's really tired. That was close. I take a deep breath and click on my messages.

**BBC Bubble Boy Forum**

**Fri August 27, 9:45 pm**

*Dear Bubble Boy,*

*Thank you for replying. I was really worried after I sent my message. I don't know why, but I worry a lot. It's late but I just wanted to tell you what I can see from my window. When it's raining all I can see is rain, but when it's sunny I can see across loads of fields. The land is really flat and it goes on for miles and miles until there's suddenly a big hill with Glastonbury Tor on the top. It's made of stone but sometimes it shines like glass. I wish I could look at it all the time but at night when I look out all I can see is black. I've got to go. It's nearly ten and I haven't been to the bathroom yet. I said I wouldn't write much. Did I write too much?*

*Hannah*

*P.S. I like Wolverine too.*

I smile and turn my laptop toward Greg. He's leaning forward with his elbows on his knees and his head in his hands.

"You were wrong."

Greg doesn't move. I tap him on the shoulder.

"What's that, mate?" He looks up and pulls his hair out of his eyes.

"You were wrong about girls not liking superheroes. Hannah likes Wolverine."

"That's good, mate." Greg puts his head back against the chair. His eyes are watering like he's just yawned. I ask him if he's okay.

"Yeah, mate. I'm just exhausted."

He reaches behind him, turns the switch, and dims the lights. I rest back down on my pillow. Greg does look tired but I don't think it's just that. I roll over on my side.

"Is Katie okay?"

Greg sighs. "Yeah, she's fine, mate."

"What about everyone else in here?"

He sniffs and wipes his nose on his hand. "Sorry, mate. I think I need to go." He stands up. "I'll catch you the day after tomorrow."

I don't know what to do or what to say. The only person I've ever seen cry is Beth; all the others have been on TV. I swing my legs over the side of my bed.

"Can you tell me what it is?"

Greg shakes his head. "No, mate. We're not supposed to."

I look down at the floor then back up at him.

"I think I know."

"Yeah. I think you do."

My throat throbs and my eyes begin to water. Greg puts his hand on my head.

"Get some sleep, mate. Big day for your friend tomorrow."

I close my eyes, lie down, and hear the click of the door as Greg goes out. I roll over onto my side. It's a big day for both me and Henry tomorrow but I don't care about it anymore. A tear falls down the side of my face onto my pillow. I never got to meet him but it feels like I did. I close my eyes tight. I think the billiard-ball kid has died.

# NINETEEN

## 11 YeaRS, 3 MON+HS, anD 11 DaYS

**The nurses smile** and talk in whispers.

"Hi, Joe, how are you doing? Just checking in on you. Nothing to worry about."

The doctors smile and tell jokes and talk about football.

"Shame about Arsenal, they always run out of steam. Hey, was that Theo Walcott I just saw limping down the road?"

I smile and talk about superheroes.

"I just watched *Guardians of the Galaxy*. Quill's on the run from Ronan and he made a truce with Rocket, who's a gun-toting raccoon."

Dr. Moore ruffles my hair. "Good lad, catch you tomorrow."

The nurses smile. "Good-bye, Joe. Be back later."

"Okay?"

I nod. "Okay."

Everything is okay.

"We just have to keep going."

Jim the security guard leaves.

Keith the security guard arrives.

Everyone keeps going.

And I keep watching my screens, the morning after the billiard-ball kid has died. I feel bad about that. It's not because I don't care about him; it's that I can't stop thinking about the most exciting thing in my life. Going outside. I check my phone every ten minutes but Amir doesn't send me a message. Where's he going to take me? It'll be too late to go and see a movie and we can't go to the shops because they'll be closed too. But even if they were open I don't think I'd want to go there anyway. I want to go outside and see real things. I don't want to get out of this room and swap it for another one.

In the middle of the morning some nurses and doctors I don't know gather by reception. They stand in little groups, talking and laughing. The lift door opens. A girl in a wheel-chair is being pushed out of a ward. Her mum and dad are walking behind her smiling. She's got an oxygen tank by the side of her, white tape on her lip, and a tube going up her nose. The doctors and nurses gather around her, then shake hands with her mum and dad. Keith walks over to them. I think maybe he's going to tell them to move on, that they're all in the way. He puts his hand in his pocket and pulls out his phone. The nurses and doctors stand on either side of the girl. Keith holds up his phone.

I think he says, "Say cheese."

They all smile.

Keith takes a picture.

A nurse hugs the girl. Dr. Hussein shakes her dad's hand.

Her mum wipes her eyes. They walk toward the doors. An ambulance pulls up outside. The girl and her parents get in the back and the ambulance pulls away. She's gone home. I glance up at the clock. There's only sixteen hours left until I go outside but I still haven't heard from Amir. I glance at my phone again.

My heart jumps when the Skype light flashes on my laptop. I look at the screen. It's a message from Henry.

Hey, Joe. How are you doing?                     12:00 PM

Jeez, I can't keep still! Like I got worms
in my belly!                                     12:00 PM

I laugh and go to reply but Henry's pen is still scribbling away.

Gonna be huge. Dad just called.                  12:01 PM

He's gonna watch it on TV with the guys
on the rig.                                       12:01 PM

Joe, you there?                                   12:02 PM

Sounds great!                                     12:02 PM

Ah, there you are! You gonna watch me too?  12:02 PM

Of course. Amir's left me instructions.          12:03 PM

Arc you getting ready? 12:04 PM

No, Amir's not here. Not heard anything. 12:04 PM

So what have you been doing? Watching the
screens? 12:04 PM

Yes. 12:04 PM

Anything happen? 12:05 PM

A girl just went home. 12:05 PM

Great! 12:05 PM

I look at the screen and think of telling Henry about the billiard-ball kid, but he seems too excited to tell him that someone has died. The pencil scribbles again.

Joe, you okay? 12:06 PM

Yes. Why? 12:06 PM

Thought you'd be hyper like me! You scared?
It's okay, I am too. Can't stop peeing! 12:07 PM

It's not that. 12:07 PM

What is it then? You should be buzzing! 12:08 PM

**I know.**                                              **12:09 PM**

My fingers hover over the keys.

**Sorry, just something happened.**                      **12:10 PM**

What?                                                    12:11 PM

**Not sure whether to tell you.**                        **12:11 PM**

You've got to now                                        12:11 PM

**Okay. The billiard-ball kid died.**                    **12:12 PM**

Aaargh! Real sorry.                                      12:12 PM

**Feel bad about being excited for going outside.**
                                                         **12:12 PM**

The pencil scribbles on the screen. Henry's either writing *loads* or he's deleted something and started again.

I glance at my phone. Still no message from Amir.

My laptop *da-lutes* again.

Joe. Sounds bad, but you got to stop thinking about it.
thinking about it.                                       12:14 PM

People die all the time. You and me will.
Could be today, could be tomorrow.

We both know if they don't fix us we could
be dead real soon.                              12:14 PM

I know.

Sorry. Bit blunt. Mum said I get it from Dad.   12:15 PM

It's okay.                                      12:15 PM

Just saying, we got to go. Could die outside,
could die on our beds ... crap, Joe,
why are we even talking like this?
We're going for the best trip ever!            12:16 PM

Sorry. Just think about dying a lot. Don't you?  12:16 PM

Yeah. But not now!                             12:16 PM

I look at the screen. Henry isn't typing and I don't know
what to write. I wish I hadn't said anything now. I wish
Henry would say something. I'm scared I've stopped him
wanting to go out, too. I hover my fingers over the keys. The
pen starts to scribble, then stops.

You've got to go! A superhero can't save
anyone if he stays inside all of his life!      12:17 PM

I giggle. Henry's right. I have to go. I can't just sit in here
my whole life, dreaming and imagining and worrying.

Switch to screen.                                12:18 PM

Why?                                             12:18 PM

'Cause I said so. And I wanna show
you something.                                   12:18 PM

We switch to screen.

"Ta-da!"

I laugh. Henry smiles at me through the glass on his visor
and raps his knuckles on top of his helmet.

"100 percent polycarbonate. What do you think?"

"I think you look like you're stuck in a goldfish bowl."

"So I don't look like a melon?"

"That too."

Henry takes his helmet off and blows out his cheeks. "It's
really heavy," he says. "And hot. Have you got yours?"

"No. Amir's bringing it tonight."

Henry leans toward the camera like he's only just seen
me. "Holy crap, Joe," he says. "You're as white as a ghost."

"I know. I'm really nervous."

"You'll be okay. It's just your anxiety. I'm anxious too."

"But your suit is designed by NASA."

"So? Yours is designed by a guy who's obsessed with
aliens. It's cool."

"You think so?"

"Of course. My suit's great but yours is going to be full of
loads of weird stuff."

"I know, but I still can't stop shaking."

"You know what to do."

I smile as Henry's face puffs out as he takes a deep breath like he's going to blow up a balloon.

"I've tried that."

"What about the humming?"

"I tried that, too."

"It's okay, I can't stop shaking either." He picks up his laptop and shakes it. "Look, it's like there's been an earthquake all day."

I can't believe he's so happy and hyper, but he always is. The only time he gets down is when the Philadelphia Eagles lose, but even then it only takes a few minutes before he's laughing again.

He puts his laptop down on his bed. "I'm serious," he says. "Been like it all day. But I can't wait!"

My phone buzzes. Henry asks me who it is. I read out a message from Amir.

"'Joe, make sure you rest. Don't worry when the temperature drops and your room starts to feel like a fridge. It should stop at 11 degrees. If it doesn't, I'll bring an icepick.'"

"Awesome! He's awesome." Henry leans over and picks up a folder. "All I get is algorithms and data sheets."

My phone buzzes again.

"What's he saying now?"

"'Don't worry if the instructions don't go in your head. I carry them in mine.'"

"See, Joe. You've got nothing to worry about. The guy's got it all planned."

"Do you really think so?"

"Of course . . . What're you texting?"

"I'm asking him where he is."

I send my message. My phone buzzes straightaway.

"What's he say?"

"He says he's shopping in Sainsbury's. . . . It's a supermarket." I take a deep breath.

Henry taps his finger on the screen.

"Hey, don't look so worried. People gotta eat. Maybe he's making a picnic for your trip. I don't need one. Gonna be stopping for a burger at McDonald's."

"Do you think they'll let you?" I think about what Greg said.

"Doubt it. Don't care. All I wanna do is go out. NASA said there's going to be so many cars it's going to be like the president's motorcade."

"Can't wait to see it."

"I'll give you a wave, or one of these." He holds up his finger. "Haha!" His eyes flick to the side of his screen then back at me. "Hang on, I think Brett's coming."

"Shall I go?"

"No, not yet, he'll be a while. Getting stuff ready for last-minute tests and stuff. Then I've got to rest. Just means I won't be able to talk for a while."

"So we can't chat after I've been outside?"

"Not supposed to, but try and stop me!"

I wait for Henry to say something else but he just looks into the camera and for a moment I think the Internet has frozen but his hair is moving from the fan.

"Henry, what's wrong?"

"Nothing, just thinkin'."

"What about?"

"It's stupid—I should be grateful. Just wish we could both go out together. It'd be fun. Both of us. Be like Halloween— me dressed as a spaceman, you dressed like an alien."

I laugh.

"Just a pain we're 3,500 miles apart."

"I know."

Henry looks toward the door.

"Couple of minutes, buddy?" says Brett.

Henry nods.

"You heard?"

"Yes."

Henry blinks, and then leans close to the screen. "Hey, Joe," he whispers. "Don't worry. You're gonna be okay."

I nod. "I think you will be too."

"Ha," he says. "We could be in a film."

I swallow hard. "Hey, Henry."

"Yeah."

"I'll pretend you're walking next to me."

"Me too, man. Oh, and Joe . . ."

"What?"

"Don't forget to breathe. Don't want you passing out and missing everything!"

"And you!"

"Catch you later!" he says.

"Catch you later."

The screen goes blank.

I lie back on my bed and look at the ceiling. My heart thuds in my chest. I can't believe it's going to happen. Me and Henry are actually going outside.

I watch the screens for a while after Henry's gone but I can't concentrate. People move around in a blurry silence and when I watch *Thor* all I can see are flames and black clouds. I try to rest like Amir told me but it's hard when all I can think about is me and Henry going outside.

It's seven o'clock when I get a new post from Hannah.

**BBC Bubble Boy Forum**
**Sat August 28, 7:00 pm**

*Dear Joe, I've just finished my homework and now I'm just checking my messages. You haven't replied. I hope I didn't say anything wrong. I just wanted to tell you I'm going to my Gran's house for her birthday. She lives in Wales. She hasn't got Internet and the one on my phone isn't great so I may not be able to write to you for a while. I told a friend that I was talking to you. She laughed and said, what was the point in talking to someone who could never go out? But I don't care. You don't have to go out with someone to be their friend, do you? I hope you are okay.*

*Hannah.*

I write a message back.

**Dear Hannah,**

Sorry I didn't reply. No, you didn't upset me. Things have just got really busy. One of the things is sad and the other thing is really exciting and I wish I could tell you what it is but I can't. I might be able to tell you after.

I'm glad you like Wolverine. I collect the comics and I've seen two of the movies. There's a new one coming out in September. My sister is going to buy it for me on DVD but I'm not sure I can wait until then.

I like what you can see from your window. It sounds really different from mine. Sometimes I dream that I'm on the hospital roof and I can see across all the lakes and parks around London. I dream a lot. I can't write much more because I have to save my energy. Something exciting is happening but I can't tell anyone. I think I already said that.

Joe

P.S. Have a nice time at your gran's.

I lie down on my bed.

I know I need to sleep and save my energy but I'm going outside for the first time in my life; there's no way I can keep still.

I pretend I'm asleep when a new nurse comes in and checks on me at midnight. She doesn't talk; she just checks the monitors. She doesn't seem to notice my heart rate. She doesn't seem to notice how deeply I'm breathing. All she does is stand at my bed for a minute and then dims the lights.

I don't remember falling asleep but it's the air conditioner clicking that wakes me up. I turn my head. My eyes are sleepy and blurry.

**Room temp.:** 18C
**Air purity:** 98%

The air conditioner clicks again. The numbers change. I blink.

**Room temp.:** 17C
**Room temp.:** 16C

It's starting to go down, just like Amir said it would.

**Heart rate:** 87
**Room temp.:** 15. . . 14 . . .

It's like it's decreasing every time I take a breath.
13 . . .
It's never been that low; the alarm should be ringing, but Amir must have overridden it. I shiver as if someone has poured ice down my back.

**Heart rate:** 91

I send Amir a message in my head. *I hope you know what you're doing. I hope you've checked everything.*

What if he hasn't? What if the temperature drops and I become tired? My white cells might decrease and my skin will start to wrinkle and fall off like a snake's. My eyes will turn to crystals, my lungs will turn to lead, my nose will start bleeding, and I'll go unconscious.

I sit down on my bed. I can't breathe and my heart is beating so hard it's like it's trying to burst its way through my ribs. I pick up my phone.

**Amir, I don't think we should do this.**

I wait five minutes. He doesn't reply. My stomach cramps. I run to the bathroom and see myself in the mirror. My face is pale and sweat is running down the side of my face and dripping down my neck.

The air conditioner clicks again. I don't want to go. I might be like a polar bear that I saw on TV. He'd been in his cage for so long that when he came out he just walked around in a circle on the spot. I wrap my arm around my stomach. It's too cold. I'll freeze. I'm going to die breathing real air. My head goes dizzy. I grab hold of the sink to stop myself from falling over. Stay calm. Take deep breaths. Take deep breaths. It's not working! I lean over and puke in the toilet.

My phone vibrates on the floor. I grab it.

**Don't worry. The temperature stop at eleven.**

I try to reply but I can't tap the right letters. I shake out my hand and try again.

**Amir, I'm scared.**

It's okay, even superheroes are allowed to be scared.

The monitors beep. I stand up and rest against the door. The figures are changing on the monitors.

**Room temp:** 11C.
**Air purity:** 98.4%
**Heart rate:** 96
My phone buzzes again.

Joe, I'm on my way.

# TWENTY

## 11 YEARS, 3 MONTHS, AND 12 DAYS

It's 2:15 a.m. The room temperature is stuck on eleven. Three workmen are outside digging under the lights. Another man is warming his hands over a big barrel of tar. I wish I could stand there with him because I'm so cold that I can't stop my jaw from shaking. I wrap my duvet around me but it doesn't matter how tightly I pull it, I can't get warm. I step away from the window and look at the screens. It's been over an hour since Amir said he was coming but he still isn't here. The service alley is dark and empty. Jim is at the reception desk reading a book under a light. Shadows pass in front of the hospital doors as car lights pass by. Jim glances up but I can't see what he's looking at. Amir wouldn't come through the front door, would he? I switch cameras. A fox limps along the pavement. Jim looks down at his book and starts reading again.

A door clicks open in the transition zone. I walk over to

my bed and pull the duvet up to my chin. The door slides back and Amir comes in. He's got a backpack over his shoulder and he's pulling a metal suitcase on wheels.

"I didn't think you were coming!"

"Of course I come." He slips the pack off his shoulder and puts the suitcase down on my bed. "I had to get parked." He nods at screen six. A car is parked in the service alley in the shadows of the building.

"But I didn't see you arrive."

"I turn out the lights."

I try to smile but my jaw is still like ice. "Amir, I don't think I can do it."

"You be fine," he says. "Once you put this on." He nods at the case.

"What, everything I need is in there?"

Amir puts his thumbs on the silver catches. "I know what you thinking but you be surprised."

The catches spring up. Amir lifts up the lid.

A blue suit is neatly folded inside.

"Have you brought the wrong case?"

"No, this is it." He lifts the suit out of the case and holds it up.

"But I can't just wear that. It's too thin. . . ." I look back in the case. "And there's no helmet or oxygen tanks."

"Of course not," he says. "They too big to get past security. This is until I get you outside."

"But it's the same as the one the maintenance man wears."

"No, it not. I show you." He rolls back the sleeves.

"Cotton and rubber with malleable titanium. Put it on."

I swing my legs over the side of my bed and Amir helps my feet into the suit. I try to pull it up but the rubber sticks to my skin. I pull harder but I can't get it above my knees.

Amir puts his hand in his pocket. "Use this. Gymnasts use it on their hands to stop them sticking to the bars."

He sprinkles white chalk on my legs. I pull the suit up and it seals me in around my waist, and then I put my arms in and pull it up over my shoulders.

"Perfect!" Amir pulls a zipper up my body and the suit seals against my skin. It's tight, like the wet suits I've seen divers wear on TV.

I put my fingers under the collar.

"It's a bit tight."

"It has to be. But you get used to it. Shukra tested it. He sat on the sofa and watched TV for two days. Then I sterilize. Here." He hands me rubber socks and rubber gloves. I put them on, look at my hands, and flex them.

Amir steps back.

"You like it?"

I see my reflection in the window. On the outside I look like the maintenance guy, but I feel like Spider-Man underneath.

"Now all you need is this." Amir passes me a metal hoop. "It's how you breathe," he says.

"But it looks like a Frisbee!"

"It's a vortex fan with a lithium battery." He points at tiny holes in the metal. "See these? When we turn it on it powers

up a shield of pure air. I show you." He connects a rubber
lead to an oxygen supply the size of a small fire extinguisher.
It looks like it would only last me ten breaths.

Amir sees the worried look on my face. "It all right. I got
two big bottles and a proper helmet by the car."

"Okay."

Amir takes the hoop and puts it over my head like he's
presenting me with a medal. I look down at it. Amir pulls
a tube out of the backpack and plugs it into the hoop.
"Ready?"

"I'm not sure. . . ."

He clicks a button. "Amir!" I gulp for breath as cold air
rushes out of the oxygen tank and up my nose.

"Oops, sorry." He reaches out. "A minor adjustment." He
pulls the hoop forward, fastens it down with a strap, and I
can breathe again. "That better?"

"Yes . . . I think so."

Amir picks up the TV remote.

"Amir, I thought we were going!"

"We are. I just check on Jim."

The screens flicker on. Jim is in reception reading his
book. "Umm, he still there."

"He goes to the bathroom at three o'clock."

"That good . . . and Phil?"

"He'll be on the twentieth floor."

Amir pats me gently on the back. "Great," he says. "That
why I make you head of security."

"Did you?"

"Of course. I ask you to watch them."

"I didn't know that was why."

"Top secret," he says. "Less you know, less you tell. Like spies."

"But I wouldn't have told anyone."

"I know. I trust you. But sometimes you speak in your dreams." He picks up the backpack. I put my arms through the loops and Amir fastens the clasps at the front.

"You ready?" He swings the pack over his shoulder.

I nod, but I don't know if I am. After waiting for so long, it's all happened so quickly—suitcase, suit, oxygen, go. I thought I'd take as long as Henry did. He took hours to get ready and that was just for a walk in the parking lot. I've got nothing. It's just me and Amir. Has he checked *everything*? What about the air temperature? What about the air quality? If it's too pure then all it takes is for someone to be smoking a cigarette next to me and I could catch fire.

"Amir, the air quality, should we check it?"

He reaches into his pocket. "I check everything." He shows me his phone.

**Outside temp.:** 11C
**Body temp.:** 37.3C
**Heart rate:** 119
**Air remaining:** 3 liters
**Air purity:** 97.5%

"So I won't catch fire?"

He presses on the air purity icon. Air—80.5% nitrogen, 19.5% pure oxygen.

"No. You won't catch fire, but I bring extinguisher just in case." He smiles. I'm not sure if he's joking.

Amir grabs my arm. "Come on. We go now."

I take a deep breath and look around the room—the monitors, the window, my bed, Theo Walcott. I've lived here all my life, had every Christmas here and every birthday. Now that I'm about to go outside, it suddenly looks smaller than it ever did before. I put my hand on my chest. After all this time I don't want to leave my room behind. All my memories are here and so are all my friends.

I want to speak to Henry.

I want to speak to Greg.

I want to stay.

I want to pee.

Amir touches my elbow. "It okay, we coming back. Now you help us find the way out."

The door slides open. I think of going back to my bed and pulling the sheets over my head but before I've had time, Amir has grabbed my hand and pulled me through. He leads me through the transition zone, past a row of plastic seats, a shower, canisters of sterilizing fluid, and tiny boxes of pills and bottles of medicine on a shelf. Then I see white coats hanging on hooks. This is where Beth gets changed. This is where all the nurses and doctors wash. I didn't know the room was so big. From what Beth told me, I thought it was a cupboard. In the corner are a pile of magazines and boxes of toys and I think that maybe they are things that people have brought in but weren't allowed to give to me.

Amir pulls me onward.

"If you stop all the time, we never get out."

We walk past oxygen bottles and stop by the door. Footsteps echo down the corridor. They get closer, get louder. We hold our breaths. They reach us, then fade away. Amir holds up three fingers. ON THREE, he mouths. He nods twice. On the third one he opens the door. My heart beats like it's trapped under my suit. A strange feeling goes through me. I know I shouldn't be doing this but I can't stop it.

I follow Amir out into the corridor. It's long and narrow with dim yellow lights that stretch as far as I can see. We start to walk. Amir suddenly stops, listening as though he can hear someone coming again.

"It's okay," I whisper. "Phil only comes up here to check on the cleaners in the morning."

Amir holds up his thumb and smiles. All the time I've been watching the screens I didn't know he was getting me ready for this. He's trained me to be a maze runner. I know all of the corridors. I know all the doors. I know the way out and I know the way back. It's like Amir has planted a map of the hospital in my brain.

We creep down the corridor past pictures of elephants, monkeys, and giraffes and doorways that lead off into the wards where the others are—the girl who pretends she's a horse, the boy who reads *The Hunger Games*. For a moment

I think we should stop and talk to them. They could tell me their own stories. I wouldn't have to hear them from a doctor or a nurse. If I stop I might get caught, or they might talk me out of going. But I have to go. They can go home when they are better. I might be like the billiard-ball kid and never get better. I can't stay here.

"We go?" Amir whispers.

I nod.

Amir walks on and we slide our backs along the wall like police on a raid. It doesn't feel real. It's like I've woken up on a film set, with bright lights on the ceiling showing us the way. We keep walking until we reach a junction: *Left* for visitors' bathrooms. *Right* for exits and wards. I look up and see a camera on the wall. I tell Amir that we have thirty seconds for it to sweep the corridor before it comes back again.

Amir nods. We jump back as the camera passes us, and then we're off down the corridor again. My backpack scrapes against the wall as we pass more doors and the corridor that leads to one of the operating theaters. Amir grabs a wheelchair parked underneath a fire alarm. He tells me to get in. I'm glad, because my legs already feel tired, even though I can feel all the adrenalin in my body like sparks. I've never walked this far, except on the exercise machines.

Amir pushes me toward an elevator. I press the call button while he checks my readings on his phone.

"Is everything okay?" I ask.

"Yes, it fine. Maybe we just increase the vortex." He reaches into my pack, turns a switch, and air hisses past my ears. I feel like Superman must feel when he flies across the sky.

Amir presses the button again but the elevator is already on its way. I hear a clang of metal and watch the number change above the elevator doors—4—5—6. I feel sick and I want to pee again. Amir puts his hand on my shoulder.

"You okay, Joe? You shake."

"I know. I can't stop it."

Amir's eyes flit from side to side like he's a scientist trying to work out an equation. He places both hands on my shoulders.

"Joe," he says. "It not too late. We turn back if you like."

"No, it's okay. It's because I'm excited . . . not scared."

"Ha. Me too!"

The cables whirr as the elevator gets closer to us: 9—10—11—12—it stops on 13. Another four floors and it'll be here. Amir starts to pull me backward.

"No, I just hiding you. We not know if someone get in or out."

He parks me tight against the wall. We hold our breaths as the number 17 lights up.

A bell dings and the doors slide open. Amir creeps away from the wall and peers inside.

"Yes, it's okay." He backs me into the elevator and the doors close. Then he *tap-tap-taps* the ground floor button rapidly like he's firing punches on Tekken.

"It overrides the sensor," he says.

I don't know if it does or not, but the elevator doesn't stop until the doors open when we get to the bottom.

The clock on the corridor wall says 3:10.

I tell Amir that Jim should still be in the bathroom. He wheels me out and we head toward the reception. Halfway along the corridor we suddenly turn down a smaller corridor signposted FIRE EXIT ONLY. There's a glass door at the end with a bar across it and there's an oxygen bottle on a trolley leaning against the wall. Amir slides his backpack off his shoulder.

"Here," he says. "You put this on now." He pulls out a white helmet.

"But—"

"It's okay," he says. "You just hold your breath. I swap it over faster than Ferrari change a wheel."

I look back up the corridor. I've got no time to think about it. Jim's going to be coming out of the bathroom soon.

"I count to three," says Amir, "Okay? One . . . two . . . three."

I take a deep breath. Amir slides the hoop up my neck and disconnects the air supply. I put the helmet over my head. Amir clicks the air line in, attaches a new tube to the oxygen bottle, and clicks the other end into my helmet— then he runs his fingers along the rubber seal and smoothes it tight to my neck. I hear a hiss as he turns a valve and the air rushes in.

"All good?" He gives me a thumbs-up. "Just breathe slowly or the visor will mist up."

"Okay, but how long will my air last?"

"It fifteen liters. It last a diver an hour. But you only little and you not going underwater."

I smile and put my hands on my head. The new helmet feels much safer than the Frisbee. I go to tell Amir but his back is turned and the door is wide open. He's fiddling with a red alarm box on the wall.

I stand by his side. The alley is dark. Darker than it is on my screens. Darker than it's ever been in my room. There's a torn plastic bag with bits of paper and food pouring out of it and three cardboard boxes stacked against the wall. I inch my feet forward.

*One more step and I'll be outside.*

I look across the alley at the brick wall and follow it up past the gutters and the roof. It's like the building is growing out of the ground.

*One more step. I only have to take one more step.*

Car lights flash by the end of the alley. Amir lifts up his hand.

"Come on," he says. "Or they see us on the monitors."

I step out of the doorway. I try to look up and see the sky. The walls and the roofs start to spin. I reach out and hold on to a metal handrail. Amir grabs hold of my arm.

"You be okay," he says. "It just shock."

A drip of sweat trickles down the middle of my back.

"Amir, it's so big," I say. "The buildings look bigger when I look up." I start to fall backward. Amir puts his arm around my shoulders.

"Let's get you in the car." He lifts his hand and presses a

button on a key fob. Red and yellow lights flash on a small
car parked by a wall. "Sorry . . . it's no Batmobile, but it get
us there."

I try to smile but my head is still spinning. Amir grabs
hold of the oxygen bottle and slowly walks me toward the
car.

"Mind your head," he says.

I get in. There's chocolate bar wrappers and empty potato
chip packages on the floor. Amir reaches in and sweeps them
aside, then puts the oxygen bottle between my legs and shuts
the door.

He walks in front of the car and gets in the other side. My
heart beats against my suit. It seems like five minutes since I
was in my room. Now I'm in a car with litter and tall buildings all around me.

Amir sits next to me and puts the keys in the ignition.

"You feel better?"

I nod. "A bit," I say. "But, Amir, you still haven't told me
where we're going."

"It a surprise. Surprise is best. Like Christmas. Unwrapping
presents is garbage if you know what you get."

I give up. I asked him so many times but he still won't
tell me. I like surprises, but just being outside is making my
heart beat twice as fast.

Amir turns the key. The dashboard lights up. The green
numbers above the radio say 3:20. Amir revs the engine. It
squeals like a cat.

"Ah, Rashid. I tell you to fix the alternator." He sighs and then presses the accelerator down. The car jumps forward. I grab hold of the door handle. Amir grins.

"It okay," he says. "We in a car, not a rocket."

He changes gears and we drive toward the bright lights at the end of the alley. A truck roars by. I sit back in my seat.

"Traffic," says Amir. "You get used to it."

Across the road, the lights are dim in Starbucks and the telephone shop. I wish I could get out and look inside, but Amir turns right and drives past the front of the hospital. Jim is at the reception desk reading his book. I look up and see all the windows . . . hundreds of them. There's so many that even if I had time to count to my floor I wouldn't be able to work out which window is mine. The car goes faster and we leave the hospital behind. Streetlights flash by—bright orange lights, one after the other, and behind them are the buildings. Massive dark buildings made of glass, brick, and metal. They climb higher and higher, thick then narrow, floor after floor, until they disappear into the sky.

We slow down at the traffic lights. Amir taps his hands on the steering wheel as we wait for the lights to turn green. The excavators are parked in a row. Mike and Andy are leaning against their van. Chris and Dave are resting on their drills under the floodlights.

"They nearly finish," says Amir. "Then the aliens come."

The lights turn green and we pull away. I peer into the hole in the road. I couldn't see any magnets from my room and I still can't see any now. My heart beats faster again.

Amir taps his head. "I know what you thinking. The

magnets get put in at the end. Otherwise they drag all the cars and vans down the hole."

He's gone crazy again.

I look back out my window and we pass more lights and shop windows with sofas and mannequins and a giant picture of David Beckham on a wall. I yawn. I've only been out for five minutes and I'm already tired. But I can't go to sleep. I can't miss anything. I rest my head against the window—more shops, more dark buildings and trash cans on the pavement with bits of plastic and food falling out onto the ground. There are newspapers in the gutter blocking the drains.

Why don't people pick the garbage up? Why don't people empty the cans? They could be full of germs. They could be full of rats. They're inside the cans, scurrying around eating bits of meat and fat. They're crawling over the trash up to the top. They're jumping out of the holes down onto the street.

I shiver and wrap my arms around myself. Here they come.

*Massive rats, giant fat rats with giant teeth and tails a meter long. I glance in the side-view mirrors. They're running behind us; they're catching us. Germs on their feet. Germs in their mouths. They're clawing at the car bumper; they're biting the tires. No! We need to go back in the buildings. We need to climb back up high. It's the only way to escape.*

Sweat runs down the side of my face. My visor starts to blur.

Amir waves his hand in front of my face. "Joe, you okay?"

I put my hands on top of my head. "No, take me back. Please take me back."

"You feel sick?"

"Take me back. There's germs in the air. There's rats in the cans."

Amir looks at his phone. I don't need to look. I know my numbers are going mad.

My legs are twitching, my hands are shaking. Rats are everywhere. I googled it once. They're only six feet away from us in city centers. They carry diseases that attack our livers and our kidneys and they're out there now. They're crawling up the exhaust into the car. They're eating at my suit and creeping up my air tubes.

I pull at my collar and try to breathe but it's like someone is sitting on my chest with their fingers around my throat.

"Joe?"

"I can't breathe. I can't—"

"Deep breaths. Slow deep breaths, Joe. Like you're standing on a beach looking at the sea."

I look back out of the car window. The rats are coming. The rats are coming. Giant rats, super rats. They breed them in laboratories.

*No. No.*

I lift my feet up.

"Take me back. Please take me back! The rats are coming. They're in the car, they're crawling up my legs!"

"They not. There no rats, Joe. I show you."

The click of the turn signal makes me jump. Amir pulls the car over into a bus stop. He leans over and puts his hand on my arm.

"You okay. Just be calm."

I try to take a deep breath. A man and a woman walk toward us holding hands. Amir points at them.

"You see," he says. "You think they walk if there giant rats around?"

I let a breath out.

"I'm sorry. I thought—"

"It's okay. It's okay."

Amir picks up his phone and increases the air flow.

"Breathe," he says. "Breathe."

"I'm trying . . . but I don't want to use up all of my air."

"No, you breathe all you like. I calculate it. 100 percent PA."

"PA?" I shiver as the sweat trickles down my neck.

"PA. Panic attack. I tell you to read the instructions."

I try to smile and take another breath but it's hard when every breath I take uses up more oxygen. I put my hands up to my collar. Amir stops me.

"No, you can't do that."

"But I still can't breathe."

"Then do this." He leans forward and rests his head on the steering wheel. He glances across at me. "Come on, you know what to do."

He closes his eyes.

I lean forward and put my head in my hands. I take a

breath. Then another, deeper and longer. Amir opens one eye and smiles. The monitor beeps slowly as my heart does the same. Amir nods slowly. The rats are retreating; the rats are shrinking. They're scurrying back up the road and disappearing into the holes. Amir closes his eyes. I close my eyes too.

We start to hum.

# TWENTY-ONE

**Outside temp.:** 11C
  **Body temp.:** 37.3C
  **Heart rate:** 120
  **Air remaining:** 12 liters
  **Air purity:** 96%

Amir is driving, following the cat's eyes in the middle of the road. My eyelids are heavy. They start to fall.

*Don't go to sleep. I don't want to go to sleep.*

I shake my head but two seconds later my eyelids are dropping again.

Amir nudges my arm. "We nearly there," he says.

"Can you tell me where we're going now?"

"The edge of the world," he says.

"Where's that?"

"The end of this world. The beginning of the next."

I don't understand what he means.

More cat's eyes. More streetlights. More headlights flashing across Amir's face.

I yawn. "Amir, am I dreaming?"

"Only you know."

The road grows wider, two lanes, then three. The buildings get bigger and farther apart. We're on a motorway. They go on for miles and miles but we can't drive for miles. This car is so old and rattly it might break down. A whale can hold its breath for ninety minutes; I can't hold mine for ninety seconds. We'd never make it back to the hospital if we had to walk from here. We'd have to get out and flag down a car or maybe the police would see us parked at the side of the road. They'd wonder what I was doing out, dressed as a spaceman so early in the morning. I won't be able to tell them because Amir will get fired and I'll get into trouble too. I hope Dr. Moore won't be too mad with me. I wonder if he would come and rescue me before my oxygen runs out. I think of asking Amir but he's too busy watching the road as we pass more cars and more buildings, but I recognize these. I've seen them before from my window: $E = mc^2$, Lucozade, GlaxoSmithKline, and Mercedes-Benz—I look ahead and see the sign for Heathrow.

*Wait. We can't go there.*

Amir flicks the turn signal.

"Amir, what are you doing? We can't go on a plane!"

Amir puts his finger up to his lips. "Just wait," he says.

"But I can't . . . we can't!"

"Trust me."

I sit back in my seat. Amir says to trust him. It's too late not to, now.

We turn off the motorway and pass thousands of cars parked behind fences. The car slows down. Amir leans forward like he's looking for a gap. "It just here," he says. "Just . . . here."

He turns the steering wheel quickly and we go down a dark track. The lights turn off and the car crawls on even though I can't see anything. But Amir seems to know exactly where he's going. He doesn't need GPS or a map or even headlights. It's like he knows every bump in the road. I think of the stowaway boy in the plane wheel who cut a hole in the perimeter fence. Is that what we're going to do? I won't be able to run across the asphalt with my oxygen bottle. My legs will have turned to jelly by the time I get there.

I turn around and look on the back seat for fence cutters, but all I see is a children's car seat and empty Coke bottles.

The car starts to slow, then stops.

In front of us is a big wire fence that stretches as wide as I can see. There's a ditch in front of it and barbed wire across the top. Amir takes the keys out of the ignition. "Come on," he says. "We get out now."

I check the back seat again.

"What are you looking for?"

"Wire cutters?"

"Ha. Why I need wire cutters?"

"To cut the fence?"

"That illegal. I don't do anything illegal." He opens the car door, walks around, and opens mine. I don't say that I think taking me out of the hospital might be illegal.

"You coming?"

I pass him the oxygen bottle.

After being in the car for so long it's like I have to get ready for going outside all over again. I swing my legs out onto the ground. My legs wobble as little stones crunch under my boots. I take a step and they do it again. It's like I'm a child trying to walk for the first time. Amir takes hold of my arm. We walk in front of the car and sit down on the hood. Amir's breath pools out into the cold air like he's smoking a cigarette. I feel the warmth of the engine through my suit. I'm not cold but I still shiver and wrap my arms around myself. I wonder if Spider-Man ever felt this cold, like if he ever got caught in a New York snowstorm. I wonder if he ever found a place like this, in the middle of nowhere, where all you can see is the dark and all you can hear is the hiss of air.

Amir points at the sky.

I look up. I gasp, and my chest seems to fill with more oxygen than it's ever held.

Above me, the sky is dark and wide and so full of stars. I turn my head. More stars. Hundreds of them. The longer I look, the more I see. I didn't know the sky was like that. I've never seen it without a window frame. I bite my lip and close my eyes. I'm scared I might be dreaming. That when I open my eyes it will be gone and I'll be staring at my ceiling.

I open them again. The sky is still there and the stars are still there and now the moon is shining on me. It's so bright and big. On my screens it just looks like a dot. I glance at Amir. He smiles, then looks back at the sky. I want to smile back, but I want to cry too.

Amir holds up his hand and squints like he's aiming a gun. "You can't touch it," he says "but you can block it out with your finger."

"I don't think I want to," I say. "I want it to stay there forever."

Amir takes his hand down. "Ha," he says. "I think you right. . . . Do you like it?"

"It's so great," I say. "Way better than TV. I can't wait to talk to Henry. I hope he gets to see it too. I hope he doesn't spend all of his time in the mall."

"Me too."

I hear a click, then the hiss of more air coming into my helmet. Amir looks at his phone, then shows me the reading. 94.4%.

"It's dropping. Do we have to go?"

He checks the other readings.

**Outside temp.:** 10C

**Body temp.:** 37.2C

**Heart rate:** 116

**Air remaining:** 8 liters

Amir nods his head slowly. "We okay. You no want to go back, do you?"

"No!"

"Good," he says "I no bring you here just to show you the stars."

He slides down off the hood and helps me back into the car. The clock says 4:45. I've been out for nearly two hours. Amir starts the car and it bumps as it crawls along between two fences. There are huge storage containers piled one upon the other either side of us that stretch forever, like we're in a tunnel. A red light flashes at the end. We drive toward it. The light gets brighter. . . . Now there are four of them with another eight white lights flashing on either side.

Amir smiles as we reach the end of the containers and drive out into an open field. He points out of the windshield. "Look at them," he says. "They been flying for over a hundred years and still they use wings! Don't they know it quicker to fly in saucers?"

We get out of the car and look across the grass toward an airport runway. A bright light shines from the control tower and a radar spins quickly on top. We walk closer. The red and white lights flash from the wings of planes. It's like there are hundreds of them. Plane after plane. Some of them are moving, some are parked in front of the terminal, and some look like they're asleep, abandoned in the middle of nowhere—*British Airways, American Airlines, Air New Zealand, Virgin Atlantic*—with orange lights flashing on top of trucks that weave in between them with cargo and fuel. Through my helmet I can hear the beeps of trucks backing up and the rush of engine turbines turning. I've watched the planes in the sky every day from my window. I've seen them on TV too, but it's nothing like this. Being locked in a room is like being deaf and blind.

Amir points at a plane being pushed by a truck.

"Engines and wings," he tuts. "Engines and wings. The aliens laugh at us. Can you hear them?" He cups his hand up to his ear. "Can you? They laugh at our TV, they laugh at our cars, and they laugh at the way we are born and die. They laugh at our planes, too. But they like them."

Amir's gone crazy again. It scares me when he talks about aliens. It's like he changes into another person. It's like there's two of him. I trust them both; it's just that I trust one more than the other.

He grabs hold of my oxygen trolley. "Come on," he says. "Let's get closer."

We wheel the trolley behind us and stop by the fence. Amir puts his fingers through the wire. His eyes are open wide and shining.

"Vasi," he whispers.

"What's that?"

"Vasi—red and white lights, visible for 3.5 miles in the day and 20 miles at night. Ha!"

"What's funny?"

"We are. Aliens don't need lights. They can see us all the time."

"Do you think so?" I look up at the sky and search for aliens.

"Of course," says Amir. "For them it's like watching TV. We *are* their TV!"

I shake my head. "Amir?"

"Yes."

"Are you sure there are aliens?"

He looks at me like *I'm* mad. "I sure?"

"Some people think that people who believe in aliens are crazy."

"Crazy?" Amir opens his eyes wide. "No, not crazy. Maybe it's just easier for people to believe lies than to believe the truth."

It still doesn't make sense to me. I go to tell Amir but he's staring through the fence.

A red light flashes on a plane in the distance—growing bigger and brighter as it gets closer toward me. The ground begins to tremble as the engines rumble through my feet. Amir grips the fence tight. His hair is blowing in his eyes. He shouts something but I can't hear him above the roar of the wind. I shake my head. He leans toward me and shouts again.

"You hang on tight or you might get blown away." Amir's coat flaps and hits against my knees.

I reach out and grip the wire. The plane is gaining speed. Faster and faster. I want to run. I want to fall down on the ground and curl up in a ball.

*Hold on. Hold on tight.*

The nose of the plane lifts up. Its back wheels lift off the ground and it flies above us, soaring in slow motion.

"Amir! Amir! I'm going to fall over."

Amir lets go of the fence with one arm and puts it around my shoulders. The fence starts to shake; the wire digs into my gloves so I can feel it on my hands. I let go quickly and hold on to Amir. I gasp for breath. The plane

is right above us. White light. Red light. White light. Red
light—with a noise louder than thunder. Its body is big
and heavy and its wings are as wide as the sky. If I could let
go of Amir I could reach out and touch it. I'd pull myself
up and climb into the wheel hold. I could survive with my
special suit and my oxygen. I turn my head. The engines are
so loud they rumble through my bones. The plane moves
away and starts to climb higher and higher. Amir's head
knocks against my helmet. He grins so wide it splits his
face in half.

*I can't believe this is happening.*

"Amir," I shout. "This is amazing!"

"I tell you," he says. "I tell you!"

The plane soars over the city and the wind dies away.
There's something thudding through my body. I let go of
the fence.

Amir looks at me. "Joe, what's wrong?"

I shake my head and put my hands on my chest.
"Nothing," I say. "I'm okay. It's only my heart."

"Ha! Mine too!"

We watch the tail light of the plane blink, blink, blink,
until it disappears into the distance.

Everything is bigger, brighter, and louder than I ever
thought it would be. A tear trickles down my cheek. Amir
bends down in front of me. His mouth is wide open and his
hair is stuck up like a troll doll.

"Hey," he says. "It supposed to make you happy, not cry."

"I am happy." I reach up to wipe my tear away. My hand

bumps against my helmet. The visor steams up and everything goes blurry.

Amir increases the air flow. "That better?"

"Yes."

Amir looks at me like he's waiting for me to say something but I can't. He told me I shouldn't cry but his eyes are
watering too. I love being outside, and I love watching the
planes, but I wish I could breathe the air and hear everything properly. I wish I could take my helmet off. Amir puts
his hand on my shoulder.

"What you thinking?" he asks.

I shrug. I don't know if I should tell him or not. I feel
bad for thinking it. I should be grateful for what we've done.

"What is it?"

"Amir, can I take my helmet off?"

He looks across at the planes, then up at the sky.

"Can I? Please. Just for one second."

He shakes his head slowly. "I'm sorry," he says. "We can't
do that. It too risky."

*But one second wouldn't hurt me . . . would it? Just one real
breath.*

Amir walks toward the car.

I could do it now. I could take off my gloves, undo the
straps, and take it off. Amir would have to be an Olympic
runner to run back and stop me. Just one second, that's all I
want. I look down at my gloves and pull at the fingers.

"Joe, I say no."

I want to do it. I want to breathe air that hasn't been

STEWART FOSTER

filtered through tubes. I pull at another finger and glance at Amir. He's standing in front of the car. Tiny bugs and moths buzz around the car headlights. Hundreds of them zing around in the air, knock into each other, and bash against the glass.

Amir walks over to me and puts his arm around my shoulders.

"I'm sorry," I say.

"It's okay."

"Just one breath."

"I know, but if you take one breath you want another and then you want ten."

He links his arm through mine and he walks me toward the car.

I stop and look back at the airfield. The planes move slowly across the runway like they're dancing to music. Out of the corner of my eye I see Amir look at his watch.

"Do we have to go now?"

Amir checks his watch again, then the figures on his phone.

**Air temp.:** 9C

**Body temp.:** 37.2C

**Heart rate:** 119

**Air remaining:** 5 liters

He bites his lip. "The time is going really fast, but I really want you to see something. How you feeling? Your heart rate quite high."

"I'm excited," I say. "I feel a bit tired, that's all."

He opens the car door. "You just sit here then and save energy." He checks the readings again. "But I think we've enough air. And we have time."

"What for?"

"For greatest show on Earth."

"What's that?"

"You'll find out. But first you rest a while. I wake you up."

I wonder what Amir has got planned. What could be greater than having a massive plane fly over my head?

Amir closes the car door. "We just sit and wait," he says.

I rest back against the seat and close my eyes. But I don't want to sleep. I don't want to go home. Lots of people would think it funny to call a hospital my home but that's what it is. That's what it will always be if the doctors never find a cure. Henry is right. We have to keep living; we have to keep hoping. It might be fun Skyping each other but we don't want to sit in our rooms for the rest of our lives.

Amir turns on the radio. I hear music quietly playing. A piano and a guitar. A man sings a song about losing his heart in San Francisco. Amir stares through the windscreen, nodding slowly like the song is playing in his head. The clock ticks on . . .

5:59.

6:00.

6:01.

The music stops. I hear the sound of birds tweeting. I look around but I can't see any birds. All I can see is the dark but it's not as dark as it was before. Is this what I'm here for—to hear the birds? I wait for Amir to tell me he's ready but all he does is take a deep breath, then starts nodding to a new song.

6:02.

6:03.

6:04.

There's nothing happening. What are we waiting for? Maybe this is when the aliens come. They'll fly across the sky and land in the field in front of us. That's what happens. I saw it when I watched an old film with Beth—*Close Encounters of the Third Kind*. The aliens landed in a place just like this with no one around for miles. They said they were friendly and didn't want to hurt anybody, but at the end a man goes into the spaceship and they take him away. If they landed here, they would take me and Amir away too. We'd walk up the gangplank like that man did and the doors would slide closed. The doctors and nurses and the police would come looking for us but the spaceship would be gone. All they would find is the car and the scorch marks on the grass.

The clock moves on—

6:11.

6:12.

6:13.

Amir put his hand on my arm. My heart stops.

"Sorry," he says. "I no mean to make you jump."

"It's okay."

He nods out of the windshield. "It's started."

"What has?"

"Just watch."

I look out across the airfield. The lights on the trucks and planes are fading. I look at the grass, the runway, and the sky. Everything that was black has now turned to gray. There's a white line on the horizon—a bright white line. I stare at it. It gets deeper and wider and stretches as far as I can see.

I lean forward.

"Didn't want you to miss it," Amir whispers. "The greatest show on Earth." He smiles and I see two crescents in his glasses. I look back across the airfield and see the tip of the sun at the end of the runway.

The sky turns red.

The sky turns orange.

The sun sits on the runway like a big burning ball.

A real sunrise.

I wish Henry was here to see this. I can't wait to tell him about it—that's if I can stop him talking about the mall. I wish Beth was here too, and Greg. I wish we could all sit here and watch the sun come out of the Earth and the sky turn blue. The sun never shines through my window. I only see it shine outside on the street.

I look at Amir in disbelief. My heart rate is 124.

"Okay?"

"Amir, it's better than okay. It's awesome! Thank you."

"It okay, maybe we do it again one day."

"Can we really?"

"Yes," he says. "Maybe the aliens turn up next time!"

I smile but suddenly I feel so tired that I could go to sleep and not wake up for weeks. My head falls back against the seat and I feel the warmth of the sun's rays on my face. I take a deep breath, then another.

Amir starts the car and we go back down the track, between the containers, and over the bumps. We turn left onto the main road and go back past Heathrow and onto the motorway. There's hundreds of cars and trucks all around us, slowing us down.

"It's okay. I calculate it—the traffic." He reaches out and turns the radio on. I rest my head against the window and try to relax as a black taxi goes by. It's been the best time of my life and I don't want it to end. But even if I had a tank full of air I'm too tired to stay out any longer. My eyelids grow heavy—*Mercedes-Benz, GlaxoSmithKline, Lucozade, E = mc²*—the sun shines on my face and the cars and buildings start to blur. I take a deep breath and my head begins to drop.

# TWENTY-TWO

## 11 Years, 3 Months, and 12 Days

**There are birds tweeting** outside my window. They're on the ledge pecking at the glass like they're saying hello and want to come in.

*Tweet. Tweet. Tweet.*

*Tweet. Tweet. Tweet.*

The sun is shining through my window onto my bed. Its rays soak through my T-shirt onto my skin.

*Tweet. Tweet. Tweet.*

*Tweet. Tweet. Tweet.*

A plane flies across the sky. I try to lift my head to see what airline it is but my head aches and my body is so heavy. It's like I fell into Mike and Dave's hole and now I'm covered in cement.

The sun climbs higher.

A plane flies across it.

The birds keep tweeting.

Am I awake or am I dreaming?

*Tweet. Tweet. Tweet.*

*Tweet. Tweet. Tweet.*

*Beep. Beep. Beep.*

*Beep.*

*Beep.*

*Beep.*

"Well, he looks quite rested."

"I know. It's just that he's been asleep all morning."

Another plane takes off inside my head and flies across the sun.

"Mmm . . . let's take a look at his readings."

I hear footsteps beside my bed.

"What's this?"

I open my eyes and sneak a look. Dr. Moore is pointing at my monitors.

"11 degrees," he says. "What's happened there?"

*Oh no. Amir forgot the monitor memory.*

Greg reaches in front of him and presses the temperature button three times.

"Sometime after midnight," he says. They both look up at the air vent.

"Best get that checked," says Dr. Moore. "But apart from that, well, his temperature's up a little, but there's little else to cause concern."

They turn around and catch me looking.

"Ah, there he is," says Dr. Moore. "He was listening all the time. How are you doing, young man?"

"I'm okay. Just tired."

"Did the cold keep you awake?"

I shake my head quickly.

"No, I didn't notice the cold. I had the covers on all night."

Dr. Moore looks over the top of his glasses at my screens.

"Mmm, maybe you're tired because you're watching those all the time."

"I've not been watching them much."

Greg pretends to cough.

"Well, I've watched them a bit."

"How about we give them a rest . . . Just for the day?"

I want to tell him I need to watch Henry but I'm so tired all I can do is nod.

Dr. Moore looks at Greg.

"He seems okay, but let's increase his fluids and keep monitoring."

Greg says something I can't hear. Their voices fade away as they walk toward the door.

A wave of energy runs through my body. I put my hand on my head. I've been outside. I can't believe I did it. I've seen the sky and the sun and the moon without having to look through glass. I've seen all the buildings. I've seen the river. I've been on a motorway.

I look toward the door. I want to tell Greg and Dr. Moore. I want to stand up on my bed and shout: *I've been outside! I've seen the sun! I've watched the planes take off and land at Heathrow!*

Shall I do it? I could do it now. I'm going to do it.

*Hey! I've been outside. I've been in a car! I went to the air-port and I saw the moon and the stars.*

No. I can't tell them. I can't tell anyone. It's like I've won the lottery but can't go shopping.

"You okay, Joe?" asks Dr. Moore.

I put my hand over my mouth in case my words jump out. I nod.

"You don't feel sick?"

"No, I'm okay."

He whispers something to Greg and they walk out into the transition zone.

I look up at the ceiling and I can't stop grinning. Did I really do it? I haven't got any proof. I didn't go to a shop and buy a souvenir or a postcard. I didn't put a stone in my pocket or pick a blade of grass. I didn't even remember my phone to take pictures of the planes. I wish I had.

I don't have any proof at all. Amir took my suit and hel-met with him. He even made me take a shower to wash the chalk off my skin. It's like it never happened. Amir said if it was a dream I was the only one who would know. I don't think it was a dream, was it? It couldn't have been. I couldn't have had a dream that felt that real. I close my eyes and another plane crosses the sun.

I roll over on my side, reach out, and check the time on my laptop. It's 1:03 pm in London. It's 8:03 am in Philadelphia. Henry will have eaten his breakfast already. If he wasn't resting I could send him a message. I'd tell him

that it I was okay in my suit I'm sure he will be okay in his.
I don't want to spoil his excitement.

My phone buzzes by my side. I pick it up.

Hey Joe. Still seeing planes?

I slide down and pull my covers over my head.

**Amir. How do you know?**

I thought maybe they stay in your head like aliens
stay in mine.

I smile.

**Amir, I'm so happy!**

Then I happy too. I just text to check you okay.

**I'm tired.**

Me too. You should sleep.

**I will. But I want to watch Henry.**

Set alarm on phone.

**I will.**

I hear Greg's voice getting louder.

**Think Greg's coming back.**

Okay. I go. I see you Thursday.

**Okay.**

Delete these messages

**I will.**

**Amir. Thank you!!!!!!**

You deserve.

**Hope you find some crop circles!!**

Me too. I send you pictures.

The door opens. Greg walks around the bottom of my bed. I slide my phone under my pillow and pretend I'm sleeping. I hate not being able to tell him what I've done because I tell him everything. He'd be really pleased if he knew I was this happy. Maybe I can tell him one day when I've been fixed for good. I could meet him in a park in my lunch hour and we could sit on a bench. I'd tell him I was working for Marvel Comics and he would ask for free copies.

I'd meet him every week and eventually, one day, I would
tell him I'd been outside when I was ill. No one would get in
trouble then; it would be too long since it happened. Amir
could get fired if they found out next week or next month.
I've seen people on TV. Sometimes people get caught and
get sent to prison years after they've committed the crime.
Amir hasn't committed a real crime. He hasn't killed anyone
or stolen anything. Some people might say he kidnapped
me—but he brought me back! They can't send him to prison
for doing that, can they?

I hear Greg's footsteps fade away.

I reach under my pillow and set my alarm, then I write
a message on a piece of paper—*Greg, come back at 8 o'clock
and we can watch Henry on TV*—I fold the paper so it stands
up at the end of my bed.

I lay back on my pillow. I've been outside. I've been outside. I close my eyes. Another plane goes across the sun.

Going outside wasn't a dream.

I've never had a dream as good as that.


"Mate, wake up."

I open my eyes. All I can see are flashing green lights and
dark shadows.

"Mate!" Greg puts his hand on his shoulder and rocks
me. "Joe!" Greg's standing beside me with the remote control in his hand. "It's past eight."

I try to blink myself awake. "It can't be . . . I set my . . . I
left you a message."

"I'm sorry, I've been busy, mate." He hands me the remote. "Amir isn't here and I don't know how to turn this thing on."

I push myself up on my bed. I'm half an hour late. Henry's longest walk lasted forty-five minutes. He'll have nearly finished by now; he'll be on his way back to his room.

I press the remote. The screens flash on. Too many buttons, too many channels. If only Amir was here to do it. I press the red start button.

All the screens go fuzzy as the decoder searches for the satellite—a man rides a camel in the desert, a woman rows a boat across the ocean, a man throws a dart against a board. Where is Henry?!

*Amir, why did you get me so many channels?*

Greg looks around the room. "Mate, did he leave any instructions?"

"It's okay," I say. "I think I can do it." I select the Astra satellite, then region 57.

The names of all the American states scroll up the screen. My hands are shaking. I scroll down to Pennsylvania and select cable channel 121.

"Ha, there he is!" Greg points at the screens.

**LIVE! LIVE! Bubble Boy at the King of Prussia Shopping Mall brought to you LIVE by WCTI TV.**

A rush of excitement goes to my stomach and can't stop myself from smiling. On the screens is a picture of a boy in a space suit walking past a fountain. It's Henry! Three camera-men walk behind him, another walks in front of him, pho-tographers run around him taking pictures, and a woman with red hair talks into a microphone.

"Here he goes," she says. "After spending all of his life in a bubble, Henry Thomas gets to go outside. The crowds are so noisy I can barely hear myself speak. Just listen to them!" She holds the microphone out.

"Go, Henry, go! Go, Henry, go!" the crowd chants.

The reporter steps out of the way and the camera follows Henry through the mall. Boys and girls wave flags above their heads and blow whistles. Men and woman smile and clap their hands. And Henry leads the way, taking slow steps like he's walking on the moon.

"Wow." I look at Greg. "This is way more exciting than watching the FA Cup final on TV!"

Greg laughs. Goose bumps crawl up my arms, cover my whole body. The camera zooms in. Henry's white suit fills my screens. As he walks it creases when his arms and legs bend. He's so big, it's like I'm walking with him. His name is written in blue on his chest pocket. NASA is written on his arm. He lifts it and waves to the crowd again.

I turn the volume up.

"Go, Henry, go! Go, Henry, go!"

The crowd chant and I want to chant with them. Children run around Henry carrying red and white bal-loons. They let go of them and they float up into the sky. Henry's mum and Matt are walking beside him, talking and laughing. Henry takes a step sideways and trips Matt up.

"Ha, he told me he would do that."

Greg smiles.

I cough. My throat feels like I've got something stuck in it. I cough again. Greg puts his hand on my back and asks if I'm okay. I nod and he hands me a glass of water. I take a sip and hold the glass up.

"What's wrong, mate?"

"Nothing," I say. I swallow. I don't tell Greg I think I can taste metal.

"And here we go," says the reporter. "The bubble boy enters the King of Prussia Shopping Mall."

The mall doors slide open. Henry walks through and the cameras follow him inside. People come out of stores with shopping bags in their hands—Nike, Levis, and Sketchers— and try to give them to Henry. The security guard takes the bags, and then hands them to another person who walks behind. It's like Henry's got his birthday and Christmas as the same time. A remote-control car races across the floor and crashes into his boots. A boy in a red RadioShack polo shirt jumps past the security guard and holds out the controls. I think Henry shrugs: his gloves are too thick to operate the controls. He turns and looks at Matt. Matt runs over and picks up the car. The boy hands him the remote, then fist bumps Henry. I laugh.

"He's having fun!" I say.

"And now for a break," says the reporter.

The picture changes.

**News from our sponsor. News from our sponsor.**

I watch a commercial of a man trying to eat a doughnut while he bounces up and down on a trampoline.

Amir might not have taken me to the mall but at least we didn't get interrupted by commercials. My trip outside was so different. Me and Amir went out in a beat-up old car. Henry's got a limo and is surrounded by people like he's a movie star. I'd have loved to have gone to the mall and got presents too. I'd love to go to Forbidden Planet and buy lots of T-shirts and comics. I'd put a T-shirt on straightaway and read the comic in the Rainforest Café. I'd like to meet lots of people like Henry has. But maybe Henry would like to see the moon and the stars and the planes, like I did. It means we've got lots to chat about.

My legs are starting to ache and my hands are shaking. Greg stands by my side and asks me if I'm okay. I tell him I feel a bit dizzy but I don't want to miss Henry. He tells me I won't and leads me to my bed.

The picture flickers. Henry is back on the screen. He's sitting down on a chair at a table outside Starbucks. The camera zooms in on Henry's helmet and the cameraman is reflected in the glass. A woman walks over to Henry and hands him a brown paper bag and a cup of coffee. He holds the cup to his mouth and pretends to drink it. Everyone laughs. I laugh too. I think how much Henry would like to do it for real but he doesn't seem to mind.

"Henry's just taking a rest here in Starbucks," says the reporter. "Let's see if we can get a word." She weaves her way through the crowd. A security guard blocks her way.

"No, ma'am," he says. "Not now, maybe later." He looks over his shoulder. Henry's only been sitting down for two minutes but he's already being moved on.

"He needs to rest."

"Yeah, mate. Maybe they're thinking about the time."

Matt runs in front of Henry and grabs hold of his hand. He points ahead. They walk toward an escalator. The photographers run ahead, get on backward, and take pictures as Henry gets on. He's smiling and his eyes are shining. It's like he's looking right at me. He opens his mouth and makes a shape like an O.

"I think he said my name."

"Yeah," says Greg. "Think he did, mate."

Henry lifts up his hand and points at a massive sign with green writing—FOOD HALL.

"I knew it!" I put my hands on my head. Then I cough and taste metal again.

Henry walks past Burger King, Snack Shack, and other shops serving Chinese food and pizzas. People are sitting on silver chairs at silver tables. They stop eating as Henry walks by. Some of them stand up and clap; the rest smile and wave. Henry stops and puts his hand up to his head.

"I don't think he believes what's happening," says the reporter. "He's having so much fun he wants to soak up every minute."

"Greg."

"Yes, mate."

"I think something's wrong."

"He's having a rest, mate."

"No, I think . . ."

Henry's mum says something to him and signals to one of the nurses.

"Maybe he just needs some water," says Greg.

"No, his drink is built into his suit."

Greg shrugs. "Then I don't know, mate."

Henry's mum and a nurse lead him to a chair. The reporter pushes her way in front of the camera and holds out her microphone.

"Henry, you must be one happy guy?"

The camera zooms in on Henry's face. He's smiles but I think he's smiling for the cameras. That's not how he smiles at me on Skype.

"Just a few words?"

Henry mouth opens but he looks too tired to speak.

Something's wrong. I know it. I look at the time. I try to work out how long Henry has been outside but I'm too worried to concentrate. I get off my bed and walk up to the screen.

*Henry, what's wrong?*

Two nurses are bending down by Henry's side. They're talking to him but I don't think he replies. He doesn't even lift his arm or move his head. More nurses arrive with medical cases and two paramedics carrying a stretcher. Henry's head falls forward like his helmet is too heavy. Maybe his blood count isn't right. Maybe his air is too pure. But

NASA would have checked that, wouldn't they?

A man puts his arm around Matt and leads him away. My heart thuds and I feel a lump in my throat. A policeman with a gun on his hip holds up his hand and walks toward the camera. Henry slumps forward. His suit crumples like all the energy's gone out of him, like someone has walked up behind him and pulled out the valve.

"Greg, what's wrong with him? He doesn't look—"

I screw up my face as a pain shoots through my head.

"Mate, what's up?"

I hold my hand up to my head. The pain shoots again. It's like an ice-cream headache but I haven't eaten any. My monitors start to beep faster. The room starts to spin, round and round, faster and faster, like Henry's flying around in a washing machine. Greg's standing over me. He's spinning around too.

"Greg, I don't feel well. I can taste metal."

My head falls back on my pillow. Sweat runs down my neck.

"You're okay, mate. Take it easy, I'm here."

"Greg, I don't—"

"Mate. Joe!"

Greg reaches over me and presses the emergency button. The world turns black.

# TWENTY-THREE

*Beep.*
  *Beep.*
  *Beep.*

**Room temp.:** 19
**Air purity:** 98.1
Heart rate: 113

*Beep.*
  *Beep.*
  *Beep.*

I've got airplanes inside my head. They're circling round, stacked high in the sky—*Air New Zealand, British Airways, Virgin Atlantic*—they go round and round and round and round. *Air New Zealand, British Airways, Virgin Atlantic.*

There's so many they make me dizzy.

*Air New Zealand, British Airways, Virgin Atlantic.*

*Air New Zealand, British Airways—*

"What's that, mate?"

". . . Virgin Atlantic." I open my eyes. The lights are dimmed. My room is full of shadows and the screens are as black as the night sky. I take a deep breath and feel a hand on my arm. Greg is beside me. He's dark and fuzzy and merges in with the wall. My eyelids fall down. I hear Greg talking to other people but I can't hear what they're saying. . . . It's like they're all talking underwater. I try to lift my head, but it aches too much and my body hurts in every place it touches the bed. I force my eyes open again and try to speak. A sharp pain shoots through the middle of my head when I cough. Greg leans over me and presses a cup against my lips.

"Try and drink, mate," he says.

I take a sip but my throat is so sore it's like I've got a hedgehog stuck in it. I cough again. Greg raises my bed. I see the shadows of doctors and nurses.

"It's happened rather suddenly."

"BP?"

"100/80."

"Heart rate?"

"117."

"Let's try . . ."

My room starts to spin. My stomach feels like it's coming up through my throat.

"I feel sick."

Greg puts his hand around my shoulders and I puke in a bowl.

"Easy, mate. Easy." He wipes my mouth. I look down at my arm. A tube comes out of it across my bed and up into a plastic bag.

"What happened?" I whisper.

"Not now, mate. Just relax."

Greg puts a wet cloth on my forehead. It's so cold it freezes my brain.

I shiver.

Greg pulls my covers up to my chin. My head falls back. The shadows move and talk in front of the window. Outside, the lights in the glass building are dull and the sky is turning from black to gray. Another plane flies across the inside of my head. I wish I could go and see them again but I don't think I'd want to go if I came back feeling like there's a bug crawling through my body. I don't want any bugs. I hate bugs. . . .

"I hate bugs. . . ."

"He's very restless. Let's try something to bring his temperature down . . . Paracetamol . . . and increase the fluids to . . ."

"I hate bugs."

"I know, mate, just take it easy." Greg's back by my side. He puts a clean bowl on my bed. I try to talk but it comes out as a whisper.

"What happened?" I ask.

Greg looks at the doctors then back at me. "We're not sure, mate. One minute you were watching Henry, the next you'd passed out."

I turn my head slowly and look at the screens. They're all blank and the red standby lights are blurred. I close my eyes and try to remember what I was watching. Henry in the mall, smiling and waving on the escalator. I wait for him to get off but the escalator goes on and on and he never reaches the top. It's like I've got a DVD in my head stuck on repeat.

I open my eyes and close them again. Henry's jumped ahead; he's outside McDonald's with people all around him cheering and smiling. Then I see Henry start to fall forward.

"Henry!"

"Wow, mate, stay still." Greg puts his hand on my arm.

"But Henry . . . ?" I swallow and screw my eyes as pain shoots again. "Is he okay?"

"Mate, please, lay still."

"Can I check . . . ? Can I message him?"

I try to reach for my laptop. My head spins again. Another nurse stands my by side and puts her hand on my shoulder. Greg puts his hand on my chest.

"Mate, this is serious. You're not well enough for that."

"But—" My chests rattles and I cough. "But I need to find out. . . . I really need to know."

Greg looks toward the doctors. "It's important. . . . I don't think he's going to rest till he knows."

I don't hear the reply but I think I see a shadow shake its head. Greg gets up and walks toward them. They nod and start to whisper.

"I think . . ."

"I know but . . ."

"Just for . . ."

"Okay. Okay."

They stop talking. Greg comes back to me. "Just one message" he says. "Just to check."

"Okay."

He slides my laptop onto my bed and lifts up the screen. I try to move the mouse but the keyboard is all blurry and the letters move up and down like they're floating on the sea. I blink. My head clears a little and I check my messages. There's two from my teachers, eleven for Bubble Boy, but nothing on Skype from Henry. I start to type.

Henry. I hope you're ok.                          10:00 PM

I wait for the pencil to start scribbling. But it doesn't.

Henry . . . message me when you can.          10:02 PM

I cough and a bright light flashes through the middle of my head. I scrunch my eyes. The light flashes again, a million times brighter than the car headlights I passed on the road with Amir. I shout to Greg. All that comes out is a croak. The lights shine again. I twist in my bed, reach for my pillow, and try to wrap it around my head.

"Easy, Joe. Easy."

A hand on my shoulder. A hand on my leg.

"Hold him. Hold him!"

Another bright light.

"No, Joe. Don't take it off. I tell you not to take it off."
Amir's standing in front of the car headlights with his hand
in the air. "Joe, I tell you. No take it off."

I didn't take it off. I don't think I took my helmet off? I
bite my teeth together as the pain comes again.

I'm at the airfield with Amir. Planes are roaring over my
head. My helmet is rocking backward and forward on the
grass.

"Pick it up, Joe. You put it back on!" Amir runs toward
me but it's like he's moving in slow motion. He looks back
at the car, then back at me. Bugs and midges buzz around
in the headlights.

Amir keeps running. Bugs fly around his legs, his body,
and in his hair.

"Joe! Hurry, they coming."

I pick up my helmet and try to put it on. My hands are
shaking and my gloves are too thick to fasten the straps. The
bugs are all around me, biting at my suit, crawling up my
arms and my shoulders toward my neck.

"Amir! Amir!"

"Joe! Joe!"

I open my eyes. I'm back in my room. Greg's standing
over me shouting my name.

I try to sit up.

"The bugs," I say. "They're everywhere! Don't let them get
me! Don't let the bugs get me!"

"Joe, there are no bugs."

Can't he see the bugs are in my room? There's millions

of them, crawling over the monitors, down my IV tube, and into me. They're biting my hands and my neck. They're going to eat me until all that's left is bones. I try to shout but they're crawling up my neck into my mouth. Doctors and nurses all around me. Bugs buzzing everywhere. They're bouncing off the ceiling and scratching on the floor.

"There are!" I scratch the bugs off my body and my head.

"Okay. Okay, let's sedate."

More hands on my arms and legs.

"It's all right, mate. It's okay."

My head starts to go dizzy. I feel something cold in my arm, like ice is traveling through my veins. I take a deep breath, then another. Fuzzy faces look down at me.

"There we go. There we go."

I feel like Spidey when he fought Morlun. He got smashed against cars and thrown from the highest towers. Then he swung Morlun around in a circle and threw him against the Empire State Building. Spidey's suit was torn and he lay crumpled on the floor. It was the hardest fight Spidey ever had. No one had hit him harder than Morlun, not even the Hulk. But he kept getting up every time Morlun knocked him down; he wouldn't give up, as long as his heart kept beating he would keep fighting every moment and, in the end, he found a way to win.

I turn my head. Something is scratching under the door. The bugs are coming back again.

# TWENTY-FOUR

## 11 YEARS, 3 MONTHS, AND 13 DAYS

**The sun is out** and the clouds are rolling slowly over the glass building. The doctors are standing at the end of my bed. Dr. Hussein has got his arms folded. Dr. Moore is holding his chin. They smile when they see me looking.

"Hey, young man." Dr. Moore walks toward me and sits on the edge of my bed. "How are you feeling?"

"Not very good," I say.

"No, you've had a tough night," he says softly. Then he looks at me for a long time like he's waiting for me to say something. I don't want to say anything. All I want is for the pain to go away.

Dr. Moore rests his notes on my bed. "Just tell me about the pain, Joe," he says softly.

"It's bad."

"I know, but where is it?"

"All over and I feel really hot."

"Okay, let's stay with the pain. Tell me where it hurts most?"

"My legs, my arms, my back. It's everywhere."

"But mainly?"

"In my head and my mouth is really sore too."

"How bad is the pain? On a scale of one to ten?"

My eyelids fall down. How bad is this pain? Sometimes it's a dull ache—that's about a four. Sometimes it's a throbbing pain—that's about a six.

I wince as the paint shoots again. "Argh—an eight!"

The pain stabs like a knife in my head, fades to an ache.

Dr. Moore taps my hand. "Joe, we need to give you something more for that. Okay?"

This must be serious. Dr. Moore doesn't usually talk to me as quietly as this. He's usually smiling and making jokes with Dr. Hussein and the only time he calls me Joe is when I've done something wrong.

He taps my hand again like he's trying to wake me up. "Okay, young man. I think you know how this goes."

"More tests?"

"I'm afraid so. It's an infection. We know that. We're just not sure where it came from. It's like investigating a crime. We have to eliminate all the suspects until we're left with the culprit . . . but we think it's fungal."

"In my blood."

"Yes."

"And sometimes it can affect the lungs."

He rubs my head gently and glances up at Dr. Hussein.

"It's taken a while," he says, "but I think we've got our man back again."

I smile. I don't feel well but I feel better. I feel better because the doctors are here.

Dr. Moore stands up. "So, Joe, this is how it goes. You need to take it easy . . . stay in bed a few days. Dr. Hussein's going to take a look at you, and then we'll do those tests and we'll give you something for the pain. Okay?" He scribbles something down on his pad.

"Is it really serious?"

"Well, you know that any infection is serious. We'll do all the usual things, like check the air purity and the ventilation system, but this really shouldn't have gotten in here. It's something new that we've not come across before." Dr. Moore turns and talks quietly to Dr. Hussein.

I know I should help them search for the infection. They're really busy looking after the other kids. I could save them time. They don't have to do all the tests or change all the filters. I could tell them the reason I'm ill is because I went outside. Every time I've had an infection before, it's just happened; they tell me it's just bad luck. But this time it's my fault. I should tell them now but I can't. I don't want to get into trouble, but most of all I don't want to snitch on Amir. He shouldn't get into trouble for giving me the most exciting night of my life.

"Hey," Dr. Moore stands above me. "Don't look so worried. We can do this. . . . You're a superhero. We all know superheroes bounce back."

I smile and try to lift my arm to show them my muscles, but it aches too much.

"Don't worry," says Dr. Hussein. "We'll soon have those muscles as strong as Thor's. . . . Now, let's take a look at you."

"I'll leave you to it," says Dr. Moore. "I'll be back later—and, Joe?" He stops by the door. "Everything will be fine. Even if it is the filters, there are back-up systems to stop the really bad stuff getting through."

I nod as he goes out of the door. He doesn't know that when I was outside all I had was my helmet. I lean forward. Dr. Hussein puts his hand on my back and taps it with his fingers. He tells me to breathe in and out. I've had this done so many times I know what to do. When he's finished tapping on my back, he does the same on my chest. Then he looks in my mouth and in my ears. He makes a "hmmm" sound, then writes in his notes. Then he sits down and asks me more questions—do I still feel sick? Have the bright lights stopped flashing in my head?

I tell him I feel a bit dizzy and that the lights have gone away. More "hmmm"s. More notes.

My head falls back onto my pillow and my eyes meet the ceiling. The pain throbs through my head every time the monitors beep. I take a deep breath and try to slow it down. Then another—seven seconds in. Eleven seconds out.

*Seven seconds in. Eleven seconds out.* Just like Amir taught me.

My heart rate slows, the pain weakens, and Dr. Hussein's words start to fade like he's walking away from me into another room.

\* \* \*

*I'm floating through the air, over the tops of skyscrapers. I touch each one with my fingertips, push gently, then float on to the next. The sky is blue but the streets are gray, and empty—there are no cars, no busses or taxis, and there are no people walking.*

*It's like everyone has left and gone to a new planet. Why didn't they tell me? I didn't see them fly past me.*

*I look ahead. Another skyscraper comes toward me. I float over it and out to sea.*

*Beep.*
*Beep.*
*Beep.*

**Heart rate:** 114
**Body temp.:** 40.1C
**Room temp.:** 19C
**Air purity:** 99.1

My room is white. Outside, the glass building is blue. There's music playing quietly.

Charlotte R. is standing beside me with a syringe in her hand. "Sorry," she says. "It's me again."

I close my eyes and feel the sting as the needle goes in.

"How are you feeling?"

"Not great." I wince.

"No, Greg said you didn't have a good night. But let's hope that's the worst."

"I'm worried about my friend, too."

"I know. Greg said he's going to try and call the hospital when he comes in." She taps my arm. "There . . . all done."

I see the time on her watch. It's 11:15. Greg won't be here until six. I can't wait that long to find out about Henry. I reach for my laptop.

"No," Charlotte R. says. "You're supposed to be taking it easy."

I give her my best *Please let me!* look.

"Stop doing that puppy thing. It doesn't work."

I do the puppy again. I *know* it will.

Charlotte tuts. "Look, I'm sure he's okay."

"I know," I say. "But I just want to check. Please."

She sighs. "I've just got to take this down to the lab." She slides my laptop onto my bed. "I'll be gone five minutes."

I give her my best *Thank you* look.

She walks back to the door. FIVE, she mouths and holds up her fingers.

I open my laptop. Henry might be tired but it doesn't take much energy to type a message. We've always been able to do it before when one of us has had a cold or been sick. We've even messaged in the middle of transfusions. I'm really ill and I can do it. But maybe he's feeling even worse than me.

I check Skype. He still hasn't replied.

**Henry, I'm really worried now.**                    **11:20 am**

I wish I could contact his mum and dad but I've only ever spoken to them on Skype when they're with Henry.

They've never called or texted me. They send me Christmas and birthday cards but I don't have an address to send anything back. But they would get hold of me, wouldn't they? They would know I am worried.

**Henry, where are you?**                                    **11:22 AM**

I look at the time. Charlotte said she would be five minutes, but it takes longer than that to go down to the lab and back.

There must be news about Henry somewhere. I switch to the Internet and start to type.

*Boy in a space suit. Philadelphia Shopping Mall.*

My finger hovers over the enter key. I want to know how he is, but I don't want to know if he's really ill. It's like when the doctors tell me what's wrong with me. I don't want to know how bad it is but I still go on the Internet and look it up.

I close my eyes, press the key, then open my eyes again.

**Bubble Boy Collapses At Philly Shopping Mall**

There's a picture of Henry slumped in his chair with his mum and the nurses surrounding him. I click on the link and start to read but it doesn't say any more than I already know, only that they couldn't do anything for him at the mall because it meant getting him out of his suit. They took him back to the hospital in an ambulance. I look at the next search result:

## Bubble Boy Burst—YouTube

I click off the screen. I've seen Henry collapse once. I don't want to see it again.

I should be resting but I can't relax when my best friend is ill. I have to do something. There are two messages on the BBC website.

**BBC Bubble Boy Forum**
**Sun August 29, 11:01 PM**
*Dear Bubble Boy,*

*I think I might have the same disease as you, but my mum thinks it's just an excuse so I don't have to go to school.*
*Marlow Trent, Essex*

**BBC Bubble Boy Forum**
**Mon August 30, 9:41 AM**
*Dear Bubble Boy, or shall I call you Joe, I don't know. Should I? Anyway I'm sorry I haven't contacted you, I've been to my gran's in Wales and she doesn't have Internet and the mobile signal isn't very good there either. What have you been up to?*
*I think . . .*

The words start to blur like I'm studying for a history test.

My phone buzzes on my bed and makes me jump. It's Beth. I haven't spoken to her since I went outside. I don't want her to worry about me or find out what I've done. I open her message.

Hey Joe. How are you?

**I'm OK.**

You sure?

**Yes.**

I know you're not.

I look at my phone and wonder what she knows. My phone buzzes again.

Greg phoned me, but I was out last night and my phone went dead. I'm going to come down.

**No, it's OK.**

But you've got an infection. It's not OK.

**The doctors are going to fix me.**

I'll check the trains.

I really want to see Beth, but she was really mad that I didn't tell her I was ill when the television people were here. She'll be even madder now.

I can get to you late this evening.

I don't know what to write. I don't want to lie.

Joe. You're quiet.

**I'm fine. Honest.**

I can get to you this evening. . . . I'll call you.

**No, it's OK.**

My phone buzzes in my hand. I said I was okay. I told her
not to call me.

"Come on, what's wrong?"

My chest goes tight. It's bad enough not telling her the
truth by text; it's even harder now I can hear her voice.

"It's nothing," I say.

"Are you feeling really bad?"

"I don't feel great."

"But there's something else? Come on, you can tell me."

"How can you tell?"

"Because I'm your sister."

I hate lying. Especially to her. But I have to tell her something. "It's Henry," I say. "He's ill."

"What's wrong with him?" She sounds worried.

"I don't know. No one will tell me."

"Can't Greg or Amir find out?"

"Greg's going to try later."

"And Amir?"

"He's looking for crop circles."

"What?"

"He's on vacation."

"Oh." The phone goes quiet. I can tell she's worried. She sighs. "Joe, you sound really down."

I slide down in my bed. I tell Beth about the mall, how Henry was loving all the cheering crowds and that they were waving and he was waving back. I tell her that it was all going great until he went down the escalator. Beth says it just sounds like he might have got too tired. I tell her I think it's more than that. He would message me if he could.

"But maybe no news is good news," she says. "That's what Mum used to say."

"Did she?"

"Yes. No news is good news and all news is bad news. When did you last watch the news and feel happy?"

"I can't . . . I can't remember."

Beth laughs. "See?"

I smile. I know she's trying to cheer me up.

"I'm sure he's fine. But we've got to make sure you are too. So I'm coming down."

"You don't have—"

"Too late . . . It's booked!"

The door slides open and Charlotte R. walks in. She kicks her foot against the bottom of my bed.

"Oops! Sorry!"

"Who's that?" Beth says.

I tell her it's Charlotte R. and Beth asks to speak to her. I pass over the phone.

"Hi." Charlotte R. looks at me and smiles. I can still hear Beth talking. Charlotte R. walks toward the door. "No, he's not having a great time but he looks a bit happier now." She steps into the transition zone.

I'm not happier but I do feel a little better. Beth might be right. No news is good news. Henry was on TV. If anything had happened to him it would be on the Internet by now. Maybe he's in his room opening his presents with Matt. They'll be playing with the remote-control car, or maybe they got two? They'll race each other on an imaginary racetrack and weave them in between the legs of the bed like Mario Kart. Matt would be Bowser, Henry would be Luigi, and if I was there I would be Mario and I'd use turbo boost to overtake them both.

Charlotte R. comes back and hands me my phone. "She's lovely," she says.

"I know, but she worries too much."

"That's what sisters do."

"But sometimes she won't leave me alone."

My phone buzzes.

"See?"

I look at my phone.

"Is it her?"

"No."

"Why are you smiling?" Charlotte R. leans over and makes a funny face. "Who's sending you pictures of crop circles?"

"A friend."

"That's a bit of a weird thing to send!"

I shrug and look at the picture again. It's a crop circle with three dots in the middle. I spread my fingers on the screen and zoom in. Ajala, Shukra, and Guru are standing in the middle of a field waving at me. I smile. They look like they're having a great time with Amir. I wish I could chat with him, but I don't want to ruin his vacation by telling him I'm ill. Besides, I might be better by the time he's back. I click on my phone and send Amir a smiley face.

Charlotte stays with me for most of the afternoon. She brings me lunch—sausages and mashed potato—but I don't feel like eating it so she gives me a glass of pink lumpy liquid instead. She says it will help build my strength back up, but all it does is make me feel sick.

She sits next to me and reads a book while I go on my laptop again. There's still no message from Henry, but since Beth called I don't feel so bad.

**BBC Bubble Boy Forum**

**Mon August 30, 3:17 am**

*Dear Bubble Boy,*

   *Do you think Arsenal is going to buy Morgan Schneiderlin? I hope they don't because he's our best player.*

   *Josh Hammond,*

   *Southampton*

**Dear Josh,**

*I think Morgan Schneiderlin is a great player, but I want Sergio Agüero!*

I press send and scroll down.

There are three more messages; the last one is from Hannah.

*Dear Joe, are you OK? You said you were excited but couldn't tell me, and I'm worried you've not replied because I mentioned your parents. I'm worried about that*

*Hannah*

I click on Hannah's last message.

*Dear Bubble Boy, or shall I call you Joe, I don't know. Should I? Anyway I'm sorry I haven't contacted you. I'm at my gran's now. I can get Internet if I climb a hill opposite her house. I usually visit her twice a year, once at Easter and again in the summer when my mum and dad are working. I walk down to the beach with her and sometimes when the tide is out we walk across the sand to an island. Do you have a gran? I know you don't have any parents because they said that in the program. I'm really sorry that happened. I should talk about something else. We're traveling back home tomorrow, then I've got to check my school uniform still fits and buy new books for school. I've just made my GCSE choices.*

*I've chosen double science and I really like art and music. Do you like those subjects? Do you take exams? Got to go now.*

*Hannah*

*P.S. You don't have to tell me what was exciting but I hope it was good.*

I smile. I'm glad Hannah wrote to me. Most of the time people send one or two messages and stop. Usually it's for a class writing competition to see who can write the best letter. They are all slightly different but then end up asking the same question: *What's it like to live in a bubble?* and after I reply they send me a photograph of their Bubble Boy project stuck to the classroom wall. I hope Hannah isn't writing a project.

*Dear Hannah,*
*No, you didn't upset me about my parents.*
*No, you didn't upset me about just being friends.*
*Two of my grandparents died, the other two went nuts!*
*Joe*

*P.S. Oh, I do take exams. I studied Archimedes' principle last week. I don't have a bath so my tutor put a brick in a can.*

*And sorry, I can't tell you what I've done. But I might be able to one day.*

I press enter. That's the last message. I look around the room. It's so quiet without Henry messaging and not having Amir buzzing around.

I click on a video of Sarah.

"Hi, Dew. Today you're going to learn about the French Revolution. How it changed and shaped the future of France and Europe."

Charlotte R. looks up from her book.

I show her my screen. "Do you want to watch?"

"No. I think I'll stick to this." She shows me the cover of her book. There's a picture of a boy running across a field on the front.

"Is it any good?"

"It's okay," she says. "It's a bit happier than the last one."

"What happened in that?"

"I don't think you really want to know."

I think that means that somebody dies.

I click play. I hear the blast of a bugle and the bang of gunshots as soldiers in blue uniforms fight outside a castle in the Battle of the Bastille. The air is full of smoke and the soldiers are screaming as they fire cannons and charge at each other with bayonets on their rifles. The flashing lights hurt my eyes. The cannons hurt my ears. I turn the brightness and the sound down and lay back on my pillow. . . .

I don't know what happened in the French Revolution because when I wake up my laptop is on the table beside me. Charlotte R.'s book is on the chair. I can hear people talking in the transition zone but they're so quiet I can't hear what they're saying. I sit up on my bed and strain my ears. The doctors and nurses always do this when I'm really ill. It's like the transition room is their meeting room where they talk about all the things they don't want me to know about. They think that I will worry too much if I know everything, and I do. But I worry about the things they don't tell me more.

I pull my covers away and slide my feet onto the floor. My body feels like lead and my legs feel like sticks. The door seems a hundred feet away. I steady myself on my mattress and edge slowly to the end of my bed. The voices get louder but I still can't hear what's being said.

My head begins to hurt and the door begins to blur. I let go of the bed and fall onto the chair by my bathroom.

"So he's . . ."

"Yes, been . . ."

I shuffle my chair quietly across the floor and press my ear against the door. I hear the rip of paper towels and the sound of water running into the sink.

"Two, this morning . . ."

"Anything . . ."

"That's all they would . . . How's he been?"

"Restless, I think maybe . . ."

I still can't hear. It's like listening to TV when pigeons are sitting on the satellite dish.

The water stops. There's a click, then the rush of the air as someone dries their hands. What are they talking about?

The air stops. I press my ear so hard against the door

that I can feel the blood thumping through my head.

"He's just too ill to cope with it. We need to . . ."—hiss of disinfectant—"a while."

"He's been looking on the Internet all day."

What can't I cope with? What's on the Internet?

"Yeah, we need to get that away—you said he's asleep now?"

"Yes."

"Okay, let's do that first."

"It's on the table by the side of his bed."

I sit up and look at the table and see my laptop.

Is it Henry? Is Henry ill? Is he—?

I push myself up off the chair and stagger back to my bed.

The door slides open.

I grab my laptop and open it up.

"Mate, what are you doing up?"

I look at my screen and click on the refresh icon.

Greg walks over to me and reaches out. I pull my laptop away and look back at the screen.

It can't be. It can't be true. It's not true.

"They've probably made a mistake! Greg? They must have made a mistake! Haven't they? Don't newspapers lie all the time?"

Greg puts his hand on my shoulder. "Mate, I'm so sorry."

Blood whooshes in my ears. I think something is going wrong with my heart. It hurts. It hurts.

"I told you something was bad!" I cover my face with my hands but it doesn't stop my tears from falling out. My lungs feel like they're bursting out of my chest. I can't breathe. I can't breathe.

Greg sits down on my bed and wraps his arm around me. I'm scared my heart is going to burst and my lungs are going to break my ribs.

Where is Henry? Where is he? They've made a mistake.

I look up at Greg. "They've made a mistake," I say. "They must have."

"No, mate. I'm sorry, but I don't think they have. The hospital made an announcement."

Greg keeps talking but I'm crying so loud that I can't hear what he says. I feel like I'm a robot that is shutting down, with my lights flickering out as I melt into the ground. Maybe it's the drugs they're giving me. They've given me too many; they're fighting each other and not the infection. That can make me feel crazy and make me imagine things that aren't real. The door slides open. Charlotte R. walks in and stands at the end of my bed.

"It's okay," Greg says. "I've got him . . . I've got you, mate." He pulls my head close against his chest.

"It hurts. Everything hurts!" I keep crying, keep shouting. I'm so confused and upset that I don't know which words stay in my head and which ones come out of my mouth. Henry's dead and I think I might die too. Maybe it's the same thing. Maybe this horrible feeling is because I'm dying too and we really did have the same thing. We both lived in a bubble. We both went outside. Now we're going to die at the same time.

We've been ill loads of times but the doctors have always found a way to fix us. The infections usually sneak up on us. They don't make us feel really bad straightaway. Was there a bug in his suit or at the mall? Maybe it was in the ambulance, but NASA would have scrubbed it clean and disinfected it, wouldn't they? I still might have the same thing. I still might die too. We shouldn't have gone outside. Our bubbles are boring sometimes, but at least they are safe.

I scrunch my eyes tight but the tears come again, and my heart surges again.

Greg wraps his arms tighter around me.

Henry's dead.

Henry's dead. I bury my head in Greg's chest. I want this pain to go away. I want Greg to squeeze me tighter and never let go. This was supposed to be the best day ever and now I just want it to end.

# TWENTY-FIVE

## 11 YEARS, 3 MONTHS, AND 14 DAYS

I'm lying on my bed, staring up at the ceiling. I sniff and wipe my tears on my sleeve. I've been crying all night. I've been crying so much that my eyes are aching and my cheeks are sore. I heard a nurse walking around my room. I saw her standing over me. But her words were a mumble and her face was a blur. She reached out and touched my arm, but I didn't feel it.

Tears roll down my cheeks and onto my wet pillow. When I close my eyes I see Henry. When I open them, I see him too. I know it's just in my mind, because where my heart should be there's a big black hole. The red charge light on my laptop is blurry through my tears. I can't stop my hand reaching out, just to check. I slide it onto my bed, flip up the top, and stare at the clocks.

It's 9:15 a.m. in London.

It's 4:15 a.m. in Philadelphia.

The minutes tick over.

9:16

9:17

I've had two clocks in my head for years. I ate breakfast when Henry was sleeping. I ate lunch when he was eating breakfast. I ate tea when he was eating lunch, and I went to bed when he was still up watching TV.

It's 9:18.

9:19

9:20

9:21

I'm missing him already even though if he was still alive he wouldn't be up yet. I wish the Skype light would shine. I wish the pencil would start to scribble.

9:22

9:23

There's nothing there. Just our last messages. I close my laptop down and look around my room. I don't feel like watching the screens. I don't feel like listening to music. I don't feel like doing anything. I've got pictures of football players and superheroes on my wall but I'm all alone. Henry might have lived inside my laptop but my whole room feels empty now he's gone.

I think about last night. I remember going on my laptop. I remember Greg rushing in. I remember my heart and my lungs hurting and crying and shouting things . . . Did I tell Greg I'd been outside? I think I did but I can't remember anything properly. I think the drugs are jumbling my brain.

I don't know what was real or what was a dream. All I know is that Henry is gone. I'll never see his face or read his messages on Skype again. I just want him to come back.

I know something is wrong when Greg calls me "Joe."

I know something is wrong when Beth bites her nails and doesn't talk.

I know something is wrong when Dr. Moore rubs his hand across his mouth.

I know something is wrong when I open my eyes and find all three of them are around my bed at the same time.

Dr. Moore sits on the edge of the bed. He puts his hand on mine "Joe," he whispers. "I'm really sorry to hear about your friend."

I look up at Beth. I want her to reach down and hug me. But she just stands there with a worried look on her face. I can't tell if it's because of Henry or because she's found out what I've done.

Dr. Moore tells me he doesn't know all the details but he does know that Henry had had a heart condition for a while.

"He looked okay the last time I saw him! And if he wasn't well, why did they let him go out?"

"I don't know, Joe," he says. He looks back at Greg and Beth like he's getting ready to tell me something bad.

They've found out I've been outside. I'm going to die. That's why all three of them are here.

"I'm sorry—"

"Joe—"

Me and Dr. Moore talk at the same time. I let him go first.

"Joe, there are a couple of things we need to talk about. First, your test results."

I hold my breath.

"Your whites are stable, but until we know the cause of your crash, we're unsure what direction the count will go in next. There are a number of options; one of them is to transfuse."

I look at Beth and Greg again. They know I don't like transfusions, but I wouldn't expect them all to be here at the same time just to tell me that.

They know what I've done.

Dr. Moore glances up from his pad with a concerned look on his face. "Young man," he says. "I think you know there's something else. We need to have a chat with you about some of the things you said last night."

My heart monitor beeps. It's gone up to 98. All my worries rush through my head at the same time—me, Henry, Amir. A bead of sweat trickles down my neck.

Greg slides the chair away from the bathroom door and sits down by my side.

"It's okay, mate. Amir's told us everything."

I do a confused look like I still don't know what he's talking about. Why would Amir tell them? I didn't know he'd been in. I haven't heard him in the transition zone or seen him on my screens.

Beth leans forward. Her face is red and her eyes are

watering. I can't tell if she's upset or angry. "Just tell us, Joe."
I think she might be both.

**Heart rate:** 114

Has Amir told them *everything*?

I open my mouth to speak, but the secret has been inside
of me for so long that it won't come out. I try again. There's
a lump in my throat and my eyes start to ache. I swallow
hard and look at Beth.

"I'm sorry."

She stands up and wraps her arms around me. "Hey, don't
cry," she says. "Don't cry. It's okay." She rocks me gently.

My chest cracks and the worms are turning in my stomach. "I wanted to tell you," I say. "I didn't want to lie."

"I know. I know." She lets go of me. "It's okay," she says.
"But you need to tell us everything now."

I nod and wipe my tears on my arm.

"So you're not angry with me?"

"Well, I wouldn't go that far." She smiles and rubs her
thumbs across my cheeks. I haven't even started to tell them
what I've done but it feels like the elephant has taken its foot
off my chest.

My mattress sinks as Dr. Moore sits down beside me.

"Okay," he says. "I just need you to tell me all the places
Amir took you."

I nod and look at his pad. There's writing scribbled all
over it, with diagrams and arrows and in the center of the

page I see the word Heathrow with a circle drawn around it.
I've never seen Amir's handwriting but it looks so mad and
scrappy that this must be his. It looks like he's written a con-
fession. They must've sat him at a desk in a room with no
windows and no doors. I've seen it in films when the police
keep people up all night without giving them drink or food.
They bang their fist on the table and make the suspect pee
in a pot in a corner. When they go to prison all they have is
a bed and a pillow for the rest of their lives.

I look up at Dr. Moore. "Will Amir go to prison?" I ask.

"Sorry?"

"I don't want Amir to go to prison. He was just trying to
help me. It wasn't his fault. It was all my idea."

My heat-rate monitor beeps again—104. It's no good.
I can't lie. My monitor is a lie detector waiting to beep on
every word.

Dr. Moore shakes his head. "Look," he says. "It's serious,
but I'm not sure it's as serious as that. Now . . . just take me
through it, step by step. The sooner we know what you've
been up to, the sooner we get to catch this infection."

"Okay."

My thoughts float around in my head. I try to put them
in order and tell about my trip outside, how I used the monitors to watch Jim and Phil. I tell him Amir made me a
special suit with oxygen tanks and monitors to make sure I
was safe. Dr. Moore tells me that Amir has given them the
suit and they're checking it for infection as we speak. Then
he listens as I describe how we drove through the streets past

the big buildings and then went on the motorway until we turned off for Heathrow.

Greg folds his arms.

Beth sighs.

Dr. Moore draws an even bigger circle around Heathrow. "What did you do there?" he asks.

"We watched the planes take off and land. It was awesome!"

Beth shakes her head. I don't think any of them want to hear that now.

"What did you do after the planes?" asks Dr. Moore.

"We watched the sun come up. . . ."

"And then?"

"Amir drove us back."

"The same way?"

"I don't know. I think so. . . . I fell asleep."

Dr. Moore puts a little check mark next to the word *hospital 6:53 am*. "Okay, Joe. Now this is important . . . did you take your helmet off at any time?"

"No."

Greg leans forward.

"Just think, mate," he says. "You need to be sure."

I put my hand on my head. I didn't take it off, did I? I know I wanted to but I'm sure I didn't. I can't think properly.

"What about when you saw the bugs, mate?"

"No . . . I don't think I did. . . . That was in my dream. . . . I don't know."

I start to cough. Dr. Moore waits for me to stop and says

he thinks that's all he needs. Beth pours me a glass of water.
I go to take it. She holds it up like she's going to pour it over
my head.

Dr. Moore chuckles and stands up.

"I think I'd better leave you two to it!" he says. I take a sip
of water as Greg follows him toward the door.

"Oh!" Dr. Moore turns around. "One last thing. Don't go
flying off anywhere. It won't look good if we have to put our
superhero in chains."

"He's not going *anywhere*," says Beth.

I know she means it.

The door opens and then slides closed. Suddenly me and
Beth are alone. She opens her mouth like she's going to say
something, then stops like she's changed her mind. Her face
is white and she looks really tired. I ask her if she's okay. She
tries to speak again, then puts her hand up to her mouth. I
don't know what to do or where to look. I hate it when Beth
gets upset. I hate it when it's my fault. I didn't want to tell
her I'd been outside like this. I wanted to tell her when I'm
well and she could be as excited as I was.

I sit up. I've already said I'm sorry but I want to say it
again.

"I'm sorry."

Beth's eyes start to water and her hand starts to shake.
She takes her hand down from her mouth. "You idiot." Her
voice wavers.

"I said I was sorry."

"Sorry?" Tears are falling down her cheeks. She sniffs.

"God," she says. "When they told me, I thought it was just one of your superhero dreams."

"No, it was better than—"

"Don't," she says. "Don't. God, Joe, don't you realize how stupid you've been? And Amir . . . I could kill him. What the hell was he thinking? Maybe you were right all along. He is crazy."

"No, he's not! He just wanted to help me. I wanted to go out."

"He's supposed to be your bloody nurse, not your taxi driver."

She wipes her nose in a tissue. She was mad when I dropped my first laptop. She was even madder when I dropped the second one, but that was nowhere near as mad as she is now.

She stands up and walks over to the window. Greg told me that when his girlfriend is mad with him it doesn't matter what he says; it's always the wrong thing, so he goes to the pub and waits for the storm to blow over. It feels like there's a big storm in my room. I don't know what to say either, but the only room I could escape to is my toilet and I don't want to go there.

I struggle up off my bed and stumble over to her. All I can hear are my monitors and the sound of her breathing.

She's right. I shouldn't have done it.

She turns her head and looks at me. Her eyes are red and her cheeks are shining.

"I can't believe it," she says. "I can't . . . anything could have happened."

"But Henry did it."

She rolls her eyes. "And look what happened to him! He had NASA; you had a crazy nurse who believes in aliens!"

My eyes fall to the ground. I wish she hadn't said that.

"I'm sorry," she says.

"It's okay." I look up at her. Her eyes look sad, like the storm has blown over.

"It just makes me mad. I don't think you thought about it," she says. "You can't just . . ." I wait for her to speak again but all she does is look straight at me.

A tear trickles down her nose.

"Come here," she says.

I turn toward her. She wraps her arms around me and pulls me so tight against her chest that I can feel her heart beating. It feels like it's beating as fast as mine. "Joe, I don't know what I'd do without you. You're the only one I've got."

I swallow hard. I hadn't thought about that. All the time I was thinking about what I wanted. I didn't think of what would happen to Beth if I didn't come back.

I start to cry. She holds me as tight as she knows she can.

"It's okay," she says. "I'm sorry too. I shouldn't have gotten so mad."

"I shouldn't have done it."

"No, you shouldn't have. . . . But I don't blame you. No one really knows what it's like to be cooped up all of their life." She lets go of me and puts her hands on my shoulders.

She's going to say something serious now.

"Promise me you'll never do it again."

I didn't want her to ask me to say that. If I say I promise I'll be lying, but if I don't promise I'll upset her.

I turn away from her and look out the window, but I'm not looking at anything. I don't want to answer. Is not saying the truth the same as a lie? Out the corner of my eye I can see her looking at me.

*Please don't ask me again.*

"Joe? Do you promise?"

"Okay," I say, under my breath. I don't really mean it. I'd give anything, anything, to do it again. Especially now that I don't have Henry here with me.

She reaches out and ruffles my hair. "Come on," she says. "Let's watch a DVD."

"What did you get?"

"*Iron Man 3.*"

I smile and feel a tiny bit warm inside, even though I still feel like there's a hole inside me from Henry being gone.

She puts the DVD in the slot while I get onto my bed. My body aches every time my heart beats. I'd been so worried about Henry that all my proper pains had gone away but now they've all come back worse.

Beth lies down and puts her arm around me.

"Are you okay?"

"Just aching," I say. "And every time things go quiet I miss Henry." My throat closes up again.

"I know," she says. "It's going to be like that for a while, but it gets better. I promise." She rests her head against mine. I think of telling her everything else I did when I went outside, but I don't think she wants to hear about it anymore because she's already got the remote in her hand.

My phone buzzes on the table. I look at it and wonder if it's Amir. It buzzes again.

"Joe, aren't you going to see who that is?"

I look at the phone. If Beth knows it's Amir she'll take it away from me.

"It's the battery warning," I say.

"Do you want to charge it?"

"No. It's okay. I just want to watch this."

"If you're sure?"

I nod even though I'm desperate to see if it's Amir.

She presses play.

I'll have to wait.

The Mandarin has just blown up the Chinese Theater. Flames are bursting out of the building. Cars are flying through the air and people are running down the street. But I haven't been able to concentrate because my phone has buzzed four times and it's just buzzed again. I turn my head slowly toward Beth. Her head is back on the pillow and her eyes are closed. I gently lift her arm off of me, pick my phone up off the table, and go to the bathroom. The fan switches on. I look back at Beth. She rolls over onto her side but her eyes stay shut. I close the door gently behind me and sit down on the toilet seat.

My phone buzzes again. I click on the messages—six from Amir.

Joe. I tell them everything.

You no worry.

Hope you okay

I have bad signal.

Are you okay?

Why you no tell me you ill?

I start to type.

**Amir, are you there?**

My phone buzzes straightaway.

Yes. I worry. Greg say you really ill.

**I am.**

Why you no tell me?

**I didn't want you to lose your job.**

Jobs aren't important. People are important. I tell the
doctors I think it a bug in Rashid's car. He not use the
air conditioner for two years.

**They're checking everything.**

Is the landing strip ready?

**What?**

For the aliens. They come soon.

Amir is confusing me. He's crazy when he's with me, and he seems even crazier when he texts. I wish we could sit down and talk properly.

**Amir, can I see you?**

Sunday. The aliens come. You watch them. Out your window.

**But I just want to see you.**

Got to go. You get better.

**But—**

My phone buzzes before I can reply.

Sunday. Bye.

He's gone already. I read his messages again to see if I've missed anything. I read the one about the bug in his brother's car. I wonder if he's right. I open the bathroom door. Beth is asleep facing my monitors. I creep over to the table and flip up my laptop. I hover my fingers over the keys.

I type "bugs in cars."

**33,900,000 results** in 0.64 seconds.

There are pictures of beetles and bedbugs crawling over car seats and eating garbage on the floor. I scroll down and click on the first link about the hidden bugs in cars.

There's millions of them, munching away through air filters and pipes—a hidden enemy of microscopic bacteria causing illnesses like E. coli, Bacillus cereus, Staphylococcus.

I click on Staphylococcus.

It's a bacteria that looks like a bunch of grapes. It causes boils, sores, and abscesses all over the skin. In some cases it produces toxins that attack white blood cells!

My head hurts and my palms start to sweat.

Is that what I've got? Staphylococcus? It sounds like a dinosaur.

A wave of heat goes through me from my head to my toes. I was right. There's a bug crawling all over my skin. I shut my laptop down and go back to the bathroom and look in the mirror. My eyes are red and my cheeks are red too. I press my fingers on my cheeks and pull them away. My skin goes white, stays white—do I have dehydration, or meningitis? My skin turns red. I'm okay. I take off my T-shirt and do the same to my body—fingers on my chest, then on my stomach. My skin goes white. *Come on. Come on.* It goes red. I take a deep breath and check for boils and sores. There's a mark on my chest but I think it's where I just pressed my skin with my fingers. I turn sideways and look over my shoulder. There's a small bruise on my right hip. I pull the waistband of my trousers down. Phew, the bruise doesn't go any farther, and Staphylococcus doesn't cause bruises anyway.

"Joe, what are you doing?"

I look up and see Beth in the mirror.

"I'm . . . I'm just checking . . ."

"What for?"

"Staphylococcus."

Beth shakes her head slowly.

"You've been on your laptop again. How many times do I have to tell you?" She gives me my T-shirt. "Just leave it to the doctors. . . . And you shouldn't be up, anyway!"

I put my T-shirt back on again. I know she's right but I can't stop looking.

"Come on," she says, "maybe you've done too much today." She walks with me back to my bed.

I lie down and look at my laptop again. I'm addicted to it. Some people, like Mike, are addicted to alcohol, and some people are addicted to chocolate and biscuits. I'm addicted to finding out about every disease in the world. I turn and look at Beth.

"Just close your eyes," she says. "Sometimes sleep is the best cure."

I'm so glad she's here.

# TWENTY-SIX

## 11 Years, 3 Months, and 18 Days

**I'm lying on my bed** watching my screens with Beth. The doctors were right. The drugs have been fighting inside me for three days. Sometimes I feel hot and want to take my T-shirt off. Sometimes I feel cold and wrap myself in blankets. And sometimes I feel hot and cold at the same time. I can't sit still when that happens. I'm having a good day today, but I might not tomorrow.

Beth nudges me and points at screen four.

Keith is talking to Julie in reception. She's laughing and prodding him on the arm. Keith is laughing too—he's standing by the vending machine with a bunch of flowers hidden behind his back. He says something. Julie looks mad and punches his arm. Keith opens his mouth wide—hey! He pulls the flowers out from behind his back—surprise! Julie puts her hand up to her mouth. Beth does the same.

"Awww, it's so cute," she says.

"I think they'll get married," I say.

"You think so?"

"Yes, you watch."

Keith hands Julie a card and they walk back to her desk. Julie smiles to herself as she reads it and then puts it down by her computer. She's got loads of cards. She's fifty today! Keith walks around the back of her desk, looks up and down the reception, then bends down and gives Julie a kiss.

"See, told you."

Beth laughs. She loves my screens. She's been watching them all the time with me. The maintenance guy came on Wednesday morning to disconnect them but all he did was look at the decoder and scratch his head. He told us he wasn't good with technology and then went away. Greg said someone from IT was going to come on Thursday instead. We waited for them all day Thursday and Friday, too. I think they must be busy. I hope they've forgotten.

Beth nudges me again. I switch to screen six.

The road crew has nearly reached the end of the road. Dave is talking to a man in a suit wearing a white hat. I tell Beth his name is Dom.

"How do you know?" she asks.

"Because he's short and bald and looks like the man who solves building problems on TV."

Her eyes are shining so bright that I can see the screens reflecting in her pupils. I love watching my screens with her. I just wish she could stay and watch them with me all the time.

Dave and Dom are walking along the trench drinking

cups of coffee. Dom points at a pipe—*move that along this way*. He holds his hands up and pulls them apart—*just to make more space*. Dave rubs his forehead and glances down the road at Mike. Mike looks down at his shovel. He's done it wrong again.

I change to screen eight. On the roof the man in the gray coveralls walks between the silver tubes with his knife in his hand.

Beth covers her eyes. She doesn't want to see the pigeons again.

"Okay, you can turn it off now," she says.

"No, it's okay. Look."

Beth peeps between her fingers.

The man walks toward the traps and bends down. He shakes his head. The traps are empty. He won't be cutting any pigeons' throats today.

"Good!" says Beth. "I hate him."

I laugh and go to switch to screen four but I hear the corridor door open into the transition zone. Me and Beth look at each other. We know the doctors are trying to help, but it's scary waiting to hear what they have got to say. I feel Beth's arm wrap tighter around me. We sit quiet and listen to Dr. Moore talking on the other side of the door. He says something about being stuck in a traffic jam; a man behind him was blowing his horn, and then he says something I can't hear and Dr. Hussein laughs.

Me and Beth look at each other.

The doctors don't usually talk this loud.

I hear the taps turn on and the spray of disinfectant.

The door clicks open so I turn off the screens.

"Ah." Dr. Moore grins. "It's good to see you two are still friends."

"Just about," says Beth.

I nudge her with my arm. Having her here has been like a holiday. She gets up off my bed and sits down in the chair.

Dr. Hussein walks over and checks the monitors.

**Room temp.:** 18C

**Body temp.:** 38.1C

**Heart rate:** 79

**Humidity:** 11%

**Air purity:** 97.0%

"All okay?"

"Yes."

"No sudden room temperature drop?"

"No," says Dr. Hussein. "All fine."

Dr. Moore looks over the top of his glasses at me.

"So, our superhero wasn't out rescuing anybody last night."

I think I've just been told off. Again!

A grin creeps across Dr. Moore's face as he sits down on the edge of my bed. "So, young man. What are we going to do with you?"

I shrug and push out my bottom lip.

"Well, tell me how you're feeling, first."

"I'm still aching," I say, "but the shooting pains have stopped and I don't feel sick anymore."

"That's good . . . and maybe we can tell you something that will make you feel a bit better."

"Are you going to let me keep the CCTV?"

Dr. Hussein chuckles.

"No," says Dr. Moore. "They still have to go."

"Can I keep the one in reception?"

"We'll see. I'll check with security."

"Can you ask about the one on the roof, too?"

"You don't give up, do you?"

I give him my best grin. Beth laughs. I wish she'd tell him that she likes them too.

"Okay, come on then. Listen." He taps my leg like he's trying to wake me up. "Some good news, some bad. What do you want first?"

"Let's go for the good," Beth says. I would have picked that too.

"Okay, well, the good news is that it looks like we've found this bug. It was in the air-conditioning in the car."

"Staphylococcal?"

Dr. Moore scratches his head. "You know, I'm beginning to think you're after my job."

"Mine too," says Dr. Hussein.

We all smile.

"Anyway, look, the bad news is that it's going to take a while to get things right. You know how it goes, just like you've been feeling these past few days . . . up and down while we balance the meds out."

I know how it goes—feeling sick, feeling heavy, feeling like my head's going to lift off my body, feeling tired, feeling dizzy, feeling sick again, feeling okay, feeling good, and then always back to bad. It only takes me a few seconds to think it but it can take days to happen. I put my head back on the pillow. I know it's going to be hard but the doctors always help me make it in the end.

Dr. Moore looks at Beth. She's smiling, but from the dark look in her eyes I can tell she's worried.

Dr. Moore rubs my head.

"Hey, come on, we'll have you right as rain before long."

"Soon be as fit as that chap." Dr. Hussein nods at my poster of Theo Walcott. "Oh, no, I forget. He's injured again!"

Dr. Moore laughs.

"Are you watching the game tonight?" says Dr. Hussein.

I try to think what day it is.

"Match of the Day?"

It's Saturday.

"It'll be on late. Maybe you'd best record it," says Dr. Moore. He stands up. "I'll pop back in later this afternoon. Will you still be here, Beth?"

Beth looks at me. We both know that she'll be gone by then. That's the trouble when the doctors think I'll get better. It means Beth can go. She's been here four days; she can't use up all her vacation days for that. She has to save them, just in case I need her again.

She stands up and follows the doctors toward the door. I know she'll want to ask them more questions about me.

Dr. Moore turns around. "Hey, don't look so down. It's good news for once."

"Yeah, I know," I say. "Sorry."

They turn away. As soon as they're gone I reach for my laptop—the doctors are right. I've got good news. I click on Skype. I must tell Hen—

I stop. My hand falls down onto my bed and I squeeze my duvet tight.

I've been sending him messages for years and he always replies in seconds. I used to tell him my bad news and he'd make me feel better. I'd tell him my good news and he'd make it even more great. I close the laptop and take some deep breaths to stop the exploding-lung feeling, to stop my heart from aching. Beth said it would get better. It's only been five days but I'm not sure it ever will.

I turn on the TV. A ferry has sunk near South Korea. It's lying on its side with lifeboats bobbing around it in the water. The news reporter says 126 people have survived but over 200 more are missing. There's a picture of Korean people and children crying in the streets. Then there's a picture of a roller coaster. A man and his little boy have been trapped upside down in it for two hours. The fire brigade have been trying to rescue them but the ride is so high that their ladders won't reach.

When Beth comes back in, a new nurse follows behind.

"Hi, I'm Chloe," she says. "I'll be looking after you for a while." She puts a silver tray down on the table. Beth pours me a glass of water. Chloe hands me two orange pills and a big white one. I swallow the orange ones easy but I cough when the white one gets stuck in my throat.

Chloe bends down.

"Okay?" she asks.

I nod. I swallow again and feel the tears in my eyes. I lie down again. Chloe picks up the tray and walks out of the door.

Beth smiles. "She seems nice," she says.

"Yeah." Chloe does seem nice, but I don't think she's going to make me laugh as much as Amir. I wish Beth would talk about him. I wish somebody would say his name. It's like he's suddenly a criminal. It's like they all pretend he was never here. I feel Beth's hand on my arm.

"Hey, what's wrong? Is it Henry?"

I shake my head. "No, I was thinking about Amir."

Her eyes turn dark like I've just said a swear word.

"I liked him," I say.

"I know, but people can't go around doing anything they want."

"But he was funny. He went home and showed me his family. He made me forget I was in here." My throat closes up again. I want to tell her I've heard from him, that he still thinks the aliens are going to land, but I don't want to upset her before she goes.

She suddenly stands up and picks up my laptop.

"What are you doing?" I ask.

"Come on," she says. "Let's not sit here all grumpy. Show me all the messages you got on the forum so far. How many have you had?"

"A few."

She nudges me. "Come on, then, let's have a look."

I flip up the lid and show them to her. She says "awww" and rubs my head when she reads the one about me not being cute anymore and laughs at the one about the man who thought he saw me in KFC. She laughs even louder at the reply. I don't tell her it was Amir who wrote the reply and not me.

I click on the new messages.

**BBC Bubble Boy Forum**
**Sat September 4, 09:15 am**
*Dear Bubble Boy,*
*Arsenal are S\*\* H \*\* I \*\* T!*
*Ha! Stuff you BBC censor guy!*
*Jake*
*London*


Beth sniggers.

"Go on," she says.

I click on the next.


**BBC Bubble Boy Forum**
**Sat September 4, 10:07 am**
*Dear Bubble Boy,*
   *If you were able to go outside, what's the first thing you'd like to do?*
   *Emma French*
   *Norwich*

I look at Beth. She's looking out the corner of her eyes like she hasn't read it.

I type.

*I'd take my sister to the movies.*

Beth shakes her head and points at the next message.
"Who's that one?" she asks.
"Hannah."
"She's sent quite a few."
"I know."
Beth nudges me. "Go on, then, let's have a look."
I click on Hannah's message.

*Dear Joe,*

*Sorry about your grandparents going nuts. Mine aren't nuts but my grandad is deaf. He has the TV up really loud and his next-door neighbor bangs on the wall.*

*I watched Mission Impossible 3 last night. It was good. I won't tell you what it was about in case you haven't seen it, but I think you probably have because I saw all your DVDs piled up against the wall.*

*I'm going to my friend Rachel's birthday party tomorrow. I don't want to go. But she's my best friend, so I have to.*

*I'll chat to you after.*

*Hannah.*

*P.S. If you haven't seen Mission Impossible 3 I could send it to you.*

*And I don't mind if you don't tell me what you did. I just hope*
*you enjoyed yourself!!*

"Awww, she sounds really nice."

"Well, she's nicer than the KFC guy!"

Beth laughs. "I expect he's okay too. . . . Are you going to reply?"

"Yeah, but not now."

"I'm glad she wrote. You need to meet new people."

"So do you," I say.

She goes quiet and looks at the screen. Her cheeks turn red. I know what that means.

"Have you got a boyfriend?!" I sit up on my bed. Beth is smiling.

"Have you?"

"I might." She pauses. "To be honest, it's where I was when you were taken ill."

"Eeeeew!"

"Haha, it wasn't like that!" She pushes me on my shoulder. "It was a party. Loads of people were there."

"What's his name?"

"Dan."

"What does he do?"

"He's a graphic designer."

"Oh . . . Amir used to be one of those."

Beth goes quiet. I'd better not say his name again.

"Can he draw cartoons?"

"Yeah. I'll get him to draw you something."

"Cool." I think I'd like to be a graphic designer, for comics. I wonder if I could do it from my room.

Beth puts her arm around me. I scroll through the rest of the messages. I'm glad she's got a boyfriend. Now when she's finished work, she won't go back to her apartment and spend her evenings alone. I hope I get to meet him, but Edinburgh to London is a long way and really expensive just to meet your girlfriend's brother. But maybe he's got a car and they can drive on the motorway like I did with Amir. It's 452 miles away. I can't imagine what it's like to drive that far. It was only 16 miles to Heathrow and that seemed to take ages.

I close my eyes. The planes don't take off anymore but I can still see the cat's eyes that were in the middle of the road and the massive buildings either side of it. They play like a film on repeat in my head. Beth's head rests against mine. I wish she could see the film too.

$E = mc^2$, *Lucozade, GlaxoSmithKline, and Mercedes-Benz.*

$E = mc^2$, *Lucozade, GlaxoSmithKline, and Mercedes-Benz.*

$E = mc^2$, *Lucozade, GlaxoSmithKline, and Mercedes-Benz.*

# TWENTY-SEVEN

## 11 Years, 3 Months, and 19 Days

**I'm standing at the window.** I sent Beth a text telling her about the dream I had last night after she left. She thought it was great but a bit weird. Then she told me that she'd spoken to her boyfriend, Dan. He's going to draw me Spider-Man. He said he'll bring it with him when he visits me. It'll be cool to talk to him; maybe he'll like all superheroes and we can watch football together too. I want to send her a text now, but it's late.

It's too late to message Hannah too.

It's raining outside. The lights in the glass building are all dim and blurry and the sidewalks are shining orange. I turn my head and look down the road. It's long, dark, and empty. The excavators and the trucks and the traffic lights have gone. Mike, Andy, Chris, and Dave's van is gone too. All that's left is a new shiny strip of asphalt running down the middle of the road.

If the aliens wanted to land on Earth, they should do it on a Sunday night like this when everyone is at home watching TV.

I hear a click behind me. Greg comes in, puts my pajamas on my bed, and then stands next to me. We look out the window and watch a man on a motorbike speed down the new asphalt.

Greg smiles. "I think he believed it, mate."

". . . Who?"

"Amir. I think he really thought that the aliens were going to land on that strip."

"How did you know that?"

"It's okay, Joe. He told me too."

"But you don't believe in them?"

"No, mate. I've told you before."

I look back out the window down at the gravity boost porthole. That's where Amir said they would land. The spaceship would hover above it, with bright lights shining down onto the road. I rest my head against the glass. Out of the corner of my eye I see Greg looking at me.

"I'll give you a penny for your thoughts, mate," he says.

"Just thinking."

". . . about Henry?"

"No. Aliens."

"If you believed in them, I could talk to you about them like I used to with Amir."

"You can still talk about them, mate. I don't mind."

"You'll laugh."

"I won't," he says.

"Promise?"

"Go on, tell me, mate."

I point at the drain cover in the middle of the road just after the crossing. "They're going to land there, but the spaceship won't touch the ground. It'll hover with a beam of light above the gravity portal. Then the doors of the spaceship will open and a gangplank will slide out and go straight into reception."

Greg stares at the drain cover. "Keep going, mate," he says.

"The aliens will walk out one by one. They won't have to wait for an appointment; they won't have to ask for directions because as soon as they get inside they will take over all the doctors and nurses, take their bodies and their minds. But they're not stealing them—"

"That's a relief."

"No, they're just going to borrow you for a while."

Greg rests his hands on the sill. I tell him that the aliens won't have to wait for the elevators or climb the stairs because they can morph through ceilings and walls. And when they do the rounds and visit us all, we won't have to unbutton our shirts because they won't have stethoscopes hanging around their necks or heart monitors in their pockets. All they'll need are their minds and their hands. "Really?" Greg looks surprised.

"They're here to cure us . . . not kill us," I say. "They just stare at us, one by one, and get inside our bodies and find the poison, then they'll take it all away. And when we're cured we all put on our clothes and shoes and walk out of the doors and then we get to go home."

Greg smiles and puts his arm around my shoulder. "Mate, maybe I should have believed in aliens after all."

I smile and look back out the window. I miss Amir talking about the aliens. I miss having him around. He took me outside; he got me Sky TV and introduced me to his family. But most of all I miss talking to him. Maybe he was crazy but he was so much fun. I wish he could've stayed. I'm tired of the nurses changing all the time. The only one that stays is Greg.

"You okay, mate?" Greg squeezes me.

"I miss Amir."

Greg sighs. "Yeah, we all do, mate. It's difficult not to miss someone like that! But maybe this wasn't the job for him."

"What do you mean?"

"I don't know. Not everyone can do it. You know what it's like."

"Kids dying."

"Yeah. Not everyone can cope with that. I don't think he could, mate."

I look down at the street. A man and a woman are walking hand in hand. They stop and look at the clothes-shop window. A car's headlights light up the landing strip as it goes down the road.

Greg ruffles my hair.

"Come on, mate. You can't stand here all night."

I turn around, pick up my pajamas from the bed, and take them with me into the bathroom. I wash and change while Greg checks my monitors and puts a fresh glass of water on my table.

The blinds are drawn when I go back out. Greg stands by the door and watches me get into bed.

"I'll check on you later, mate. Maybe catch some football in the morning."

"Okay." I slide down under the covers.

"Night, mate."

"Good night."

He dims the lights and slides out the door. I hear the sound of water running, then the click of the transition room door. Greg will be walking down the corridor. I lie back and remember all the things I saw on my adventure— all the lights and doors, and the pictures of elephants and giraffes stuck to the walls. I'd like to see them again. I'd like to meet the kids who drew them.

I jump as my phone buzzes. It'll be Beth telling me she's got home. I reach over and pick it up.

They come yet? The aliens?

Amir, where are you?

On the landing strip.

My heart starts pounding. Is he really here? I slide my feet off my bed and walk over to the window. There's a man wearing a hat walking down the middle of the road. He stops and crouches down and smoothes the asphalt. What is he doing? If a bus comes along he'll get flattened like a cartoon cat and I won't be able to go out and blow him back up.

The man reaches into his coat pocket and gets out his phone. He looks like he's typing a message. Then he looks up at me.

My phone buzzes in my hand.

Well, it look like it ready!

Amir, is that really you?

Who you expect, David Beckham?

I laugh. I can't believe he's here, even if he is here to see the aliens land and not me.

He stands up and walks over to the bus stop and rests against the wall. He types and then looks up at me. My phone buzzes again.

How are you?

I'm OK. What about you?

That good. I'm good. I look forward to the aliens.

**It's been really quiet without you.**

But you got Sky TV!

I smile down at my phone and try to think what to write next, but I don't want to text. I've spent my life talking to people through screens. I want to talk to real people.

**Amir can you come up?**

I can't.

**Why not?**

He points at the CCTV cameras on the lamppost.

Too much security

**But we did it before.**

That why we can't.

**Why not?**

You ever see anyone rob a bank twice?

I nod. He's right. Maybe we were lucky last time. If Jim
had read a short chapter in the bathroom or if Phil had
gotten bored and checked the building backward, we might
have gotten caught before we'd gotten out of the reception
doors. I wish he could come in. I know everybody thinks
he's done something wrong, but it wasn't a crime.

My phone buzzes again.

Ah, what the hell!

Amir's standing at the curb.

I come. You guide me.

**Yes!**

I clench my fist.

**Brilliant!**

I turn away from the window.

**I'm just turning the screens on.**

I can't stop grinning to myself. I walk over to the table
and pick up the remote. The screens flicker on and light up
my room. On screen six, Jim is in the waiting area reading
his book and eating sandwiches. Phil is on screen nine. He's

walking down the corridor toward the Bluebell Ward tapping a rolled-up newspaper against the wall. It looks like he's whistling.

I check all the other screens. Most of the corridors are empty. On the twelfth floor, a nurse is talking to a porter. On the tenth floor, an African lady with a headdress is talking to a doctor outside the Butterfly Ward. I don't think I have to worry about them. They won't know who Amir is unless the hospital has put up a wanted poster of him on the notice board.

Jim clips the lid on his sandwich box. He stands up.

**Joe? Can I go?**

**One minute**

Jim puts the box on the reception desk and starts to walk toward the food hall.

**OK. Now!**

Amir runs across the road into the reception area. He looks left, then right, then gives me a thumbs-up to the camera. I chuckle to myself.

**Hurry. The next corridor is clear.**

**The elevator?**

I switch to screen eleven. There's no one waiting for the elevator but I don't know if there's anyone in there.

**I can't tell.**

OK. I use stairs.

Amir pushes the emergency exit doors open. We're not robbing a bank, but this is really exciting.

Okay. I on your floor.

I check screen twelve. There's a cleaner mopping the floor. My heart pounds in my head.

**Stop!**

What wrong?

There's a cleaner.

On the screen I see Amir peer out into the corridor like a mouse escaping from a cage.

That okay. It Janet. She deaf.

He creeps behind Janet and disappears from view.
I can't help him from here because this is the last camera before my room.

I sit on my bed. I can't wait to see him. He's made me feel better already. I know he won't be able to stay for long or be able to work here again, but it will be so great to talk to him.

I wait for the door to click open. It should only take a minute but it seems so much longer than that. Maybe there's a doctor or a nurse reading the notice board or looking at the kids' paintings on the walls. Or someone sitting outside guarding my room like when they put policemen outside rooms to stop reporters getting information, or to stop gangsters with machine guns bursting in to kill the patient. Maybe he's turned back?

The transition room door clicks open. I hold my breath. The water is running. It stops. Then I hear the hiss of the disinfectant. My door opens and I scramble off my bed. . . .

Amir walks in. His face is wet and his glasses are steamed up. I breathe out and Amir grins.

"Sorry it take long," he says.

"Was there someone outside?"

"No. I burst for bathroom and two nurses talk about Justin Bieber."

I laugh. He's only been in my room for a few seconds and he's already made me smile. He walks over to my table and wipes his glasses with a tissue and puts them back on. I want to hug him, but we've never done that.

"I missed you," I say.

Amir nods. "I miss me too. You okay?"

"Yes." I'm not really, but it's like all my aches and pains have gone now he's here.

"I okay too." He checks his watch. "Fourteen minutes," he says. "Then Greg come back. You got new nurse?"

"Yes. She's nice."

"Does she believe in aliens?"

"I haven't—"

"She should." Amir walks past me and I sit down on my bed. He looks out of the window down onto the road.

"It could be smoother, but I think they land okay."

I lay back on my bed. I'm so glad he's actually here, but suddenly I feel tired.

He turns around and looks concerned.

"You okay?" He walks toward me.

I try not to yawn.

"It's okay. I tired too." He sits down in the chair. "Because I worry about you."

I smile wearily. I don't want him to worry. "I'm okay," I say. "The doctors have found what it is. I'm tired because of the meds."

Amir looks at me, then glances at the screens. Phil is talking to a porter on the twelfth floor. Jim is sitting by the big plant reading his book. All the other screens are quiet.

I can't tell what he's thinking, and after all the time I've spent wishing he was here, I can't think of what to say. Amir puts his hand inside his overalls and pulls out his phone.

"It's okay," he says. "No bugs. I spray it." He leans forward. "I show you pictures."

I strain my eyes to look at the screen.

"I stand on a big white horse and take this one," he says.

It's a picture of a crop circle. I tell him it's great, and then he scrolls down.

"This one I take in Wiltshire, this one I take in Somerset, and this one I take in Berkshire on the way home. Oh! . . . And this one I take at Legoland." He shows me a picture of Ajala, Shukra, and Guru on a Viking boat.

"It's great," I say.

He smiles at me, then looks at the ground. After talking so much, he's suddenly gone quiet. I try and think of something to talk about, but I haven't got any pictures to show him. All I've done is lie on my bed and watched TV.

Amir looks up at me. He's smiling but there are tears in his eyes. "You should have told them," he says.

"I couldn't. I told you. I didn't want you to lose your job."

"No. I did my job."

"What do you mean?" I try to think clearly but my head hurts.

"I take you outside."

He's confusing me. His job was to be a nurse, not take me outside.

"Amir . . . I don't understand."

He shifts his weight on the edge of my bed. "I see you on TV . . . last year . . . your documentary. *Bubble Boy.* Me and my wife, we watch you stuck in your bubble. . . . She upset, so I say, no cry . . . I take him out of his bubble!"

"You saw me on the BBC show?"

"Of course. I no just watch Sky!"

I shiver. Goose bumps grow on my arms. Is he saying

what I think he's saying? Did he plan this all along?

"It take me a year. It would be sooner, but I have problem with your suit and Rashid had trouble hacking into CCTV."

I put my hands on my head. I don't believe this. Amir grins at me.

"You think I just turn up? I speak to best brains in London. But I very careful. Everyone know about you. I tell them I a qualified nurse and need help and Rashid get a research job at the All India Institute of Medical Science."

This doesn't make sense. Amir didn't come to the hospital to work. He came here to take me outside?

"So you came here just for me?"

"No. I come for the planes and the aliens too." He gets up suddenly and walks over to the window. "It the best view in London. Apart from London Eye but that never still." He looks at his watch, then down onto the street. "I don't think they come tonight." He suddenly sounds sad.

I walk over to the window and stand by his side. The streets are dark and empty. The buildings cast long shadows across the road and onto the pavement. Everything is still. The only thing that moves are the red lights on the planes circling over Heathrow. Amir looks at his watch again. I don't want him to go yet. It feels like he only just arrived. I look down at the portal.

"I saw them," I say.

Amir turns his head slowly.

"In my dream."

Amir smiles. "I like dreams," he says. "Everyone should have them. They pictures we paint in the dark."

"What do you mean?"

"They the best place," he says. "We do what we want. You're a superhero in your dreams. I'm an alien in mine."

"Are you?"

"Of course. That why I so tired. I fly round the galaxy every night. It take a long time."

I chuckle. I'm not sure if he's joking or not, but he's making me laugh again. I love it when he's like this, but it makes me wish he would never leave.

"Will you come back and see me?"

"Yes. Maybe not lots. But I text." He looks down at the street and shakes his head. "It the workmen fault. I think they put the magnets facing wrong way."

He checks his watch again. I wish he could wind the hands back thirty minutes so we could start again. I want to talk about the planes. I want to talk about Henry. I want—

"Must go."

I've been dreading him saying that.

He turns away from the window and starts to walk toward the door. I don't want him to go, but I don't want him to get caught either. He points at the monitors.

"Don't forget to turn them off."

"Okay."

He puts his hand on the door then looks back at me. "Hey," he says. "No worry. I be back soon."

I nod and take a breath. "Amir . . ."

"Yes?"

I swallow hard.

"Thank you."

He smiles at me. "No need."

He slides out the door. I turn and look around the room. It's empty and quiet now. I hope he doesn't leave it too long before he comes back. I pick up the remote, turn the screens off. I don't know if I'll still have the CCTV, but I'm sure he'll figure another way of getting up here. Maybe he'll surprise me and one morning I'll wake up and see him outside my window in the cleaning cradle like Rashid was. I can't believe Amir did all this for me. He must have gone home from work and stayed up all night planning and making everything. No wonder he was always tired.

I walk across to the window and look down at the street. Amir steps onto the pavement. He looks up at the sky, then walks down the middle of the road. I wish he wouldn't do that. I wish he'd stay close to the shops like everyone else. But he doesn't seem to worry about traffic. He just keeps getting smaller and smaller until he turns the corner at the end of the road and disappears.

I look across the roofs of the buildings. The orange clock is flashing on top of the Lucozade building. The strip lights are flickering above the cars in Mercedes-Benz. And up in the sky, red lights are flashing on the planes above Heathrow. I shake my head and can't stop myself from smiling. I think of me and Amir standing by the fence with the wind blowing through his hair and the roar of the planes. I'm glad he came back. He's not going to be like all the rest of the nurses that come and go. After everything he's done for me I think that maybe he's a superhero too.

I turn away from the window and get into my bed. The air conditioner clicks in. All I can see are shadows of the furniture and the red light from the monitor reflecting like tiny fires in my screens.

Flash. Flash. Flash.

*Beep. Beep. Beep.*

Flash. Flash. Flash.

*Beep. Beep. Beep.*

Flash. Flash.

*Beep. Da-lute!*

The message light is flashing on my laptop. I should go to bed but I won't be able to sleep until I know who it is. I reach over and click on the screen.

*You have a new message.*

**BBC Bubble Boy Forum**

**Mon September 6, 12:34 AM**

*Dear Bubble Boy,*

*Sorry to bother you so early but me and my brother have been up arguing all night. We just want to ask you a question. Who do you think would win if Superman and Spider-Man had a fight? My brother thinks Spidey would win. He says all Superman can do is fly really fast and burn through sheet metal with his eyes. But I think Superman would win because he could*

burn through all Spidey's webs and all he'd have to do is pick
him up and fly him into space and Spidey wouldn't be able to
breathe and he'd die.

What do you think?

Chris and Ben Milton Keynes.

I smile.

This one is easy.

Dear Chris and Ben,

Spidey and Superman wouldn't fight. They'd be friends. All
they want to do is try to save the world.

# EPILOGUE

*Da-lute!*

*Da-lute!*

I squint my eyes in the dark. The Skype light is flashing. It says there's a message from Henry, but it can't be. Even NASA can't bring Henry back to life. I pick up my laptop and hover my mouse nervously over Henry's name. Maybe it's Brett, but he's only ever spoken to me on the screen. It could be that someone's picked up Henry's laptop while they were clearing his room.

I want to look, but I don't want to look. It could be a ghost! No. Ghosts can't type, can they? Their fingers would go straight through the keyboard. Who is it? I wish it was Henry.

I click on his name.

*Hi Joe, are you there?*                                    *12:01 AM*

I shiver and goose bumps travel up my arms. It's only five
words but it sounds like Henry.

The pencil scribbles again.

*Are you?* 12:02 AM

I stare at the messages.

**Brett?** 12:02 AM

*No. It's me, Matt.* 12:03 AM

I blow out my cheeks.

**Matt. You scared me.** 12:03 AM

*Why?* 12:04 AM

I go to type, but I can't tell Matt I thought I was talking
to his brother's ghost.

*It's OK.*
*Did you think you were talking to a ghost?* 12:05 AM

**Yes.** 12:05 AM

*Haha! Henry told me you would think that.* 12:06 AM

**Matt, where are you?**                          12:06 AM

*At home. Henry said I could have his laptop. It's great!*

                                                 *12:06 AM*

**Ha. How are you?**                              12:07 AM

*I'm okay. I miss Henry.*                         *12:07 AM*

**Me too.**                                       12:07 AM

**I used to message him every night.**            12:08 AM

*I know. He told me.*                             *12:08 AM*

*Mum said he's okay. No bubbles in heaven.*       *12:08 AM*

I smile and want to cry at the same time.

*Can I talk to you on here instead?*              *12:09 AM*

**Course. I'd like that.**                        12:09 AM

*After school though.*                            *12:10 AM*

**Okay.**                                         12:10 AM

*I've got to go to bed soon.*

*Henry told me to send you a message.*
*I've got to find it.*                    12:10 AM

I smile. Here it comes. It's probably a picture of Henry giving me the finger.

*Here it is.*                             12:11 AM

He sends a link to click on.

**What is it?**                           **12:11 AM**

*Don't know. He just told me to send it.*   12:12 AM

*I've got to go now. Mom says I gotta go to bed.*   12:12 AM

**OK.**                                   **12:12 AM**

*Chat tomorrow? After school?*            12:12 AM

**Sure.**                                 **12:12 AM**

*OK. Bye, Joe.*                           12:13 AM

**Bye.**                                  **12:13 AM**

*Are you still there?*                    12:14 AM

**Yes.**                                                         **12:14 AM**


*I got to keep the remote-control car too!!!!*         *12:14 AM*


I smile. The pencil stops scribbling and the light is gone.
I scroll up and click on the link.

A video starts to play.

Henry is sitting on his bed looking right at me. It's like he's
still alive. He blows out his cheeks and makes his face go fat.

"Ha, what? Were you expecting the finger?"

"Yes," I say, but I know he can't hear me. My eyes fill up.
Henry looks just like I remember him. He doesn't look like
he's going to die.

"Hey Joe, this is gonna be weird. Just me talking to you,
but maybe I'll imagine what you would say and fill the gaps.
That okay?"

I sniff and wipe my eyes on my sleeve.

"Hey . . . this is supposed to cheer you up, not make you
cry! Did I get that right?"

I smile.

"I'm not gonna talk about being ill. I'm sure Brett has
told you about that. Just wanna show you something. Come
on." He stands up. "Connect your laptop to your screens.
I'll give you a minute."

I slide my feet down onto the floor and take my laptop
over to the cables.

"You done yet? . . . Great. Now switch your screens on."

"Wh—"

"Don't ask, why! Ha! I bet you did!"

I look around the room. It's like there's a sensor picking up all my thoughts and sending them to him.

I turn my screens on. They all stay blank except for screen one in the top left corner. It flickers and then Henry appears, waving at me. It's amazing. It's like he's actually here.

"Hey, Joe. Watch this." Henry walks to the edge of the screen. "See you in a second!" He disappears. Screen two flickers on. Henry jumps into the middle of it.

"Ta-da!"

I laugh. How did he do that?!

He holds up a finger. "One second," he says. He crouches down and jumps into screen three.

"Ha. What d'ya think . . . it's cool, right?"

I nod. It's cool.

He walks into screen four, then pretends to make a massive leap and arrives back on the other side of my room in screen five.

I step backward and bump into my bed. He's jumping all around my room.

"Like it? Told the tech guy from NASA about your screens and he showed me how to do it." He walks into screen six and he's walking in a park, in screen seven he's on a beach, in screen eight he's in a field full of cows.

This is amazing!

Henry keeps walking. In screen nine he's standing in front of Buckingham Palace.

"Just around the block!" he says. He jumps again. In

screen ten he's in front of the Eiffel Tower, in the next he's holding the camera on a roller coaster, in screen twelve he's in the middle of a baseball park.

I put my hand up to my face. I'm smiling so much my jaw aches.

Henry stands up and pretends to dust down his trousers. "You finished gawping?" he says. ". . . One last thing before I go."

I walk over to him. I don't want him to go. I could press pause and freeze him and he could stay there on my wall forever.

"Hey, don't get upset. This is the best bit!" He takes a TV remote out of his pocket and puts his finger over the green button. "You ready?"

I nod.

He presses the button.

"Here you go, Spidey!"

The screens go blank. I walk in front of them, waiting for him to reappear, but all I see is my reflection. I sigh. Maybe he didn't have time to finish his video before he died.

I pick up the remote, then stop. There's a little flicker of light in screen eleven. I press my face so close to the screen that my nose is almost touching it. Orange and red lights begin to glow. They start to mix together and grow bigger. I look at screen ten, then screen nine. The orange and red lights are bubbling in them too. They start to spit and spark across the rest of the screens, bubbling like a volcano. The speakers rumble. I hear Henry laughing somewhere.

"Hang in there, Joe!" he shouts.

What's happening?

I have to lean back against my bed. Pieces of earth break apart and fly across the screens from one to another and disappear off the edge. My heart jumps in my chest. This is the most exciting movie I've ever seen.

"Hey, Joe, you might want to cover your eyes for the next bit. It gets really bright . . . Oh . . . you might want to cover your ears, too."

I wrap my arms tight around my head. The noise rumbles deeper and longer, so loudly that I can feel the vibrations on the floor a little bit. I sneak a look under my eyelids. The light is white bright, like Superman and Cyclops are fighting and burning each other with their laser eyes. I close my eyes again and wrap my arms so tight across my head I can feel my heart beating in my ears.

Then suddenly, silence. Nothing.

I unwrap my arms away from my head. The only sound is the wind from the air conditioner and the beep of my monitors. I open my eyes slowly. I check the floor for bricks and earth, but all I see are the tiles.

"It's okay, you can look now."

I lift my head.

"Wow!" I suck in air like the Lizard's tail has just whacked me in the stomach. There's hundreds and hundreds of little lights on the screen, shining out of tiny windows. My eyes start to water and the lights go blurry. Henry walks onto screen twelve and holds up his arm.

"Like it? 6,500 windows. 102 floors."

I blink.

"I love it!"

Henry gives me a massive grin. He's the only person who knows I'd love to live where Spider-Man hangs out— right at the very top of the Empire State Building. I put my hands on my head. Henry turns and faces the camera. He's still grinning and his eyes are sparkling. He looks up at the Empire State, then back at me and shrugs. "Guess I can't stick around here all day."

"No." But I wish he could.

Henry lifts up his hand. "Don't cry."

I won't.

"See you around, Spidey."

Henry fades away. The lights on the Empire State twinkle in the dark.

The building's so big I can see in through every window. I drag the chair away from the door but when I stand on it I still can't reach the top. I look around my room. I could stand on my monitors but I might damage them. I could climb onto the windowsill but I'm scared of falling off. The only way I can reach the top is if I stand on my bed.

I try to move the bed, but I don't want to wake up anyone sleeping below. But I don't want to be stuck on the viewing deck either. Maybe if I try quietly, no one will hear.

I walk over to my bed and bend down. The brakes click as I unlock them from the wheels. I put my hands on the bar at the end of my bed and pull it gently. I'm not very strong, but little by little the wheels move across the tiles until my bed reaches the screens. I climb up onto it until I'm standing beside the lightning rod. This is where Spidey goes to catch a breather, to look out over the city. He sees the skyscrapers reaching up into the sky, the cars with their flashing lights and all the people walking along the sidewalks like ants. A warm feeling grows from my feet through my stomach to my heart. I might not be able to go outside but I can still see the world from my room. I can watch all the people on CCTV. I can see if they need my help if they are in trouble. I can watch them all from my bed, just like Spider-Man watches everyone from the lightning rod.

I reach out and touch a screen. I want to tell everyone what Henry has sent me. I can't wait to tell Beth. She'll love it. I think Greg and the doctors will like it too. Maybe I'll tell Hannah. Maybe one day she'd like to visit me and see it. I'll look at the building every night before I go to bed and I'll remember Henry and maybe one day if the doctors fix me I'll go to New York and see it for real.

I glance at the clock.

It's after midnight. Greg will be coming back to check on me soon. He told me to rest. I climb down off my bed and push it back against the wall.

I pick up my phone. He might not be awake but I have to tell Amir.

**Amir, guess what?**

I wait for a few seconds for a reply. The light on my phone screen goes out. It's too late. I put my table and pick up the TV remote. I look up at the Empire State Building one last time. The lights flicker like candles in its windows. I wish I could hang out all night like Spidey, but I'm tired and need to sleep. I press the off button. The screens zap off and my room turns black and dark.

**Heart rate:** 82

**Body temp:** 37.4

**Room temp:** 19C

*Beep.*

*Beep.*

*Beep.*

The monitors never stop. Superheroes' hearts never stop. They don't die. They don't even go to sleep. They might get knocked out by a massive punch but it only takes a second for them to bounce back.

I close my eyes. My room might be dark now, but in the morning, when I wake up, it will light up again.

# ACKNOWLEDGMENTS

**My shining lights:**
Lobes and Tal

**My guiding light:**
My omnipresent friend and editor Jonathan Bentley-Smith

**Bright lights:**
Special thanks to . . .

My agent, Nicola Barr, for falling in love with Joe and *Bubble*.

All the chocolate frogs I ate in the last year.

My daughter, Lois; Sam Drew; and Jade Craddock for helping me over the line.

Rachel Mann, my brilliant editor at Simon & Schuster, who pushed and cajoled me, and splattered my manuscript with red ink, until we finally got a story worthy of all the superheroes up and down this land.

And finally a big thanks to David Gale, Simon & Schuster, USA, who loved *Bubble* so much that it got to go to America, too.